For ONCE
In My
LIFE

ALSO BY COLLEEN COLEMAN

Don't Stop Me Now
I'm Still Standing
One Way or Another

For ONCE In My LIFE

COLLEEN COLEMAN

Bookouture

Published by Bookouture in 2018

An imprint of StoryFire Ltd.

Carmelite House
50 Victoria Embankment
London EC4Y 0DZ

www.bookouture.com

ISBN: 978-1-78681-495-1
eBook ISBN: 978-1-78681-494-4

To Shannon,
The most free-spirited, fun-loving, adventurous, kind-hearted and hard-working person I know. There's not a corner of the earth you haven't seen or a cocktail you've turned down. Love you so much and couldn't be more proud to call you my sister.

PROLOGUE

There are very few things in this world that bring me as much joy as weddings do. I mean, how can you not love a giant, fairy-lit, all-day, all-night party where you get to dress up, dance, drink bubbly and watch two people you care about vow to be best friends forever?

If sharing a peak emotional experience surrounded by all the ones you love and admire is 'overrated', 'overpriced' or 'over the top', you just haven't been to a really good one yet. Which is what I told my fiancé Adam when he suggested we elope and spend all our savings on cocktails and jet skis. I waggled my finger and spelt it out in no uncertain terms that was never going to happen for us. There hadn't been a wedding in my family since the 1930s. Our big day, in the quaint little church at the top of our town, surrounded by all our friends and family, was to be La Shebang Totale.

So, today is my wedding day. Sorry, typo! I keep saying that, but of course I mean *our* wedding day. Even though it's me who has planned everything down to the smallest detail. A DNA test would now confirm that I'm at least sixty-six per cent Bridezilla. But it will all be worth it because you only want to do this once, right? And once it's done, there's no going back, so you may as well throw everything you have into getting it as close to perfect as possible.

And I've promised Adam that it will be the best day of our lives. I can't believe it's actually here. May 29th has been the centre of the universe so long, it feels surreal that it's come, that the sun rose and this morning started like any other ordinary day. Which, of course, it isn't. From now on May 29th will never be just an ordinary day. It's our wedding day, and this time next year we'll open a bottle of champagne that we've kept back from our reception and exchange paper gifts to mark our one-year anniversary and we'll look back on all our amazing, dream-like photographs and remember what a perfect day it was, and how frazzled and nervous we felt, but how it all played out beautifully without a single hitch in the end. We'll cosy up on the sofa and reflect on all we've achieved and everything we hope for in the future. May 29th will be our day to remember our love, thank the heavens above for bringing us together and toast the two of us, Lily4Adam4Ever.

So, I have high hopes for today. I'm wearing a hand-made gown shaped like a cupcake (but elegant; I know, but trust me) and I've got a bouquet of the most beautiful fresh, wild flowers I've ever seen. My real hope is that my future groom's eyes will well up with tears of joy as he watches me walk towards him. And I'm hoping everyone I care about will be there to witness me giving my heart to the person I love. I'm also hoping that the saying 'Dance like no one is watching' will be something people take to heart once the band starts playing. And I hope that when I look back on today, only the most joyful of memories will spring up in my head.

Relax, I know a wedding is only the sparkly tip of the iceberg. I know it's so much more than just a pretty dress, live music and a free bar. To me, a wedding day is the beginning of the most intimate earthly relationship you'll ever have. In two minutes, when I walk down that aisle and recite my vows, I'm really saying 'I do' to a lifetime commitment with the one I love. I'm saying 'I do' to a lifetime of challenges, of obstacles and rainy days, and I'm saying 'I do' to a lifetime of highs and laughter and support and sunshine.

The person who's waiting for me, right now, at the end of the aisle is the person I'm going to experience all of life's blessings with for the next fifty years or more, if we are lucky. He's the person I'll buy my first house with, the one who I'll spend lazy Sundays with and the one I'll have children with (or another dog, if that's more appealing).

And this formal Church ceremony is going to be so special, but I really can't wait for the after-party. This beautiful long, wrapped ivory gown has a trick up its sleeve. Once the music starts, I'm going to whip off the frilled layers of tulle and organza and have that first dance with my husband in a gorgeous, beaded minidress. Complete with vintage lace garter of course.

Hopefully, my best friend Hannah may feel well enough by then to give a toast that'll make me cry and then I'll do the chicken dance with my granny and maybe even convince my mum to sing. I hope I will feel love in ways I've never experienced before, and that nothing but happiness will fill my spirit, but most of all I hope that happiness is one that doesn't go away as I ride off into my happily ever after.

My granny stands beside me at the church steps. She steadies her own royal blue fascinator and dabs her eyes with a tissue. 'It's eleven on the dot, Lily.' She nods towards her watch. 'It's time. Are you ready?'

I smile at her, hook my arm into hers and take my first sure steps down the aisle. I had planned that Hannah would be my maid of honour but she came down with a violent episode of food poisoning in the early hours of this morning and my back-up bridesmaid was too hung-over to step in, so it's just me and my grandmother, which is absolutely fine as I feel such love and pride emanating from her as she tightens her grip around my elbow. It's actually worked out even better that we can share this together, just the two of us.

With each step, I see all our guests beaming at us. We don't rush; wanting to take it all in, to see everyone and everything in this perfect suspended moment.

Is this really it?

We approach the final pew, and my grandmother lets me go. I kiss her and thank her and then I pause. Taking a second to compose myself, to take a deep breath, because when I take my next step towards him, Adam will be facing me. Seeing me as his bride for the very first time.

His back is still towards me and, at this moment, time feels as if it is slowing down, because I'm waiting for him to turn around, but he's not moved. He's still facing the altar as if he doesn't realise that I'm even here. Maybe he is crying? Maybe he's overwhelmed with emotion! Ah Adam, you big romantic! And now all I want to do is rush up and wrap my arms around him and say 'Don't worry, darling! It's okay, it's our big day! Nothing to be scared about, I'm feeling it too, it's just excitement.'

But I hold back, pressing my fingernails in to my palms as I wait for the last note of the song to end, just like in rehearsals, and then I take four steps towards the altar with a huge smile on my face and butterflies in my stomach. I can't wait to see his reaction. Adam and I setting eyes on each other for the first time as bride and groom.

But here's the thing.

He doesn't turn to me.

He doesn't move at all.

Adam is standing stiff beside me, staring ahead, tears pooling in his eyes. His face is grey, beads of sweat on his brow and the top of his lip.

'Adam?' I whisper. 'Are you okay?'

He shakes his head. Closes his eyes slowly and then, with a deep sigh audible to the whole church, he walks away from me towards the sacristy.

I hear murmuring and shuffling amongst the congregation behind me. This did not happen at rehearsals. Heat creeps into my chest and a bolt of panic courses through me. Why is this happening? What is going on? If I don't know, then who does?

The priest leans in towards me, his voice low and grave. 'Lily, I think we need to take a moment in the sacristy. You go follow Adam and I'll deal with your guests. I'll tell them he's feeling faint.'

Relief washes over me. 'Of course, thank you, Father Quinn! I'm sure that's it. My bridesmaid is ill as well, so maybe it's a bug.'

The priest raises his eyebrow. 'Brace yourself, Lily, I'm not too sure it is.'

In the sacristy, Adam is sitting on the lone wooden stool. He's taken off his jacket and his black bow tie falls undone. His collar is unbuttoned and wide open. His eyes are bloodshot. He looks terrible.

'Adam, talk to me. What is it? I need to know.'

He doesn't answer but just keeps wringing his hands over and over.

'I just can't do it,' he whispers to the ground.

Okay. He's got cold feet. It happens. We can get through this.

'Of course, you can, Adam! Everyone is here! It's just stage fright, it's easy to get nervous.' I bunch up my tulle and organza layers and hunker down in front of him, trying to catch his eye, trying to get close, trying to de-escalate this random crazy spanner in the works and get us back on track, in front of that altar and onto the rest of our lives.

Adam shakes his head and pinches his eyes.

'Adam, look at me!'

He won't look at me. He lowers his head even further.

'Adam, you can't be serious. This can't be happening! We can do this. All you have to do is come back out that door with me and we can do this! Everyone is waiting, everything is ready… Don't you dare bail on me…' I say, a hint of hysteria now in my voice as I realise this is serious. Something is really wrong.

But why? We're here. Everyone is here. We're at the church. This is *not* a rehearsal. I'm in a veil for God's sake. And he is in his suit. On the other side of that curtain, there are a hundred people sitting in morning suits and pastel dresses, waiting for Adam and I, waiting for us to look at each other lovingly, recite our vows and throw confetti!

He better have diarrhoea. He wouldn't do this to me, right? Not now. Not like this.

I squeeze his knee. 'Adam?'

'I can't go ahead with this,' he says, gazing past me as though he's looking at someone else entirely, his face slowly creasing up in pain. Or is it pity?

'What do you mean exactly, why can't you? What can I do? Let me help you, Adam, whatever it is, we can sort it out *after* the wedding okay? Let's just get through the next few hours and whatever it is, I promise, we'll sit down after all this madness has passed and talk it through? C'mon. I love you! I want to be with you! This is our big day… right?'

I look at him in his tuxedo, like he's getting ready to say I do and kiss me till death do us part, yet the expression on his face doesn't correspond with that at all.

Then something shifts. His eyes flick upwards and there's something different about him. Something deep and dark and bad that's coming, I can feel it. I just know before he says another word that this wedding day isn't going to be going on Pinterest. Maybe it isn't going to happen at all. Certainly not in the way I envisaged it would. And then he says the seven words that will change my life forever.

'I'm not in love with you, Lily.' These seven heart-breaking words garble with the tears in his throat.

'No,' I tell him, my eyes searing into his. 'That's not true. It's just all the craziness, all the pressure, the weight of expectation weddings bring. That's all. You don't mean that.'

I hold his hands in mine, but he won't release his balled-up fists; tight, clammy and white. He pulls away from me, stands up and opens his eyes wide.

'Lily, I can't go through with this because I've met someone. And I've fallen in love with her.'

My knees buckle beneath me and I slide backwards on to the floor.

And there I stay. Frozen. Paralysed with shock and confusion.

'What has anybody else got to do with anything? What do you mean? Adam, what are you talking about?' My voice is dangerously close to a wail, a deep, howling, child-like wail.

'It's Hannah. And she loves me. No one ever set out for this to happen or for you to get hurt. We didn't mean for it to end up this way, but it has and I'm sorry, but it's the truth and I can't go through with this charade another second.' He swallows and meets my eyes for the first time.

'Hannah? As in my Hannah?' I'm shaking my head. 'Not my Hannah, she would *never*…'

Adam presses his palms together. 'Why isn't she here then?'

'Food poisoning…' And as soon as I say it aloud I realise how untrue it is.

'As I said, she's just as sorry as I am…'

I search his face, his eyes. For some sense that this is all some terrible joke, a dreadful misunderstanding. He winces. I'd like to say his eyes are full of shame or regret but they are not. They are full of pity, of commiseration. He runs both hands through his hair and stands from his chair, walking towards the small stained glass window, as if a prisoner imagining his release.

And just like that everything changes. It's the happiest day of my life. And then, in a moment, it's the worst day of my life. He tells me, *I don't love you. I don't want this. It's all over and I'm taking your best friend with me.* And suddenly the room feels very small and the air very heavy and my dress feels very tight and I need to get as far away from here and from Adam and from candles and flowers and organists and my caved-in world as possible. So I hitch up my dress and I just manage to put one silver-heeled foot in front of the other, out the sacristy door, through the heavy curtain, down the aisle, past the gawping guests. I exit my wedding day alone, without looking back, without any more pleading, without any more hope that this can ever work out. For once in my life, I have no idea what's supposed to happen next.

CHAPTER 1

3 Years Later

Happy Jobiversary to me, Happy Jobiversary to me, Happy Jobiversary to mee-ee...

Seven wonderful years. Seven years ago today, I remember my granny telling me, that if I got taken on, I should give my first job the six-month test. Can't hate a new job too soon; can't love it too soon. There's a honeymoon stage, a trial-by-error stage, an 'is this it?' stage, a warrior stage for new colleagues and bosses to dance around each other in the ring, self-conscious about smiling or shouting too soon, trying to balance being firm and fair and friendly and familiar all at once. Not wanting to give away too much of themselves or show all their cards too soon. Except...

I showed all mine.

Straight away.

Every single one of them.

I couldn't help it. For me it was love at first sight, the second I pushed my way through those double doors and stepped into this electric little newsroom; buzzing with energy, phones hopping and keyboards tapping away. The legendary editor, JJ Oakes, welcomed me with open arms. He told me that all I needed was a genuine interest in people, the courage to follow my instincts and a knack of getting to the point. No mention of high grades or further education. I knew in that instant that this was me. This is where I belong.

The newsroom at the *Newbridge Gazette* was alive with urgency and purpose and fun and excitement and passion and I wanted to be part of it from that first flutter. Call it instinct or naïvety or pure dumb luck, but I decided there and then that if somebody would just give me a chance to do this, then I'd never let them down. I'd do it with all my heart.

Getting paid to write?

Getting paid to snoop?

Getting paid to meet many weird and wonderful people and ask them your own questions, listen to their own answers?

Getting paid to drop everything and drive to the scene of a major breaking story? And hang around nosing legitimately as it unfolds?

Oh yes. Yes, yes, yes please.

This was a job I knew I could do; in time, maybe even do it well. After all, I'd done similar stuff for my mum all my life. She had no patience for the dull or the detailed; if it didn't amuse or inform her, she switched off, so it often fell to me to edit all external dreariness, filter the banal admin of everyday life and cut out the boring bits. Few bank statements were ever opened in our house. We used them to line the kitty litter tray.

So, I tried out my best I Can Do That, Let Me Do That, Pick Me, Pick Me dance, and my amazing boss and mentor JJ Oakes, said yes. In gratitude, I paid close attention to everything he taught me, and I soon tried out some new moves of my own. And he liked them. He gave me a promotion and a desk and even paid for my driving lessons out of a professional development budget. And when I passed, he granted me a company car and even more chances to prove myself. And I loved him for it and swore my allegiance to this little paper. That was seven years ago. I didn't need six months to figure it out. I didn't need six seconds. I'm here to tell you that trusting my instincts really paid off: my job is awesome.

And I wasn't alone feeling this way. The whole news crew felt it too, we were a team, a family, in it together, doing what we loved. When the shit hit the fan, we all gave up evenings, nights, weekends, sleep, sanity and a degree of hygiene to share takeaways at our desks, drink neat gin from mugs, spray ourselves down with Febreze and tap into our deepest reserves to meet that deadline. To make a great local paper. We were the peoples' paper, stories for them and about them, no story too big or small, if it was happening within our readership, we ran it! It's what we did, and we loved it. The success of the *Newbridge Gazette* was our success. It reflected who we were and it was such an adrenaline rush! That's what got my heart pumping. Here in this fourth-floor office is where I found my calling, where I published my first article, where I met my first group of real friends. It's where my life really began.

So Happy Jobiversary to us, dear *Newbridge Gazette*. I love you, I mean that.

I hope to God it's not our last.

I'd be lying if I said things are still awesome, though. They're not. Things around here have been weird for a while now. Since our latest external consultancy report recommended we 'cease trading with immediate effect'. That confirmed how badly Gareth, JJ's successor and current Editor in Chief, had run the newspaper into the ground, filling it with page after page of planning permission and tender applications and second-hand car sales. What my mum would call the 'boring bits'. I was relegated to page ten, a single page devoted to human interest features and community social events. One page, just enough space for two photos and 950 words of content. All my old friends and colleagues left, unable to stand it any longer: Gareth's totalitarian rule, his egotism and incompetence. I would have gone for the

Editor in Chief job myself except the timing was all wrong; I was still getting over Adam jilting me at the altar and running off with my best friend. Exactly the gossip-tastic kind of heartbreak that you want when you work at the local paper. I can see the church that staged my worst nightmare from my desk. Well, I used to be able to, before I stuck a big, leafy plastic plant in the way to block it from my view.

But, anyway, I wasn't exactly in the right frame of mind to sit in front of a panel and field questions on sales strategies and circulation figures and future operating models. I was barely keeping my head above water. Struggling to work out how I was supposed to be successful, fit, happy, well rested, clean, be a good daughter/reporter/friend, and remain sober with only twenty-four hours in a day to work with. I wasn't my 'best-self' at the time.

So when much to everyone's disappointment – especially mine – JJ retired, Gareth put himself forward for JJ's old job. He blinded the panel with his bullshit, over-promised and under-delivered. We lost our best staff, the quality of the paper suffered, and people noticed – namely the readers. Sales plummeted and continue to do so at an alarming rate. Gareth still refuses to acknowledge it has anything to do with him and his leadership; he refuses point-blank to seek help. Why would he possibly need help, right? He gets angrier and angrier every passing week, scapegoating each step of the way, so it never appears his fault. So instead of excitement or purpose, what we've got now is a distinct shiftiness in the air. And it appears infectious, toxic and suffocating for those of us who love this place, want to save it and make it work. But as long as Gareth is in charge as Editor in Chief, it's near impossible to see how that will happen.

I hear you. If things are so bad, then why am I still here?

Where else would I go? This is where I belong. I've never really had the desire to go anywhere else, everything I was after was right here: great job, great community, great town. If I couldn't make things work in Newbridge, then what chance did I have as a stranger starting from scratch in some other place? And, if I'm brutally honest, I don't want to risk another big, fat 'no', personally or professionally. Been there and done that, got the lousy T-shirt.

How am I dealing with this? Well, I keep a very low profile and try to stay out of the office as much as I can. The situation reminds me of *The Lord of The Flies*. We know rescue isn't likely and we're done crying about it. Now, primal strategising has kicked in, it's everyone for themselves. Each looking at escape routes, at the best place and time to jump, gauging who we should cling to as our best chance of survival. With our current readership at an all-time low, some of us will be sacrificed, devoured and cast aside. Everyone has taken on that sidelong look that means if it comes to it, they'll eat you. And lick the bones.

Take yesterday, whenever I ventured near Gareth's office door to check on a lead or offer an idea for a story, he slammed shut his laptop. When I asked if he was feeling okay, he coughed into his fist and made strange rubbery faces at me with a garbled, incoherent commentary. And despite his raspy protestations and gum-baring, he didn't look okay at all. Sweaty… well, sweatier. And pale. And the raised red line of an itchy scalp that began at his forehead had flaked all over his shoulders, which hasn't happened since we were sued for defaming the Chief of Police over a year ago. Gareth's doing. We had one suspected burglary in the town and Gareth ran with the headline 'Crime Up 100% Under New Police Chief'. Up 100% only because there hadn't been a burglary recorded in living memory. I told him I thought the headline was ill-advised (and the Chief of Police is really nice and IMHO does a great job for our little community), but Gareth's not keen on my input. Or my presence. Or me generally. So yes, instead of the proverbial calm, we have this weird cannibalistic shiftiness before the storm. And, frankly, I'm done with it. I'd say I'm ready for the storm. Or the Apocalypse or Armageddon or whatever will happen next. Whatever shape it takes, it's got to be better than the stasis we've got now.

It's not just Gareth's attitude that makes me nervous about the future. In the top corner by the big windows overlooking the car park, sit the wild-haired, wild-eyed ad-sales team; most of whom are his after-work drinking buddies. Swivelling on chairs, phones ever-hooked into the crook of their necks, even they are now throwing back ibuprofen like smarties to combat the throbbing mix of hangover and looming target pressures.

Mark is the Head of Sales: he's tall, tanned, bearded and built like Action Man and he's been here about three years. He's barely spoken to me since his first *Gazette* Christmas party when he drunkenly made a pass at me and I told him in very clear terms that I wasn't interested, and that I never have and never will get involved with anyone from work. Too much potential for mess and complication. And humiliation, of course. The fallout after a break-up is hard enough, can you imagine if you had to face them every day in the office too? It's just a no-no on every front.

The thing is, my work is my safe space. Outside, everything else is erratic and emotional and unpredictable and completely out of my control. But here, I know where I stand, I know what's expected of me and I know I belong here and I won't be doing anything to mess that up in any way. To Mark's credit, he keeps his distance from me and has never tried it on again, but as a result of that I don't really know a lot about him despite the fact he's now one of the longest serving on our team.

And then there are the temps. A constant stream of random admin strangers circle the main office space at all times, appearing and disappearing with the same bits of paper, darting around pretending to be preoccupied so we won't get suspicious while they attend castings or complete their online degrees on company time. They are not attached to the place like we are, well, like I am. They don't care if it sinks or burns or collapses. When you try to engage with them, they appear horrified, murmuring low sentences that begin like condolences and then just trail off as their eyes wander to random points on the wall. It's like being an extra in a zombie movie as we stalk around each other, looking pale and stricken, doing the same thing over and over, almost alive but not quite.

Watching all of this happen, day in, day out, is breaking my heart. Current headline mood: 'Unhappiness Up 100%'.

If only Gareth would piss off. If only somebody else could step up and take over and lead us forward. If only I wasn't the only one prepared to fight for it.

I get that the others don't see it this way. They probably have rich and varied lives outside these office walls, lots of exciting career options to explore. To them this is probably just a place to clock in and clock out; an honest way to pay the bills. And the only news this newspaper cares about right now is its own precarious future. The *Newbridge Gazette* is limping along its last few steps, one-legged, dragging its debt-ridden body towards some kind of terminus. But how, when and what that end will look like is still anybody's guess.

There's been no shortage of guessing. We're reporters after all, professional gossip is our *raison d'être*. A huddle of the guys can always be found by the water cooler, swaying on the spot with blown-out cheeks, their hands shoved down the backs of their trousers, fantasising about how they'll spend their redundancies. By now, I've heard everything, from cycling the world to creating their own craft beer, to just playing non-stop FIFA in their pants and living off deliveries.

I won't burst their bubble. The fact is, if there is no money in the pot to run this paper, then there's no money for redundancies. We'll be let go with a sad shrug, a handshake and an hour to clear our desks.

It's been like this for weeks now. Limbo. Navel-gazing. Ear-picking whilst doomsday prophesising. They've given up on the idea that someone, anyone, even one of us with an army of media-savvy saviours, could still swoop in and save us from extinction.

But I haven't. Not yet.

Because if there's anything I've learnt from my experience, it's that there's no point in peering into the future, no point in speculation or second-guessing or imagining you are going to logically follow a series of events which will lead you to arrive at a particular destination. And as for all their contemplations of escape routes and Plan B's, there's not much point to that either.

Every day, I fight back the urge to storm over there and tell them all to stop their arse-scratching, shut the hell up and get back to work. Don't they understand that hanging around whining and moaning isn't gaining us any new readers? Don't they get they are compounding a very sad and stressful situation by doing even less than they did before? And that that's pretty much what got us into this situation in the first place?

I'd also like to point out that not only is their approach ineffectual, it's also irrational. You can spend the best part of two years planning everything out, perfectly, to the finest, tiniest detail. You can know every single thing from the cup size of your back-up bridesmaid to your fiancé's cousin's husband's sister's nut allergy to the choreography of every step of your first dance. You can even get a formal warning from the security guard at Boots for trying on every shade of lipstick to find the perfect one to pronounce those fateful words 'I do'. And then, guess what?

None of it happens.

So, I don't waste time supposing and guesstimating about anything until it actually happens any more.

And perhaps that's why I'm the only employee who still does any work around here, and thinks maybe, just maybe, our story isn't over just yet.

So Happy Jobiversary dear *Gazette*. This year my only wish is that we get through it. Together.

CHAPTER 2

I'm an hour late today because I spent this morning visiting an old man who turned ninety-eight (or thereabouts), won the lottery and nearly died the next day. I know, right? So, this story had to be covered; classic Page Ten news.

I drove 20km to visit Mr Clark in his hospital bed. I kept my head down as I searched the wards, worried that I'd run into my ex best friend Hannah who used to work there as a nurse. I imagine she's still nursing locally, but maybe not, we haven't had any contact whatsoever for three years now, so who knows what she's been up to or where she's moved on. She could be married to Adam with kids and a brand-new life abroad for all I know. In a way, I hope she is, just so I can't bump into her, this morning or ever. I haven't heard from either of them and that's the way I want to keep it. I have no social media accounts. I don't want to see them drink cocktails or ride jet skis. That's the past and I need to try my best every day to remember that and keep moving on, so the fewer reminders, the better. Thankfully, a very friendly receptionist offered to help me when she could see me looking lost; we turned into a private room across from her desk and my stomach finally stopped flipping with dread.

Mr Clark wasn't at all what I expected on meeting a newly minted millionaire. He's mad. As in furious, wishes he'd never bought the goddamn thing as he checked the numbers, discovered he was a winner and then, next thing he knew, he's strapped down in an ambulance, a lump the size of a beef tomato in the middle of his forehead. He was especially worried about leaving his slow-cooked stew behind as well as a stray kitten he'd taken in. So that was my light-bulb moment on how to get the exclusive scoop on the oldest millionaire in town.

'How about you give me a statement and a photo and I promise to nip straight by your house, save your stew and feed your cat?'

Mr Clark struck out his hand and we made ourselves a deal. 'His name is Chaplin,' he told me, slightly brighter. 'He looks just like Charlie Chaplin. You'll know him because he's white with a little black patch over his mouth like a moustache.'

I smiled, and we chatted animals for a bit. I love them, but when Adam moved out, he took our bouncy Dalmatian, Oreo, with him, so I've been living by myself pet-less for much longer than I'd like. When you've got an animal in your house, it never feels empty. Their warmth, their routines, their presence becomes such a comfort, such a close and constant companionship. I had planned to adopt a rescue pup, but when my granny became ill I shelved all ideas of that as all my attention turned to her. Maybe it's something I'll look into again sometime. I really miss Oreo – I'd say I miss him more than Adam most days.

And I get it; Mr Clark lives alone like me, so he's the only one he can count on and I couldn't help but warm to him for caring more about this little creature than the lotto millions he's yet to collect. He grabbed a scrap of paper from his bedside locker, scribbled down his address and handed it to me.

'Ah, I know where you live, Mr Clark, I'm just at the back of your field, I'm the little two-bed cottage with the thatched roof.'

He squinted at me. 'Thatched roof? Are you any relation to Edith Buckley?'

'She's my grandmother. As in she was when she was alive…' I told him.

He nodded and clicked his tongue. 'So your mother was that wild redhead?'

I shrugged. She'd been called worse. 'Yes. I'm afraid so.'

A half-smile tugged on his thin grey lips. 'Every year, October time, when she was a teenager, I'd catch her in my field in the middle of the night, picking magic mushrooms. Off her head she was. Stubborn too. Reminded me of my own son, always drama and calamity. I called the police on her, set the dogs on her, reported her to your grandmother – who was a respectable lady, mind – but there was no stopping that redhead from harvesting those mushrooms.'

Hmm. I'd like to say she grew out of all that.

'Well, she lives in the States now, so I doubt you'll be seeing her around.' I explained, eager to get off the subject of my mother. For someone so good at not being around, she has a knack of still cropping up everywhere, especially in unexpected conversations like this. I mean, my mother isn't a serial killer or anything. She's no Mother Teresa, but she's all right. She's just not very maternal. If anything, she's actively un-mumsy. She views all traditional relationships as frumpy and old-fashioned and overly sentimental. She's the polar opposite to me – she does attention, adventure and applause. I guess I'm more cautious. I like stability, routine, the quiet life: no alarms and no surprises. She left me with my granny here in Newbridge when I was ten, so she could pursue her singing career. Which worked out. For her. She's a professional 'recording artist' with more albums under her belt than I can count on my fingers. Maybe somewhere along the lines she wanted us to be more like friends than mother and daughter, but that hasn't worked out so well. She can act more like a demanding older sibling, competitive and self-absorbed. But that might also be down to artistic temperament after all. She is a singer, a really good one, but it comes with a big dollop of diva, which means I don't always want people to know I'm her daughter. That's the thing about doing this job in the smallish community where I grew up from such a young age. The plus side is that everyone knows everyone. The down side is that everyone knows everyone. And their mother.

I straightened up and poised my pen to paper, leaning in for my exclusive statement.

'So, Mr Clark, tell me, in your own time, what would you like everyone to know about the newest millionaire in the country?'

'I want everyone to know…' he began. Deep breath in. 'I want everyone to know…' Deep breath out. 'I want…' His eyes closed and his chin dipped, his face slackening with every passing second.

OMG. Was he dying? Was he dying right now?

I looked around. For someone. Anyone. 'NURSE! NURSE!' I shouted while I panic-pressed the red button for help. God, I'd even call Hannah over here if I saw her! But there was nobody. Nobody else at all. Just me. Me and Mr fading-fast Clark. 'EMERGENCY! Over here! MAJOR HUGE EMERGENCY RIGHT THIS SECOND HERE!!'

Squeaky plastic soles thudded down the ward, and a broad, starched nurse elbowed me out of the way, checking Mr Clark's pulse, listening in to his breathing, his chest, then studying his chart. She straightened up and nodded with a satisfied, tight-lipped smile. 'Nothing to worry about, painkillers have kicked in, that's all. He'll be able to rest now.' She drew the curtains around his bed.

'But I was going to get an exclusive statement for the *Newbridge Gazette*. It's not just a local story, it's national interest, even international interest. Once this story breaks beyond Newbridge, everyone will want to know all about Mr Clark. Who is he? Where did he buy his winning ticket? What's he going to do with all this new-found wealth? Mr Clark is ninety-eight. I imagine he's the oldest lottery winner and multi-millionaire there's ever been. That's HUGE! And I had the perfect headline.'

This is the biggest local story we've had in ages. This kind of breaking news is exactly what the *Gazette* needs to boost our ever-falling figures. And morale.

She continued to pull at the curtain, her face unmoving.

'I really need a statement, Nurse. He is my headline story, page ten! Couldn't you just wake him up again? Just for five minutes? Two minutes? Give him a quick shot of something just to perk him up temporarily? I can't take a photo either now, not while he's asleep like that.'

We both looked down at him, a few bubbles of spittle on his bottom lip, oblivious to us, to everything, whistling away with every deep, peaceful breath.

She shook her head and blinked at me slowly. 'Yes, well I very much doubt that gracing the local rag in his gown and slippers is on Mr Clark's bucket list now, do you?'

I looked down at the scrap of paper he'd handed to me just before he turned into Rip Van Winkle. His handwritten name and address, evidence of our little deal he dozily reneged on. By the sound of his heavy snoring, this was no catnap and I had to admit, I was disappointed. I couldn't wait to hear what Mr Clark had to say as a lottery winner. What was the first thing he was going to do? Eat an amazing meal at a famous restaurant, go on a round-the-world cruise, throw a huge party for all his friends and family? Imagine suddenly having the means and the freedom to do anything you wanted.

I ran my fingers through my hair. I'd harboured a vague hope that this story would give the *Newbridge Gazette* the lifeline it needed. That maybe even Gareth would lift his head from his keyboard and say 'Well done, Lily, nice one.' Being the first to report on a major local story would have made us the talk of the town, surely it would've seen our paper fly off the shelves, lifting our spirits. Even for just an instant.

The nurse cleared her throat and yanked the curtain over. 'I suggest you call back later when he wakes up.'

If he wakes up more like.

This was the biggest story that could happen in our town and I'd failed to get it.

What a morning and I haven't even made it in to the office yet. A little deflated, I make my way back to my car, humming the tune of Alanis Morrisette's 'Ironic' and glancing at my phone to check the time. It's after nine. I should have clocked in well over an hour ago now. I sit in the driver's seat and smooth out the scrap of paper Mr Clark gave me, folding it carefully and tucking it into a special pocket of my wallet. Maybe he will wake up and give me that story. I can't see any sign of other reporters here so maybe all is not lost on our exclusive just yet.

But I can't face going in to the office, especially without a story. I'm already late, so I may as well take a detour to check on Charlie Chaplin. Yes! Why not? If Gareth wants to bollock me, he'll do so no matter how late I am, so what difference will another half hour make?

I'm off to find a kitten and save a stew. In that order. Stomach rumbling, I turn my key and hit the road to Mr Clark's cottage, the thought of my little detour giving me a much-needed something to look forward to.

CHAPTER 3

'Morning Mary! So, what have I missed?'

We share our cleaner, Mary, with the rest of the offices in this building, which means she can be hard to catch. She has polished this floor and wiped these railings for nearly thirty years, and I'm still convinced she's a top-secret spy with a very poor sense of direction, hence why she gathers intelligence in Newbridge, mainly for me. She's my best ear to the ground and like a morning Twitter feed, she tells me what's trending in the area. And she is spot on one hundred per cent of the time. She wouldn't dream of ever telling me her sources, but whoever they are, they're solid. I'd nearly say she knew Mr Clark won the lottery before he did.

Mary glances over each shoulder to be sure no one else is in earshot and then hands me a Post-it note in her hallmark loopy handwriting. 'Never a dull moment round here,' she says. 'The theatre club are doing an open call for auditions; they want a shake-up, new blood, fresh meat. The new director has taken over, ripped up the *Fawlty Towers* script and told them they are doing *A Midsummer Night's Dream*. Never heard of it. He's very up himself, this new fella, Julian he's called. Moved here with his husband Luiz, a sound engineer from Brazil. They have a "vision".' Her tongue slides over her top lip. 'They want everyone who is anyone to access high-quality theatre and not miss out just because they live on the wrong side of the motorway.'

I smile at Mary; she doesn't half get people to open up. She could teach Piers Morgan a thing or two.

She taps the Post-it note. 'What else? Ah yes, red bobble hat found in the first pew at the church. Good quality, cashmere I believe. Not cheap, so we're looking for a stylish Catholic female in upper income bracket, aged sixty-plus. Possibly recently bereaved as one candle was lit near the scene. Suspected time of loss approx. 3.30 p.m. If no one claims it by next Friday, it'll be redistributed or destroyed.'

This is what I love about this community; a lost bobble hat constitutes a public appeal.

I squint down at the last point. Her penmanship is a little rushed, so it's hard to work out the letters.

She peers at the Post-it note herself. 'High importance this one! A reminder from the dog warden – the red disposal box beside the park gates is for dog poo, not for posting letters! He found four small parcels and a postcard in there yesterday. So that's more of a public service announcement.'

I fold the Post-it note in two and pop it into my top pocket. 'Thanks, as always, Mary. Come up and see me later for a cup of tea if you like.'

She nods and waves me off. No doubt already on the hunt for the next big story.

I enter the lift to the *Newbridge Gazette* offices and use the five-second ascent to straighten myself up in the panelled and unflattering elevator mirror. I smell of iodine and I've forgotten to wear eye make-up again, so I look like Gollum. But everyone I work with is used to that and they're used to me, so it's not like they'll look up from their screens as I whizz by. I lick a finger and smooth my eyebrows into place, smell my armpits – which are passable – and notice a long ladder in my black tights working from my knee downwards. Typical. I must have nicked it as I knelt down on the gravel to coax Chaplin out from under Mr Clark's car. This just means I'll be forced to stay seated most of the day and if the hole expands so much that I look like I'm wearing fishnets, I'll slide them off and go bare-legged, treating my lucky co-workers to a glimpse of my spiky, sunless legs.

The lift slows to a halt and just before the doors open, I sneak a peek into my handbag and smile. Of all the unexpected things that may have tested me and tried to throw me off course this morning, this one has proved a pleasant surprise. So, today of all days, I'm aiming for invisibility and for everyone to ignore me and gloss over my lateness and torn tights and drugged-up-looking eyes and lack of lottery story. Today is a day to just show up, keep my head down, then clock off and get me and the contents of my oversized handbag home.

Stepping out of the lift, I'm relieved and also a little surprised to see our open-plan office is a hive of activity. Something is going on; I hope it's news, as in real news. Maybe Mr Clark has woken up and wants me to come back for that exclusive!

I turn excitedly towards the huddle by the water cooler.

'Nice of you to join us this morning, Lily,' says Gareth, zoning in on the ladder in my tights.

I tighten my grip on the handle of my handbag and purse my lips at him. 'I was following up a story. Should have something later today. If not, I'll come up with something else,' I tell him, thinking about Mary's tip-offs. None of which really scream at me that they're going to save the fate of the paper, but it's this kind of community content that keeps our remaining readership ticking over.

As there's nothing special or newsworthy happening after all, just the usual boy's club, I sidestep the water cooler and move towards my desk. But just as I dip my head and step forwards, an uncharacteristically fast-moving temp cuts across me, handing an email print-out to Gareth.

I watch as the blood drains from his face. He reads it twice, turns it over and then raises it up in the air. 'What the hell? When did you get this?'

'Yesterday, sir. It was marked urgent – you know with one of those little red exclamation marks in the subject line, so I thought I better bring it to your attention straight away.'

'Yesterday? Twelve hours later is not STRAIGHT AWAY!'

She shrugs and chews her gum.

'Right, whatever. There's no time now. It's fucking McArthur,' he says, handing the paper to the nearest of the water-cooler gang. 'Read that – does it say what I think it says? That she's actually coming. Here. In person this time?'

All ten fingers scratch at his scalp. Gareth's neck is now a different colour to his face, darker, purpler. Veinier. Reminds of me of why I don't eat turkey.

The water-cooler guys pass it around, nod, hands on their hips, all eyes down.

'Are you sure?' Gareth tries again, his voice now a high pitch. 'As in one hundred per cent sure?'

Mark has the letter now, he casts his eye over it, reaches out a hand and places it on Gareth's dandruff-dusted shoulder. 'Two hundred per cent. It's here in black and white. She wants to meet with the Editor in Chief regarding all aspects of business, the current operating model and a scrutiny of all accounts to date. She's bringing her accountant and a "transformational consultant". They should be here any minute.'

Transformational Consultant. I see him mouth the words, rubbing his chin hard. I don't blame him for being worried, consultants don't drop by with a bouquet and box of chocolates to congratulate you on the fine job you're doing.

'Transformational?' he mouths again, this time with a little volume. I think his throat is shrinking. It sounds like it is.

True, 'transformational' is new to me too. Maybe it's a euphemism for bringing in the heavies to beat you up and leave you disfigured because you've cocked up the share value.

'Sounds to me like the gig is up, Gareth,' says Mark in a low, slow voice. There's a glint of excitement in his eye and I can tell he's already thinking of new ways to spend his imagined redundancy cash, the dilemma of classic deep pan or hot-dog stuffed crust etched across his face.

Gareth, breathing heavily, his chest rising like the Hulk (but more puce in colour), crushes his empty plastic cup in one hand, firing it at the bin that's positioned in front of him, but still, it falls short and he misses his target. He stares at the crumpled plastic on the carpet, the temper rising from his neck into his jawline and creeping into his cheeks. He throws his hands up in the air as if it was the cup and the bin at fault, like they've conspired against him. Like everything is conspiring against him and he is utterly faultless and yet again foiled by the universe, by life, by us. And I don't pretend to be arty or deep, but I think, yep, that pretty much sums this whole thing up.

Gareth walks over to the bin and kicks it, turning to the lip-biting huddle. 'I know what you are all thinking, you know. You're thinking Lily should have got the job over me. That I shouldn't have been so dynamic, so radical. You just wanted to plod on with your small-minded news for your small-minded paper. Well, it's easy to stay the same, easy to stay in your comfort zone, in a rut. I took risks, I changed things…'

He changed things all right, just not in a way that that anyone wanted. However, I can't help but catch what he said about me just then. I never knew that Gareth saw me as a potential contender for the position of Editor in Chief. I think this is the nicest thing he's ever said to me. Even though he didn't mean to.

I feel a sudden pang of guilt and sadness for all the trees whose lives have been wasted under Gareth's editorial direction. Maybe I could be a decent Editor in Chief one day? Lord knows I know what *not* to do.

He faces me for the first time since being promoted as my boss two and a half years ago, a crazed half-smirk on his lips. 'Happy now, Lily? Bet you think you're ready to be Editor in Chief of the shittiest regional paper in the country? Believe me. You're welcome to it. It's all yours.'

'What?' I ask. 'You're quitting? Abandoning ship, just like that?'

He clicks his fingers at me. 'That's right. Just like that.'

And even though I want Gareth to leave more than anything, the fact that he's willing just to walk out and feed us to the lions infuriates me! If it wasn't for the *Newbridge Gazette*, I may never have got out of bed again after what happened with Adam. Never faced the world again. It has been an anchor, a refuge. It's never let me down. So I'm proud to be here, to have stuck around, because I take issue with abandoning things. I can't bring myself to do it; it goes against everything I believe to be the mark of a decent person, to just give up and run when things get tough. Maybe because I know what that feels like first-hand.

So instead of backing down and biting my tongue and hiding behind my screen like I normally would, I look Gareth straight in the face and say what everyone's been thinking for the last two years. 'This is your mess, Gareth! All of it is your mess.'

Carefully, I place my bag down on the desk and walk over to him, feeling the heat rise from the pit of my stomach with every step. This isn't even a decision about whether to let Gareth have it, it's coming and I can't stop it, I won't be able to swallow this anger back.

I hold out my open palms and twirl on the spot. 'At least have the decency to face the music and try to make it better! This is not a shitty regional paper! At least it wasn't before you took charge. This place used to be fantastic. How can you even sleep at night? Knowing you caused all this, that you've killed the paper and you're going to leave everyone in here without a job? And you stand there, shouting at us, telling us all how crap and pathetic we are yet you're not even brave enough to even stay and meet with McArthur?'

He presses the heels of his hands together, a manic grin on his face. 'Believe me I sleep just fine. You can't polish a turd, Lily, this paper is *done*. You're on your own, I've had as much as I can take of this cultural drip-tray. Not my circus, not my monkeys any more.'

And with that, he snatches his coat and his laptop bag from the desk and storms out the double doors. Ding Dong Gareth is gone.

The doors swing closed behind him and we all wait a second, suspended in disbelief, half expecting him to burst back in, at least to shout at us, blame us, punish us. But the doors settle in place and stay shut.

I realise it's happened. He's actually left.

And the mood shifts, the atmosphere lightens.

He really is gone. He's quit. It's over. We are on our own.

I hear a nervous laugh break the silence, and realise it's me. I catch the incredulous smiling eyes of everyone now sighing their relief, stretching out their arms, unfurling after the long hard winter of Gareth's reign.

I take a deep breath, blink my eyes and reach into my bag... and lift out my lovely new little buddy Chaplin and introduce him to the *Newbridge Gazette*. The under-new-leadership-we're-not-going-out-without-a-fight-*Newbridge Gazette*. The worst is over. Now we've got a chance. There's still time. Still hope.

I spin my little black and white kitten around to orientate him; much like us, he's probably relieved to come out of the shadows and feel a sense of freedom again. After all, what else could I do? I couldn't leave him there underneath the car waiting for Mr Clark to return at some unknown point. He could be in hospital for days, weeks even. No, it was my duty to take in Chaplin and with Gareth gone I don't need to hide him away for the day.

'So what now?' asks Mark, twisting the tuft of his beard and bringing me back to the situation at hand. I wait for someone to answer, but Mark's looking at me. 'Lily? What now? McArthur's going be here any minute. What should we do?'

Oh-kay. It looks like they expect me to know. Everyone's now turned in my direction, waiting, eyes on me. I guess this is my chance. My chance to save the paper, if it has any chance at all.

I suppose I should be thrilled. Ecstatic. This is my chance to be Editor in Chief. In the footsteps of the great JJ Oakes. That's what I always wanted, what I always thought would happen one day. But that was before La Shebang Totale and all that followed, when I was full of optimism and confidence and…

I pinch my eyes and try to stem this flow of thought, of memory. My head feels very light all of a sudden. I grab a drink from the water cooler; everything is happening much too fast, everything is changing much too quickly. I gulp down the cool water, trying to focus, to anchor myself, to take a minute to register that this is really happening.

'We could take a vote?' I offer, opening my eyes. 'On who meets with McArthur? On who takes over as editor? So we can at least appear like a professional outfit when she gets here?'

My name echoes around the room and a sea of hands fly upwards.

'Looks like a unanimous decision.' Mark shrugs one shoulder at me. 'Lily? Are you happy to meet with McArthur as acting Editor in Chief?'

Am I happy? Am I ready?

Mark looks down at the watch on his wrist. 'Lily? What do you say?'

I hear a soft meow from Chaplin as he sidles up against my leg. I scoop him up and watch the smiles break the faces of my colleagues. It is the first time I've seen everybody smile. There are some people here I've never really seen at all.

'Lily? What do you say?' Mark asks me again; he needs an answer. We all do.

'I say okay. I say let's do this.'

And the room erupts in applause.

Chaplin in the crook of my elbow, I climb up and stand on the Editor in Chief's desk. *My* new desk.

'Right, this is a new page for the *Newbridge Gazette*. Everything begins now. We are going to save this paper. We will restore it to its former glory. *Exceed* its former glory.'

Mark grits his teeth, flexing his jaw. 'With respect, Lily, I think we need you to go in there and negotiate our redundancies. This is the ideal time to get out. Local papers are a thing of the past. We can't compete with social media and national news streams. McArthur knows all about our plummeting sales, she's here to shut us down. And, I for one, am happy to take the money and run.'

But there's no way I'm giving up now, now way I'm backing down.

'Then you should,' I tell him sharply. 'You should take the money and run, Mark, because we have a lot to do and we can't carry anyone who's not with us wholeheartedly.'

He runs his fingers through his hair, 'I mean, don't get me wrong, I'd love it if someone came with a magic wand and could turn this whole situation around. I like it here, I grew up in this town, but we can't fight the inevitable; local newspapers just don't have a place in today's world. It's over. The internet is not going away. How can we compete with national news, world news, fake news...'

'That's exactly it!' I cry. 'People are getting tired of knowing who to trust online, tired of being bombarded with news that doesn't hold meaning for them personally. Society is looking much more inwardly, buying local, supporting small business and seeking out ways to invest in their immediate surroundings. In-depth, factual, accurate reporting, that uses official sources as its basis is what they pay for and what we deliver. You can get your Facebook friend's ill-informed opinion for no charge. You can read conflicting internet stories all day, every day and still not know what to believe. We are potentially at the start of a revolution that could see the local press have a resurgence. This could be the most important time for the *Gazette* yet!'

I survey the dozen staff members in front of me, their faces full of anticipation. Or is that trepidation? Why is it that contrary feelings often look exactly the same?

'So, by committing to working your asses off to save this paper and its 126 years of history, you are completing a circle that brings innumerable benefits to the people who live and work in your community.'

Silence. Lip-biting. Thoughtful inhalations and wrist-grabbing.

'Oh – and just to clarify, the *Gazette* has no money at all. If this paper folds, we're all out on our ears. There'll be no redundancy, no severance package on the table to help cushion the blow. No craft beer kick-start. No cash for pizza and FIFA in your pants. Just a goodbye and good luck as they turn out the lights and close the door for good.'

I wait, holding my breath in my chest, expecting some to bow their heads, murmur their apologies and shuffle backwards out the door. But they don't. Nobody does. Not even Mark. Not even the gum-chewing temp. I raise my eyebrow at her, just so she's sure.

'I'm Jasmine,' she says as she steps forward, reaching up and tickling under Chaplin's chin. 'I knew that email was urgent. I just hated Gareth's guts,' she tells me with a wink, opening both hands to receive Chaplin as I climb down from the desk.

'Well, Jasmine, great to have you on board,' I tell her as I hand her Mr Clark's purring little fluff ball and knit my fingers together as I take in just what happened. 'So what does everyone else think? Are you with me?'

Shrugs, smiles, nodding, resounding yeahs rise from the huddle.

Oh-kay. She's staying. They're all staying. Maybe I underestimated them. Maybe they love this place as much as I do. Or, more likely, they're skint. Either way, it doesn't matter why they're here, we're in it together. Ready or not.

I've convinced them to stay and that this place is worth fighting for, but can I convince McArthur? Is it already too late? Wanting to save the paper is only the beginning, how we're going do that is another matter entirely.

My hand grabs the back of my neck and I suddenly feel a little dizzy. I think I got carried away; I think I've set our sights too high; I think I've just climbed into a pressure cooker and sealed myself inside.

I spot Mary through the glass panels. She gives me a thumbs-up and a wink. There's a look on her face that tells me she's watched this whole thing play out. I stand, dazed and overwhelmed a moment. Until I hear a knock on the glass and Mary claps her hands together as if to tell me to get a move on. I blink myself alert and clap my hands in the same gesture.

'Right, folks, tidy up your areas, we're expecting the owner of the entire company and some very important people anytime now. And I don't know what they will ask of us, but we have to be ready, we have to show them that whatever it takes, we're prepared to do it. There is still hope, guys, but we've got to fight.'

Mark cranes his neck towards the car park. 'Black Mercedes just pulled up. Two guys getting out the back... one's young, one's bald... and now a small, silver-haired woman.'

That's McArthur and her team.

Here comes the storm.

CHAPTER 4

McArthur and her team burst in without greeting or introduction, parading past us all with stacks of files and folders. They head directly to the conference room shutting the door firmly behind them. They're scary. This is scary. I take a long, deep breath and try to summon the courage to point myself in the right direction and put one foot in front of the other in their wake. I'm the Editor in Chief. It's my job now to do stuff like this. The whole staff is counting on me. They put their faith in me. I can't let them down at the very first hurdle! I repeat affirmations over and over in my head, as advised by Tony Robbins, Rhonda Byrne and all the other Law of Attraction guru books my mum left under the sink in the cottage loo.

This is going to work, this is going to work, this is going to work...

But despite signalling the universe, what if it doesn't work? What if all my pleas and promises fall on deaf ears and they shut us down anyway?

Well, then something else will turn up, something else will turn up, something else will turn up...

But it might not be in local news or within commuting distance from the cottage or with enough salary to cover my basics. I've already accepted two pay cuts in the last few years, which makes me the only Editor in Chief to date to take on more responsibility for less cash. But still, this isn't about the money. I don't need much to live on here in Newbridge these days. I live simply, I eat simply, I dress simply, i.e. I eat the same stuff in the same order wearing roughly the same clothes week on week.

I wasn't always this way, as my lovingly catalogued archive of *Jolie* magazines would suggest. I used to pore over them, often over the kitchen table with my granny, finding inspiration for everything, from how to make home-made preserves to how to wear animal print without looking like mutton, and from achieving frizz-free hair to in-depth features on how people overcame tremendous obstacles to achieve their wildest dreams – housewives that became opera singers and gap-year students that found ways to raise thousands for charity. *Jolie* magazine was my absolute favourite. My gran bought me a subscription every year for my birthday, so I never missed one. I think that's why she encouraged me to go for the job at the *Gazette* in the first place, that maybe it could lead to writing for a glossy publication like *Jolie* one day. She was sweet like that, always believing that I could do well, that things would work out if I kept trying my best.

But so much has changed since then. After my disastrous wedding day – heavily inspired by the beautiful weddings I'd seen in *Jolie* – I dropped out of socialising altogether, for two main reasons. Adam and Hannah were my closest friends and the only ones I used to go out with and my granny became ill, so I stayed close by to care for her until she slipped away, one golden autumn evening, in her sleep. I didn't renew my *Jolie* subscription. I'd no real need for new lipsticks or sky-high stilettos or reading up on must-see holiday destinations. Instead of making me happy, it just made me feel worse. So now my weekends roll like this: I read books, I sleep, I potter around the cottage. My only real indulgences are chocolate and stationery. I cannot resist a creamy caramel heart or a hazelnut swirl or a pretty new notebook, but what I do need is a purpose, a job, a place I belong. Because the *Gazette* is the only slice of life I've really got going on. We have to show McArthur that, whatever it takes, we're prepared to make the changes and put this paper back in business. I accept my life isn't much, but it's comfortable and safe and it is mine. All mine.

And without the *Gazette*, I don't know what it would look like. And I do not like the idea of that.

I slope off to cool down and check myself out in the full-length communal toilet mirror. I'm not strutting catwalk confidence today. *Jolie* readers worldwide would recoil in horror. I finger-comb my hair and pin it into a makeshift chignon with a refashioned paper clip. My face is okay as long as I keep smiling. Torso will do, draped in standard-issue office wear: light pink blouse, black jacket and skirt suit. But things go downhill from there – my tights are ripped, and in terms of projecting the right message, I may as well go in with spinach stuck between my teeth. I could slip them off and turn them round so that the ladder is at the back of my calves and I might just get away with it and go unnoticed, but I then risk making the hole much bigger in the process of taking them on and off again. No, too risky. I rummage in my bag for inspiration and, lo and behold, a black felt-tip marker finds its way into my grasp. I smile at myself in the mirror. Something did turn up. If I can't fix my tights, I'll have to blend the ladder into the background. And so I do what any girl would do in a professional do or die situation: I colour in my leg.

I'm impressed with my black-out camouflage artistry. The ladder is now undetectable, unless you're on your hands and knees scrutinising my hosiery. And if it gets to that, then the *Newbridge Gazette* is well and truly done for.

As satisfied as I can be with my appearance, I head out of the toilets, but instead of taking a seat outside the Conference Room, I pace up and down the office, restless with knowing just how important the next hour or so is. Jobs like this are rare outside the cities. Even more rare for the likes of me as I'm not a 'proper' journalist – as in formally qualified. What I am is a super-nosy administrator with lots of energy who happens to be passionate about reading and writing. I left school with a fistful of C grades and a report that celebrated my averageness. And as

JJ is now retired and Gareth has jumped ship, I have no solid references to go forward with.

So starting over somewhere else is not an option; I need this job. I need to convince McArthur that there's life in this paper yet.

I brainstorm possibilities, what can we do? What can be done? I sit back down, take out my little notebook and start scribbling down ideas and bullet points.

But I don't get very far because I hear raised voices outside and look out the window down to the car park. A tall, dark, messy-haired man is waving an arm in the air whilst in deep conversation with a gesticulating ponytailed blonde in yoga pants. Something in the way they are shaking their heads while talking to the sky, to the ground, to their own hands, tells me they are not arguing over a parking space. It looks heated, emotional. The blonde girl's fingers are set claw-like, as if she's about to pounce on him and tear him apart. A security guard emerges on to the car park and I'm relieved someone is around to de-escalate. I have to say, this kind of public argument isn't rare outside our local pub, The Black Boar, at closing time on a Friday night, but it is extremely unusual in an office car park in broad daylight midweek.

I turn from the window; I don't like rows and I don't like playing voyeur to other peoples' misery. I was once the girl that everyone was gawping at; I felt every blatant pitiful stare and every uncomfortable darting glance. On the street, in the supermarket, in the café, people I hardly knew gave me unsolicited advice about 'moving on' and 'bouncing back'. Yet people I had known for years and who I considered to be my friends avoided me altogether. Maybe they didn't know what to say, or maybe they felt they had to take sides and chose Adam and Hannah over me. But I've learnt to shut this particular circuit of thought down. No point. No resolution. No joy. That's why I would rather run a story on the have-a-go hero that wrestled a seagull to the ground when it attacked a one-armed man's chips. I like that kind of thing. It makes me smile. Reminds me to look out for the often unreported best in people. And I figure I can't be the only one who feels that way.

I hear the door click and watch the handle turn from the inside. The sight of it sends my nerves into sudden overdrive – I want this so much, my stomach is sloshing like a washing machine; a loud, annoying washing machine that needs servicing. Dear God, I hope she can't hear it.

McArthur's straight silver bob rounds the door. 'I have to say, you don't look much like a Gareth. Where is he then?' she booms in a smoky, no-nonsense voice.

I straighten my back and swallow, trying to keep my voice steady and in control, not like I'm delivering further damning news about how chaotic and crazy things have become. 'Gareth's gone. He walked out on us this morning. I'd like to say I'm sorry to see him go, but, actually, leaving us is the best thing Gareth has ever done for this paper. So, I've stepped in to meet you instead.'

She narrows her eyes to study my face and I feel her try to size me up.

I thrust my hand out in an attempt to avert her gaze from my torn tights. 'My name is Lily Buckley. Acting Editor in Chief as of this morning.'

'Right, the plot thickens. I mean, does anyone know what's actually going on around here from one minute to the next?' She sighs and turns in to the office, still ranting with her back to me. 'The office is clearly as out of order as the figures. This paper is just one giant headless chicken…'

I follow her in and sit on the chair in the middle of the floor, now facing McArthur as she sits behind the long walnut table. A stern-looking man is already standing to her left with an overflowing stack of papers in front of him. He does not even acknowledge me.

McArthur glares at me and knits her fingers together. 'Look, I'm not here to pull any punches. I was hoping it wouldn't come to this, but the way things stand, I can't see an alternative. You hire people to run something, you trust them, you leave them to it and what do they do? Strip out all that was good and replace it with dull, boring, irrelevant junk.' She flicks a silver strand away from her face. 'Well, today that stops. I've brought in my most trusted advisors to work out what the hell's been going on and where the hell we go from here.'

I nod to this tour de force, the real-life Mags McArthur with her swirling platinum bob and dark plum lips. No wrinkles. No eyebrows. Her pale blue eyes peer over the mounds of her cheekbones like a jungle cat. And I then nod towards the guy behind her – smart blue suit, heavy-set, bald, mid-fifties – who doesn't look up at me at all but sighs and rubs his nose with the back of his hand. He's immersed in stacks of cardboard folders, two laptop screens, a calculator and an open filing cabinet. His entire hairless head is glistening with perspiration.

'That's Jennings. He's my accountant and a dog with a bone right now.'

Jennings and McArthur continue to flick through ledgers and print-outs from accounts, crossing out entire pages with red pen, squinting and circling tiny typed numbers, lots of head shaking, lots of lip biting. All I can do is sit still and wait. Which is really hard and awkward. I cross and uncross my legs. Try not to pick my nails or breathe in an annoying way. Which is hard when you're gasping for air in a room that is too stuffy and too quiet. How long is this going to go on for?

'Where the hell is Christopher, our oh-so promising transformational consultant?' McArthur queries Jennings.

'Last I saw, he had some rather urgent-looking business with Victoria in the car park.' Jennings pushes out his bottom lip. 'Looked… and sounded… rather intense from where I was standing.'

He must be referring to the man arguing in the car park. Who knew *that* was the transformational consultant who was supposed to save the paper?

McArthur rolls her eyes and shakes her head with blatant exasperation. 'All that nonsense belongs in the bedroom, not the boardroom.'

My sentiments exactly. I think I'm going to enjoy working closely with Mags McArthur. If I get the chance, that is.

'Christopher claims that he is desperate to move up the ladder, totally committed to this process and then we get this.' She signals to an empty chair beside her. 'Anyway, back to business.' She socks her fist into her other hand and glances down at my personnel file open in front of her, a snigger on her lips. 'Liliana Bluebell Buckley.'

A flush of red rushes into my cheeks. I hate that my mother gave me this ridiculous middle name, like she was naming a pet or a doll or something else that only reflected her own whims and quirks. Bluebell was actually supposed to be my first name, but after a tense stand-off, thankfully my grandmother talked my mother out of it on the steps of the birth registration office. Her other top choices were Infinity and Aura. No thought to the fact that I'd be branded by this name for the rest of my life; even as a second name I've never quite got used to the interminable wincing from everyone in authority – passport controllers to bank clerks. Being taken seriously in this industry without university qualifications is tricky enough without this 'fanciful name' distraction. People squirm when they read it aloud to me. Correction, we squirm together.

'I prefer Lily,' I tell her.

She nods and peers back down at my file and just then the door opens and in comes the messy-haired man from the car park. He looks even messier than before, his glasses are lop-sided and I see they're broken at the hinge, almost to the point of snapping off altogether. He doesn't really fit the profile of what I imagined a high-flying transformational consultant would be. I thought he'd be older and slicker and more meticulous about his corporate appearance. But hey, what do I know? McArthur and her team are the experts. Maybe he's here because he is so different from the normal grey-suited blank-faced consultants. The ones that sit on their laptops, don't say anything for three days and then rip us to shreds in a lengthy report which no one quite understands. Maybe this guy breaks the mould. Maybe that's why he's so 'transformational'.

'Ah, Christopher, you've made it.' McArthur frowns. 'Wasn't sure you could fit us in, so we started without you. This is our current Editor in Chief, Lily Buckley.'

I stand up to shake his hand. He doesn't flinch. I can only presume that he doesn't realise that Gareth has left and been so swiftly replaced. Or maybe he doesn't care?

'I'm Christopher. Pleased to meet you,' he says in a very well-spoken voice, gentle and deliberate, slightly breathless. 'Apologies for being late, I had some unexpected business to attend to, I'm afraid.'

Mags McArthur shoots him a look. 'I can guess.'

I realise that I'm staring, his bright, beautiful smile eclipsing the bed-head and crooked glasses. For some reason, I am still holding his hand, and he smiles politely as he lets go and I sit back down, my cheeks now flaring red.

'Late and tardy? Perhaps you have more to learn than I thought. You geeky types can get away with it when you're hidden behind a screen all day, but not here! That was the whole idea, to give you real-world experience. Meet real people up close and face to face. For God's sake, what the hell happened to your glasses?'

Christopher blushes and takes them off whilst running a hand over his loose dark curls to smooth them down. They spring up again despite his efforts.

McArthur blows out her cheeks and turns to Jennings. 'Transformational Consultant, eh? You're going need to transform from your bed to this office a lot quicker if you want to stay on this Fast Track Leadership Programme. You're here now, representing me and representing my interests, so smarten up, you hear me?'

My heart clenches in my chest for poor Christopher. Somehow, I always believed that 'Head Office People' never, ever got a dressing-down, that they were flawless and beyond reproach. But I can tell by the way Christopher is listening intently, taking in every word, that he's new to this role, maybe a little out of his depth too and may have even more to prove to McArthur than I have. And that's saying something. But still, his heady title of 'Transformational Consultant' was enough to send Gareth running. So, as far as I'm concerned, Christopher is already doing a fantastic job.

McArthur pouts and motions for Christopher to sit down and join us. He swings himself behind the table, still holding his wonky glasses out in front of him, puzzling at the broken hinge.

I catch his eye and point to the desk tidy right by his hand. 'Sticky tack please,' I whisper.

He furrows his brow in confusion, pushes out his bottom lip, but still, he does as I ask and passes it over to me.

'And glasses,' I add, palm out in front of him.

And again, he co-operates.

With my trusty black felt-tip, I colour in the sticky tack and then mould it around the broken hinge of his glasses, evening out both arms. I hand the glasses back to him, he slides them on and smiles.

'Straight and secure.'

McArthur curls her lip in bemusement. 'Well, that's rather clever, Millie.'

'Lily.' Christopher corrects, his eyes on mine. 'I think I can take things from here.' He slides a hand over to my file and pulls it towards him. 'If I may?'

McArthur blinks her permission.

'So, Lily, tell me your strengths and weaknesses,' he begins.

Okay, this is it. My chance to prove myself, to show them that not only am I willing to take on the Editor in Chief position, but I'm ready for it. I can do this.

'I'd have to be honest and say my weakest area is anything political, or sport-related. And while I can produce tag lines, headings and short pieces, I haven't much experience of writing long articles.'

None, actually. I tried a few, but Gareth sent them back to me saying they weren't right for us and maybe I should remember that it's adverts that pay our wages but I don't want to undersell myself before I've even had a chance to show them what I could do, if only they'd give me the opportunity.

'How about features?' Christopher asks.

I pause a moment and glance at McArthur and Jennings. They're not looking at me at all, both head down in paperwork.

I swallow and answer Christopher with a smile. 'I've had lots of ideas but none of them made it to print unfortunately, so I've not published any features yet. Mostly I cover local news and events, social and human interest pieces. But I'd love to. I would absolutely love to write features. I've been gagging to do them since forever!'

'Gagging?' he repeats, eyebrow raised. His eyes are distracting: dark green, with flecks of light brown, like olives.

'Yes. I mean to say, it's an area I am keen to develop.' My cheeks flare red. This is an interview. I've got to appear professional, use the right words, sound like I've got the skills and the experience they need. I take a sip of water to compose myself.

He nods and rubs his chin, listening to my every word, scribbling down notes in a notepad just like mine. From across the table, I can't make out anything he's written. Although his spoken words are soft and clear and perfectly formed, his handwriting is as erratic and indecipherable as a doctor's prescription. 'Please continue.'

For a second there, I forgot that I am supposed to be the one doing the talking.

Focus Lily, focus! But I can't remember the question. I've been dreaming about olives. I never noticed how gorgeous and rare a colour they were till…

'Your strengths…?' Christopher prompts.

'Yes! My strengths are that I am enthusiastic, organised and hard-working and loyal as a dog. I have a good ear for a story and a knack for getting to the point. I am fully committed to this paper, and can work long hours, weekends, holidays. I can travel at short notice… the perks of having no partner or kids to look after, and I can be deployed anywhere at any time.' I swallow and smile through the bittersweet reality of my availability. But it's true, I live by myself and my job's the only commitment I've got, so why not try to turn that into a positive?

'And resourceful,' adds Mags, tapping her fingernail on the desk. She's obviously been paying attention all along, the ultimate multi-tasker. She slides my file back from Christopher. 'It says here that you cut your teeth under JJ Oakes? I rang him this morning to find out about the staff and your name stood out. He was particularly adamant that I should hold on to you. He tells me I'd be mad to let you go.'

Good ole JJ. 'That's kind of him.'

'You've been here…?'

'Seven years.'

'And you've been Editor in Chief for?'

'Just before you guys arrived.' I glance up at the clock. 'Almost ninety minutes now.'

Christopher raises a smile. 'So, let's cut to the chase… you think the *Newbridge Gazette* has a future?'

'Yes! Absolutely! I think it has so much more to give.'

Jennings jolts around from the filing cabinet and shakes his head so fast that his chins are out of sync. 'Wrong. So very, very wrong.' He spreads out a stack of old newspapers across the table between us, some curling at the corners with age. 'It's beyond terrible. In terms of our entire media portfolio, the *Newbridge Gazette* is our weakest link by far. The figures are a humiliation, they are that low. I mean, look at these stories, these headlines – "Man still alive hours before death".'

Uh-oh. I was worried this might happen. We're not perfect. We've had clangers. Editing not as tight as it ought to be. Gareth offloading too much to work experience teenagers, so he could take an extra hour for lunch. Communication breakdowns, sloppy systems, lack of direction, shitty coffee. That's low. As low as it gets.

Jennings shuffles through for more. 'Ah, here we are, the infamous Page Ten.'

That is my page! I hold my breath and dig my fingernails into my palms...

'"Local Cemetery deemed a Death Trap".'

'That headline got the stinging nettles cut back... it's much better now.' I know because my lovely granny is buried there.

But Jennings keeps going. '"OAP reveals his 2ft courgette".'

'It was massive. It was longer than my arm...' I push up my sleeve to my elbow and stretch out my left arm for full effect.

I glance at Jennings' clean short nails and soft, uncalloused hands, guessing that as he is from the city he may not fully appreciate how hard it is to plant and grow anything from scratch and keep it alive. I tried a herb garden last year and it was annihilated by slugs. The only plant I now own is plastic. So, hats off to that OAP. Two foot is bloody impressive!

'And then there's this,' Jennings winces. '"Toilet Curse Strikes Again!"... I don't even want to know.'

Christopher takes the last paper from him and continues reading. He laughs out loud and bites into his knuckle. '"Dog that looks EXACTLY like Chewbacca – exclusive pictures inside!"'

I redden. That one was mine too. But it was well-received. And I stand by it because that dog was cute. It deserved coverage; even during election week.

McArthur straightens her back. 'Okay, enough already. I've pored over every edition that's gone out over the last twenty-three months, and you know what? Page ten is the only decent page in the whole paper. At least it offers something engaging, something innovative. The rest is just so… dull, so boring, tedious and bland, it reads like flat-pack instructions.'

This sounds like praise but I can't be sure by her tone. Or her face.

She heaves a deep sigh. 'Lily, you've been here seven years, you can't say you think the current situation is working?'

I open my mouth to answer but stop as Christopher slaps his hand down on the table, chuckling to himself.

'This page ten stuff is great, how about this one – "One-armed man applauds kindness of strangers", or this one "Woman who ran naked into a cactus! Pictures inside!" It's like *The One Show* meets *Viz*. Genuinely, I love it. It's got character, I think it's great.'

The consultant from London thinks my page is great? Genuinely?

I try to read his expression, but there is no trace of sarcasm. His eyes are still creased in a smile. He should be an eye model. That green is mesmeric.

He laughs again before turning the page. I feel a swell of gratitude and pride. Actually, I shuffle in my seat and try to control my next breath, slow it down, don't give away too much, don't appear amateur. But the truth is, this tiny spark of praise, of encouragement, has made me feel a little emotional – but I cannot let that happen! Not here, not in front of these hardballers, at my first meeting, on my first morning as Editor in Chief!

I blink rapidly and shift my eyes away from Christopher's lovely, soft, smiling features and focus on a spot on the wall behind his head. I've got to hold it together because I could so gush right now. I could fling back this chair, run around to his side of the table, grab him by the shoulders and say thank you, thank you, thank you! Thank you for being so kind about my work, for 'getting' this, for 'getting' *me*. For making the last three years not feel such an epic failure on every front. That I was doing something meaningful, something worthwhile. It feels a really long time since anyone's 'got' me, or cared to try. And it's taken me aback a little more than I realised it ever could. I didn't know I was missing that but it feels so lovely, now I know I certainly was. I swallow and focus on McArthur. If anyone will snap you out of succumbing to a deluge of the feels, it's her.

McArthur isn't laughing or smiling, she just keeps flexing her fingers as if she might punch something. Or someone. 'You are a proper city boy, aren't you? There is a world outside zone 2, Christopher, and these stories, this coverage, is our bread and butter.' I'm quickly learning that McArthur is harsh, even when she agrees with something. I wouldn't like to see her reaction if you got something wrong. 'The latest market research says our readers want more of this, they want more human interest stories. Those that still buy the paper do so for page ten alone! But the rest, I mean, how many second-hand cars can there be?'

Wow. That's good! That's superb! Page Ten is the *Newbridge Gazette*'s way forward! And even McArthur seems to be on board. I've got to move with this one positive aspect immediately before they lose sight of it.

'OK. Is the *Gazette* in a crappy place right now? Yes!' I say, straightening my collar and acting like I'm a serious journalist, ready to cut the bullshit and lay all the cards on the table. 'But it's still got what every other paper out there hasn't got – a community that will get behind us if we listen to them and act on what they are telling us. It's the paper for people who don't necessarily read national newspapers. It used to be part of the tradition around here for people – and those people are still here! They still want to know about the lives of their friends and neighbours, they want to connect and support each other. And that's where we come in. It's what we do. We can make that happen. We're small and we're proud and we have the least direct market competition out there.'

Jennings coughs into his fist.

I speak up a notch louder, because I'm not finished. If I get Jennings on side, maybe I'll have a better chance with McArthur. 'And, okay, our figures are lower than recorded in the previous years. But that's just because we lost our way, we forgot what we were about and instead we treated our readers like idiots and padded out the pages with ads and announcements and boring bits. But now we're all on the same page, we can get it back on its feet! This is not the time to shut up shop. We are truly unique, and we serve the uniqueness of our community. Who else can say that? Not the *Mail*. Not the *Herald*. Certainly not the *Chronicle*. Just us, because we are truly independent. And I think now is the time to build on this and relaunch and come back better than ever.'

Now its Jennings' turn to take my CV. It's hard to read the expression on his chubby, studious features, but I sense interest, possibility. I seize on it.

'This paper just needs someone who believes in it, someone who understands that a regional platform is an invaluable resource. The *Newbridge Gazette* is an everyman newspaper. No story is too low or too high to reach for.' I hear JJ Oakes' voice booming in my ear. And for the first time in ever so long, I feel a little spark of hope returning. Maybe it's not too late for things to get better. Maybe we're just at the beginning of something special. Maybe this is exactly what we've all been waiting for: a second chance.

Jennings meets my gaze head on, shifting his weight to his back leg. 'No offence, Lily, but you've never been an Editor in

Chief before. You're too young. You're inexperienced – you've never worked beyond these four walls. And,' he runs a finger over my CV, 'your education, it's a mishmash of diplomas and short courses and evening classes… With respect, it's hardly reading English at Oxford, is it?'

Christopher swallows hard and opens his mouth to speak, clearly offended on my behalf, but I don't need him or anyone else to stand up for me. I can do that for myself. Especially when this man doesn't even know me.

'With respect, Mr Jennings, why on earth would we need someone from Oxford to tell the readers of Newbridge what's going on… in Newbridge?'

He doesn't answer me. But he does look a little taken aback at being questioned.

'And, for the record, I do most of my work outside of these four walls. I was at the hospital this morning interviewing a lottery winner. Yesterday, I was at the opening of the new train platform. Every single day, I am out and about finding the stories that people want to read about.'

Jennings pauses and hooks his thumbs into his belt, pressing his chins against his neck. Mags stifles a tight smile.

I continue, 'The *Newbridge Gazette* needs someone who believes it can succeed. Someone who has not forgotten that it used to be at the top of its game. Stuff has gone wrong, but it's survived and we can learn from our mistakes. And I know you have little reason to believe in me, but I work harder than anyone else. I'm in first and out last each day and I devote myself completely to my job. You can ask anyone.' I pause to catch my breath. 'I know I haven't been Editor in Chief long, but I learnt a lot under JJ Oakes and I just know I can do this if you give me the chance. You said yourself that people want page ten and page ten is what I do. I *am* page ten.' There! Have that!

I am met with three blank faces.

Mags swings around to Christopher, who appears lost in thought. Or zoned out? She nudges him. 'Christopher, perhaps you have some thoughts? Observations? Contributions? Insights?'

'Yes.' He clears his throat and makes a steeple of his hands. 'Many, many of all of those things.'

Okay, we've clearly lost him. Christopher has mentally left the room.

McArthur breathes through her nose. 'Well come on! Spit them out, boy.'

He shakes the glazed look from his eyes and opens his mouth. I don't think he's been listening to me rambling on and I imagine he's just going to make up some corporate gobbledygook right now to dig himself out of this.

My heart sinks a little. What a shame! For a second there I really thought he was interested, that he was different and that maybe we could even start to make a difference. Like Jennings, he obviously thinks I'm not up to this, that they need someone with more qualifications, more potential. They probably have someone already in mind from the London office ready to swoop in and kick ass.

He takes his jotter in one hand and adjusts his wonky glasses. 'Well, everything Lily said makes perfect sense – we do already have an established circulation, no known competitors at present. However, we have also faced increasing production costs and a tough print advertising market. Our biggest challenge is re-engaging with our previous readership while also attracting new readers. This should make us financially viable once again. But how likely is that in a short turnaround time?'

Is that a yes or a no? He's talking in riddles. Consultant riddles.

Jennings opens his hands and bites down on his bottom lip. 'I'm pleasantly surprised; that's a good grasp of it, Christopher – well done.' Then he turns to me. 'So, you heard it there, Lily, despite your passion – which I must admit that I admire – it's the end of the road.'

End. Of. The. Road. I go to say something, except I can't find the words. Because there are times in life when you put *everything* into something and it vanishes like it was nothing, just completely valueless, and then there are no words. Or you don't have the energy to find them.

'If you'd be so kind as to allow me to finish…' Christopher cuts across him. 'If we incorporated a presence in the digital space, we might just be able to fix things.'

Fix things as in make them better or fix things as in sell us off or shut us down? I can't figure out if he's backing me or not.

McArthur turns to face Christopher, clearly intrigued by what he has to say. 'Go on.'

'Move the paper online and establish a digital edition to increase reach. That way we can generate more content and appeal to wider and more targeted audiences with minimum costs. Pictures, photos, features, interactions, competitions, social media networks… we want to take page ten and expand it. More photos of the gargantuan vegetables, and the naked cactus lady, it's exactly what we need.' He says, his glasses now lopsided again as he gets more animated. He's talking so quickly, scribbling down notes and doodles with arrows and circles everywhere, running a hand through his hair with excitement.

Excitement! He sees it, he feels it – if this paper has any chance, it's Christopher. I've got to say, I'm excited too, and relieved. As much as I want this to work, I could really use someone like him to support me. Managing the team as well as the content and development is a huge job alongside everything else I'll have to do as Editor in Chief – it would be amazing if Christopher got stuck in here, to have someone to bounce ideas off, someone to run things by, someone to get excited with…

'It'd need an ambitious and fearless Editor in Chief, I couldn't implement this alone, Lily?' he turns to me, his green eyes bright with possibility and something else indiscernible. Hope?

This morning everything seemed to be sliding from bad to worse, but now, there's this. Maybe this is the beginning of something better, not just for the paper but, I daresay, for me? I spend so much of my life at work, that feeling happy here could have a ripple effect. It's time for a change, a change for the better, and I want that more than I realised.

With both thumbs, Christopher taps and scrolls at lightning speed on his phone before turning the screen to me. 'Our stats say fifty per cent of residents in this area are under thirty-five years old. We need to reflect that and carry content that engages them. We want to reach out to the bored commuter, the student dreaming of their gap year, the office worker wanting some excitement and escapism while they have their sandwich in the park.'

Everyone is nodding now, even Jennings, our bald accountant. He turns to McArthur, with what looks almost like a smile on his lips. 'It's got legs, in fact this could be a nice platform to advertise the other networks too.'

McArthur slices her hand through the air to silence us. 'Okay, I've heard enough. I've made my decision. This is what works for me. Christopher, we know you're clever with tech and talk, but if you ever want to progress to the next level, you need some grassroots experience.' Her finger points out to the main office. 'And you can't get more grassroots than what you've got out there. You'll work with Lily to bring about a…' She looks to Jennings.

A revolution! A 360 degree change! An incredible, life-enhancing paradigm shift!

'Twenty-two per cent increase,' he replies without blinking.

'A twenty-two per cent increase in the next four weeks. That's about twelve thousand new readers,' McArthur confirms.

Christopher raises an eyebrow. 'That's three thousand new readers every week? In a semi-rural area? That's pretty challenging by anyone's estimation.'

Thinking on these figures, I wonder if I've pulled a Gareth here and over-promised only to under-deliver. No matter how much I want this to work, is it possible to achieve this? Is it just wishful thinking that we can really pick up so many new readers in such a short space of time with the resources we've got? Is this do-able or have I even deluded myself on this one?

McArthur leans towards us. 'Bottom line. If the *Newbridge Gazette* has the future Lily says it has, it really needs to prove that; not just to me and Jennings, but to the shareholders who are fully awake to that fact that they are haemorrhaging money at this rate. Twenty-two per cent in four weeks, any less than that and it's game over; for the *Gazette* and for your Leadership Programme.'

I dart a glance over to Christopher and try to offer a reassuring smile. Not only does he have to prove himself in a new role with a team that don't know him, but he's got a very tough, black and white target to reach in an insanely tight amount of time. And if he doesn't succeed, he's failed his leadership program and the paper really does reach The. End. of. The. Road. I shudder at the thought. What will I do? What will that mean for me? Rejection after rejection at interviews based on my lack of qualifications. That's if I even get any interviews.

Um, no pressure then.

Christopher pinches his lips and nods.

McArthur takes a deep breath and directs her eyes to mine. 'Lily, you'll remain our new Editor in Chief for the time being until we know where we stand. You need to make a name for yourself. If the *Newbridge Gazette* is going into unchartered territory, then so are you.'

I brace myself. If she's given Christopher that high-wire remit, then she's not going to let me off lightly. I have absolutely no idea how this woman's mind works. She could ask anything of me, and the way things are looking, I bet I'll say yes. What choice do I have?

She taps her fingers against her chin before continuing. 'I want a weekly column, feel-good, fun Friday kind of thing; personal, original, fresh content. Human interest. There's an appetite for that and we need to supply it before someone else does.'

That sounds amazing! It'll almost be like writing for *Jolie*, although obviously without the glamour or the scope or the status or the travel opportunities or the goodie bags... But it's more than I've been allowed to do so far and it's right here in Newbridge. So that's good enough for me. I lean into the table, eager to hear more.

Jennings grimaces as if he's about to pass wind, then shouts out, 'Buckley's Bucket List!' A smile breaks his lips and McArthur nods beside him, rubbing his shoulder.

'Not bad, Jennings, turns out you are more than a numbers man. Very catchy, straightforward, says what it is on the tin. I like it.'

Jennings is grinning like a laughing Buddha.

McArthur continues, 'It needs to be serialised so they keep coming back for more. So, every Friday, I want to see a four-page feature, complete with engaging photos, quotes, all that sort of thing. That's where we'll grab the attention of this new under-thirty-five reader profile. Bucket lists sing adventure, fearlessness, indulgence...'

'This is great. More than great.' I scribble in my notebook. 'Spa days? High Tea at the Ritz? That kind of thing...?'

McArthur stops nodding and pinches her dark plum lips. 'No. This isn't Day Out With Your Granny, Lily. We want interesting, daring, things that you haven't done before. Things that you wouldn't even contemplate doing unless your life depended on it or you actually thought you were going to die anyway. Push yourself beyond your limits! That's why it's a bucket list, it's supposed to make you feel alive.'

Okay... What does that mean then? Snuggling up to big furry deadly spiders? Throwing myself off great heights? Singing to a crowd? Streaking across a football pitch? But before I even get a chance to process, never mind express my concerns, her watch beeps and flashes red.

'Right, I've got to go check my blood sugar.' McArthur slides her chair away from the desk. 'Lily and Christopher, good luck. Four weeks today, I want to see a promising online presence and a twenty-two per cent increase, okay?'

'Okay,' we echo back in unison. What other answer is there at this stage?

Okay, okay, okay. I don't really know what I've agreed to or how she is expecting us to hook in twelve thousand new readers in less than a month, but I do know what'll happen if we don't pull it all off.

Well, looks like we made it by the skin of our teeth, hopefully buying enough time to get us back up and running. But this chance hasn't come without cost. As Editor in Chief I've got a team to motivate and a new colleague in Christopher – a very attractive, very creative 'transformational' consultant – who has even less experience than me and just about as much at stake. I've got to liaise and work with him to achieve a massively ambitious target in very little time. It's hard to know where to start.

I glance over at Christopher and we share a tremulous smile. What the hell have we got ourselves into?

Almost everything is riding on the success of Buckley's Bucket List. It'll either save our butts or kill us off altogether. I shake everyone's hand and sidle into a quiet toilet cubicle for just a bit of peace, privacy and space to process all that's happened. I kick off my shoes, wriggle out of my torn tights and pull out the paper clip from my makeshift updo, finger-combing the knots out of my long, brown hair.

Despite it all, I'm happy. Genuinely happy. Because when I woke up this morning, I made a wish. I shut my eyes tight in the shower and silently wished for just one more chance to make things work.

And it looks like it's been granted.

CHAPTER 5

After such a crazy day, I leave the office for the weekend and skip home for an hour to settle a sleepy Chaplin into Oreo's old blanketed basket in the kitchen. Taking a quick shower, I change into jeans, boots and a clean vest top then short-cut across the field on foot to The Black Boar. It's the closest pub to the office and is an alternative meeting room and therapeutic hideout to imbibe and relax. Or imbibe and rant.

This is where we used to take new staff joining us and take old staff leaving us. So, it makes sense we would go tonight, I guess we're having Gareth's leaving party without him, but also it gives us a new start as a team. We've been through a lot and the fear and low morale isolated us from each other so much that we need to forge a new way forward. Believe me, there are worse ways to try to get people to work well together.

I shiver, remembering the time Gareth made us complete a lengthy questionnaire to determine what kind of workplace animal each of us was. He turned out to be a 'lion' (surprise!). And I turned out to be a 'monkey', which I had to act out in the middle of the circle. Complete with noises and gestures and facial expressions – apparently an advanced technique to overcome inhibitions and build trust and respect at a primal level. I blush at my naïvety; in those early days, I always did as I was asked, believing that he had our best interests at heart.

So, we're not doing any more of the contrived ice-breaker crap designed to make people feel stupid. Instead, we are going to sit around a corner table at The Black Boar. Everyone there of their own accord. This is important. Because I know from experience, you can't make people do things or want things or feel things that they don't want to. I remember my own lesson in that very clearly. My classroom was a summer's day in the sacristy at our local church – my wedding day. You can't make someone feel for better or for worse and you can't make them even pretend to feel it just to get through the ceremony and the reception so 'we could at least save face in front of one hundred of our nearest and dearest and then talk about whatever needed to be talked about on honeymoon'. Nope. It can't be done.

I don't think you ever forget lessons like that. I also learnt that double-wear waterproof mascara is a good bridal choice if you think you'll get a little teary and emotional on the day, but that it can't hold up to gut-wrenching sobbing.

It's getting darker now as I pass our office on the other side of the street and, looking up, I see the conference room lights are still on. It must be Christopher working late, getting prepped for our first meeting on Monday morning. It crossed my mind to invite him to join us for a drink tonight, but then I decided against it. These are odd and extraordinary circumstances; the *Gazette* on the brink of closing down one minute, then a last-ditch maverick attempt to save it the next. A radical restructure, new targets, new teams. It's a lot to take in. Bet even Mary didn't see this one coming.

And even though Christopher looks about my age and I think he's quite nice – I love how he's excited about getting started and making a go of our new-look paper, he has lots of great ideas and he's very attractive – I can't forget that he is still part of McArthur's team. He is still a consultant with the power to make or break us. Even though I'm Editor in Chief, he's from the London head office. He's here for a clear professional purpose, number-crunching and acting as McArthur's eyes and ears over the next four weeks. The most important four weeks the *Newbridge Gazette* has ever seen.

So, I think it's best I keep a respectable professional distance, otherwise the next four weeks could become either awkward or overly complicated, which is the last thing any of us needs right now. I'll take care of the team and re-energise the layout and content of the paper. He can work on the online stuff and accounts and our new readership. We'll work together on the bucket list feature as I'll need his input on what will work with new audiences and how to maximise our reach. And if McArthur wants pictures, I guess he'll have to come with me to do all these activities because I won't be in a position to take pictures of myself. Whatever the hell it is I'll be doing...

That's another thing, what to put on this goddamn list? I've drawn a blank since McArthur slammed the first three ideas I fired off as senior citizen day trips. I'll need his help with that too.

I arrive outside the pub and look through the steamed-up windows at the merry throng inside, all relieved to have knocked off from work, excited to begin the well-earned weekend. I catch sight of Jasmine, the cat-loving temp through the window. She's laughing and pulling faces with the IT guy. They're all in there, and I exhale a breath I didn't realise I was holding in.

I bite down on my lip, suddenly thinking maybe I've made a big mistake not inviting Christopher? I could just nip over the road right now and let him know where we are? If he fancied a quick drink? Just to be sociable? And then if he declined, I would understand completely, but at least he wouldn't feel left out.

Jasmine spots me and raps on the window to wave me inside. Then she sticks out her tongue, pinches her nose and throws back a dark-coloured shot.

No, I did the right thing. Rocking up with Christopher may frighten him off. And frighten them off. Yes, I'm the new boss, but they know me, and they know I'm trying to save their jobs. They may not trust Christopher. I don't even know whether to trust him myself yet! I'm hoping he's not another Gareth who can turn it on for interview and self-advancement but throw the rest of us under the bus if needed. We both need to get that twenty-two per cent increase to save our skin, our careers, and this paper. The *Newbridge Gazette* needs us to have a clear-headed, single vision not six double-vodkas and a gobful of pork scratchings.

All hands on deck! Eyes on the prize! Onwards and upwards to victory! I hear ole JJ Oakes shout in my mind. He was a master motivator; a man we wanted to work our asses off for, we wanted him to be proud of us.

I can't let Christopher see us at anything less than our best. What we don't need is McArthur's 'transformational consultant' to think we're a load of amateurs who have nothing better to do than go to the pub on a Friday and spend our free time boozing. That would look unprofessional. And I imagine a bit sad and hick compared to the cool London scene to which he's accustomed. So, it's best we keep that to ourselves.

I glance up one last time at the light on in the office, a huge part of me yearning to be up there too, brainstorming and action-planning. But I know that I need to prioritise, and right now is the crucial time to bring this team together if we're going to get anywhere. So, I turn back to the heavy wooden pub door in front of me, I take a deep breath and push my way through.

'Same again for the corner table and a large red wine for me please,' I ask the barman. My team is in rowdy form already – but in a good way. Laughing, drinking, listening, chatting like friends, they look happy and relaxed and excited and well on their way to drunkenness. A positive, encouraging sign for the weeks ahead when they'll have to rely on clear communication and support. And possibly have to share roll-on deodorant and toothbrushes if we fall behind schedule.

I spot Denise the barmaid who has been here since I was a teenager when I used to lug my mum's speakers in, setting up her stool and mike, tuning her guitar for her Folk Festival guest appearances. For all her faults, my mum was a born performer with an amazing voice – distinctive, smooth but sensitive, crackling with emotion but controlled. Even this country pub would fall to a hush once she started to play and sing. It was widely recognised by agents and punters alike that once Marilyn Buckley was your headline act, you were guaranteed a full house.

Denise winks at me. 'Good to see you back, Lily.'

'Good to be back,' I reply and realise that it does feel good. After everything over the last three years – the wedding, work, my mother – it feels like things are finally beginning to settle down into normality, and it does feel good to be out of the house and out of my pyjamas on a Friday night. I pay for the round and carry the tray over to the table.

'Yay! Make way! Here she comes, bearing gifts!' Jasmine smiles at me brightly, shoving strangers out my way and jumping up to dole out the drinks. 'Large Chardonnay! For you, Amy?' she asks.

Amy, a new reporter who has just been with us a few weeks, downs the rest of her current Chardonnay and wipes her hand across her mouth, smearing her bright coral lipstick. 'Oh, yes please. Cheers, much appreciated!'

I've only ever came across Amy in the loo where she reapplies her make-up on the hour. But I've never heard her speak or smile like she is doing now. We wave our hellos and she returns giddily to her conversation.

'Nice cold pint bottle of cider? Any takers?' Jasmine offers.

A short guy with red hair, one of the ad-men, raises a finger. 'Guilty as charged,' he reaches over to take his drink and thanks me. 'Already feeling like a cloud has lifted, wouldn't you say?' he grins.

We exchange pleasantries and I tell him how happy I am that everyone made it tonight, how pleased I am that we're going to get a chance to show what we can do. I say 'pleased', I mean relieved.

I turn to find Mark and hand him his beer.

'Thanks for this, Lily. And for your speech earlier. Gave me some food for thought. I just want you to know that you can count on me. I'll do whatever I can to help the paper back on its feet. Just one word of warning.'

'Yes?' I ask warily. I don't like the sound of 'words of warning' and I can feel my stomach clench with dread at whatever he's going to tell me next.

'Watch out for that "transformational consultant". I did a bit of ringing around. He's a completely different league; nominated for a Global Innovators award, just finished his MBA. Anyone selected for that leadership programme is there because they're ruthlessly ambitious. You don't slave away for sixteen hours a day to win friends and look out for the team. So, all I'm saying is watch your back. He's here for one reason only – to make himself look good for McArthur.'

I raise my glass to my lips, unsure of what to say to that. Should I be thankful that Mark is giving me some insider info? Or has he got a chip on his shoulder about Christopher and all that he's achieved so far? I want to shake my head and tell Mark that I don't think this tallies up. That the man I met this morning has been nothing but kind and passionate. But then again, I thought Adam loved me and that Hannah would be my best friend forever. So maybe I'm not the most perceptive on this kind of thing. Maybe Christopher does have a ruthless side. Maybe he has completely dazzled me with his charm and brilliance and I've had the wool completely, and willingly, pulled over my eyes?

But for now, I've got a job to do. And that's deliver drinks to my thirsty team.

'Rusty Nail?' I call out. 'Scotch and something?'

A hand breaks through the mob and I weave my way towards Dylan the IT technician. He's the one with the long, skinny ponytail and colourful Japanese tattoos that begin at his jawline and cover every inch of his exposed flesh. Another colleague I've never really got a chance to speak to before, he's usually head down with huge headphones on, but now he smiles at me and I see his small, pointy teeth for the first time. He offers me his seat, which I accept gratefully, and I dish out the rest of the drinks to more smiling, thirsty recipients and finally take a big glug of my own.

And it goes down a treat.

'Last orders! Ladies and gents, last orders before midnight please!'

I can hardly believe it when Denise the barmaid rings her bell. I guess it means I've not stopped drinking and giggling for nearly three hours. It turns out that Jasmine and Dylan are a couple, due to get married in just a few months, so there's no way they wanted the paper to fold, not only because they need every penny but because they met by the *Gazette* water cooler a year ago when Jasmine started temping and they've have been together ever since. Mark is in the process of building his own house, so he also needs the paper to stay afloat to make sure it reaches completion. Amy worked for another regional paper, *The South-Eastern Star* which collapsed last year, making her unemployed for six months and meant she had to move 300 kilometres away from friends and family to start afresh at the *Newbridge Gazette*, so the last thing she wants is to do that all over again. *The South-Eastern Star* was a great paper with first-class reporting. I bet Amy has a lot more potential than Gareth gave her credit for. Maybe we have more in common than I gave her credit for. It seems like the shiftiness I interpreted as apathy was good old-fashioned terror of the unknown.

Well, we're all in the same boat there. My last few attempts at change and adventure backfired spectacularly, so I'm not interested in life outside of this little paper in this little town and I don't want to make myself vulnerable to the whims and decisions of others, because that's where you get hurt. When you take risks on other people, on other places, you lose control of what you want your life to be like. Then people don't stick to their promises and they chop and change and crush your dreams and you are left completely alone and exposed. And devastated. Like someone has bombed out your heart and all you can do is riffle around in the smoke and rubble, trying to find a way to piece it all back. So, my intention now is to stay put, to stay safe and to stay here in my bombproof bubble of Newbridge, in my cosy little cottage by night and at my *Gazette* desk with the plastic plant by day.

We raise our glasses into the air and toast our new chapter… which will begin bright and early on Monday. But for now, we're here, so I make an executive decision that we have one last drink for the road. I swipe a handful of pork scratchings from Mark's open packet and dash up to the bar to conclude an absolutely belting staff night out.

'Same again!' I holler over to Denise. 'And throw in five packets of crisps please!'

She gives me the thumbs up and starts pouring. 'Just made it in time there, Lily, cut it very fine indeed.'

I look up to the clock just as it strikes midnight. I laugh and squeeze in beside the seated drinker at the bar.

'Tell your mum we said hi! I got her last album – best one yet.'

'Thanks, Denise, I haven't seen her in ages, not since my granny's funeral in fact, so last summer? But I'll pass on your kind words over the phone, she calls at least once a month.'

'Just once a month? My mum calls me ten times a day!'

I'm kind of stumped; I don't really know what say to this, so all I can do is offer a shrug. The truth is, since my granny died, my mum has called even less than before. Sometimes she just sends me a photo: a new city skyline, a screenshot of a great review, a glass of wine at the end of a long gig.

'Of course, it's different when your mum is a big singing sensation right? Touring and late-night shows, and the US time difference. I guess it's easy to lose touch.'

I nod, rearranging the drinks on the tray. 'Well, I'll save up your lovely compliment and pass it on to her the next time she's having a bad day. It'll really cheer her up to hear you liked her new stuff. You know what she's like.'

Denise rolls her eyes knowingly. 'One crazy diamond,' she says, and I laugh out loud. Denise is used to my mum's backstage diva antics. *Change the seating, dim the lighting, the sound's not good enough, the temperature is too hot, the wine is too warm, the mirror in the toilet makes me look old...*

And then I stop laughing. Because there are a pair of olive green eyes staring straight into mine. And a mess of dark hair. And two soft parting pink lips with an incredulous half-smile.

I lean in closer, squinting as the light seems to dart and dance in my blurred, wine-riddled vision.

Uh. Oh.

It's him.

It's definitely him.

It's Christopher, sat right up at the bar. All by himself. Pen in hand, working on something...

'Hey, it's you. I wasn't expecting to see you in here,' he says, smiling and swinging around to face me.

My hands fly to my mouth, and in doing so I knock over Dylan's Rusty Nail, the Scotch and Drambuie drenching the bar and seeping into the open notebook Christopher has in front of him, and now spilling on to his trousers.

'Oh my God,' is all I can say... along with *I'm sorry* over and over.

He jumps up from his seat and lifts the Scotch-soaked note-book into the air.

'I'm so, so sorry. Denise! Towel please!' I can't believe this has happened, my worst nightmare realised. To be half-drunk and clumsy and smelling of deep-fried pork product in front of my new colleague, manager, consultant… bloody green-eyed MBA global award nominated, ruthlessly ambitious transformational consultant Christopher! The one who holds the future of the *Newbridge Gazette* and my career in his hands.

I feel tears surface. I know the options: fight, flight or freeze. I always freeze. Sometimes I freeze and lose the power of speech. Other times I freeze and scream. Also, I've covered freeze and cry, freeze and beg rescue. This is freeze and gape soundlessly. But my mouth keeps opening and closing, goldfish style. Mute and slack-jawed, I nod and wipe my hands down my face.

Denise slides me the tray of drinks, including a fresh Rusty Nail, across the counter, and I throw her a twenty quid note with instructions to keep the change.

'I better go,' I say. 'Think I've disrupted you enough…'

Christopher tilts his head. 'Seriously, it's nothing, I've already wiped it from my memory.'

That's kind of him to say but I doubt it very much. So much for keeping up appearances. I tried my hardest in that office today to look competent and credible only to undo it all with some drunken spillage. Great.

Up until five minutes ago, I was actually thinking I could do this. That I could be a boss and motivate a team. That I could make a go of this second chance we've been given. But I haven't even written one word and I've already screwed up. No wonder Christopher is an up-and-coming fast-track leader. He's working on a Friday night, coming up with new ideas. Ideas I should be coming up with. And then he finds me in here, shouting for last orders like a fishwife, only to then stumble over him and drench his work in booze. Brilliant impression I must have made on him. I can imagine what McArthur and Jennings are going to say when he tells them first thing Monday morning.

'Are you okay?' Christopher asks me, this time the half-smile gone from his lips and genuine, tender concern on his face.

I nod, arms pinned stiff at my sides, unmoving like a mannequin's. Am I okay? I am mortified.

I look to his notebook. 'I'm so sorry! This couldn't be more awful. I know what you must be thinking, what a complete mess I am…'

He puts his hand on my shoulder. 'Whoa! Slow down, it's fine! Really! I was in having a few drinks myself – it's Friday night, you're having a drink like ninety-five per cent of the world, no big deal. Actually, I'm really pleased. When I heard I was coming to Newbridge, well, I had to look it up, never heard of the place in my life. I admit, I didn't expect much. But this place is fantastic; the atmosphere, the music, this local beer is incredible… Is it like this all the time?'

I search his face for traces of sarcasm but I can't find any. He's sincere this guy, I can sense it despite what Mark said earlier. Of course, my judgement could be a little clouded. But right now, it's what I want to believe. This is a fresh start after all.

I nod. 'Weekends always, but it's even busier when the festival is on. Can't get in the door in here, never mind a get a seat.' I pause as I take sight of his sodden notebook once again. It's ruined. Not only the notebook but all the pages and pages of handwriting in there. What if they were really important ideas? Or passwords? What if they can't be recovered or replicated? I know how devastated I'd be if I lost loads of precious work this way.

'I feel terrible about your notebook. Really I do, I can't apologise enough…'

He lifts it up and shakes it slightly. It's soaked through, and just as I suspected his handwritten notes are now blurry with

Scotch. 'Just a jot pad, no problem. I was just scribbling down bucket list ideas actually. Trying to come up with something inspired that would impress Mags and the readers... and you, of course.'

'Impress me?'

'Well, you're the one who has to go through with it.'

I press my fingers into my temples. Maybe he doesn't think I'm as drunk as I think I am? Or maybe I'm not that drunk? No, I am that drunk. Unless, do pork scratchings absorb all the alcohol from your bloodstream? Or maybe Christopher really doesn't care about my current level of intoxication and can't help himself yabbering on about our new project?

I shift my weight on to my left leg and squint sideways at this really handsome, really smart, really well-spoken guy in front of me who wants to talk about work on a Friday night with his half-cut editor. This is definitely the alcohol clouding my judgement. I think of Mark's warning. Maybe he's tricking me? Getting me to trust him? Can consultants be really gorgeous, nice guys or is that naïvety on my part? Professional and romantic naïvety. Wine-thoughts. I'm definitely having rambling wine thoughts, believing someone like him could be... Never mind.

I blink several times to try and snap myself out of whatever ball pit of stupid ideas I'm swimming around in. Getting hopes up that are never to be raised again. Because... well, I don't want to think of that right now. Rules are made for good reason. Workmates are out of bounds. I think so and McArthur thinks so. And what about that angry blonde who was arguing with Christopher in the car park? McArthur said that those antics belonged in the bedroom not the boardroom, surely that must mean they were – are? – involved? One thing is for certain, McArthur wasn't one bit impressed. Maybe that's why she gave him such a severe dressing-down when he did arrive? Calling him geeky and tardy and in need of transformation himself? I mean, that's so harsh! It all feels too complicated and mysterious and speculative. And all of that spells trouble. Spells heart-grenade.

I take a deep breath and straighten up. I don't want to think of anything right now other than getting out of this conversation with a shred of integrity.

'Take a look yourself if you don't believe me.' Christopher hands me the soggy paper and I squint to make out the blurred words numbered down the page.

Life-changing adventures, Travel, Charity, Sports, Cultural, Culinary, Before your next birthday, Before you get married, Before you die, Unique ideas, Awesome ideas, Most popular ideas…

He leans over my shoulder and trails a finger down the list. 'Trust me, it's not the Scotch, my handwriting is illegible at the best of times. So, from what we've we got here, I've researched them all to find stuff that is affordable, accessible and practically possible to achieve this week.'

This is too good to be true. Where's the catch?

'So no budget for diving in the Great Barrier Reef, I'm afraid… but skydiving we can do,' he tells me, grinning.

Right, there's the catch.

I shake my head. 'No, skydiving we cannot do.'

There is no way I can hurl myself to death fully conscious. Even if I wanted to, my body would seize up and I'd freeze and I'd just stay stiff and shivery and immobile until everyone got bored, gave up and started thanking me for wasting their time while the plane started its descent.

'No, no, no,' I say, wagging my finger. 'That can't happen.'

'Oh yes it can, I checked online, there's a place just half an hour from here, the Skyfall Centre. It'll be a tandem jump, so you'll be attached to a qualified instructor, a quick and easy introduction to free fall. We can get you up and down and back to your desk to write your feature all in a few hours.'

So he was just trying to soften me up after all, letting me believe that he was ordinary and real and down-to-earth and one of us, but really, he wants me to throw myself face first out of a plane, so he can show McArthur how much of a great leader he is.

'Ah!' he flashes me a smile and picks up a sticky pen and scribbles something completely illegible on the soggy notepad. 'Just had an idea! How about we make it a sponsored event to show some goodwill and raise cash and awareness for a local charity – that's a good thing to do and will help us engage some of that twenty-two per cent – let them know the *Newbridge Gazette* is back with a vengeance, what do you think?'

'I love the charity idea but not the crashing to my death idea. Sorry, Christopher, it's too much. And as much as I love my job, I can't will myself to do that. I'm afraid of heights. And I'm afraid of falling. And I'm also really afraid of dying and what you're suggesting covers all three of those, so skydiving is out for me. Back to the drawing board.'

He squints back at his notebook, trying to read the smudgy writing.

'Have you any other ideas in there?' I ask him, gesturing vaguely.

'We get new jobs.'

I dart him a look and a smile breaks his lips.

'I am joking!' He twirls his pen in between his fingers and then pats his notebook. 'Limitless ideas in here. I'll keep scribbling away and I'll be back to you Monday and I promise we'll find something, hopefully something, that not only you want to do but sets your heart on fire, something really exciting.'

I smile and thank him. I want to tell him that I know exactly what he means about limitless ideas when you've got a pen and notebook. It's just the way my brain seems to work; I'm able to write things down that I'd never, *ever* dare say. Sometimes I read back what I've written and can't believe that was me. Can't believe those words are mine, can't believe the feelings are mine. Often, I don't even realise what I'm feeling at all until I sit down and write it all out. It's my favourite way to communicate, just me and the page. The page that always listens, the page that never judges. The page that can be folded up and kept for decades, the page that can be torn and tossed in an instant. I'm beginning to wonder if Christopher is the same, I see ink marks all over his fingers. I'd bet he's a head-to-page kind of writer too. Maybe he realises himself on the paper just like me.

I feel a tap on my shoulder and turn around to see that it's Jasmine. 'Where have you been? We're dying of thirst over here! You've been gone ages!'

Christopher holds up his hands and dips his head slightly. 'Entirely my fault, please, excuse me. I didn't want to hold you up. Back to the drawing board it is. Forgive my intrusion, I didn't mean to take you away from your friends; have a lovely night.'

Jasmine opens her mouth to say something, but I shoot her a look. I'm afraid it's going to be a) we're not friends but work colleagues, which will let Christopher know that he was the only one in the office I didn't invite, or b) an invite to come and join us, which would just be the worst, because he'd see all of us in our full inebriated state and that would make Monday morning's staff meeting a very awkward affair. Thankfully, Jasmine gets the message and grabs the drinks tray. I say my goodbyes and wish Christopher a lovely night too, apologising again for spilling the drink on him and refusing the skydive. Bloody hell, how much more could I have done to sabotage myself in the first instance?

'Ping me anytime if you have any other ideas,' he calls out as he offers me his card with all his numbers and contacts. 'Otherwise, enjoy the weekend and see you on Monday.'

I head over to the corner table, where Mark and Dylan are arm-wrestling topless, Amy's asleep in the corner and Jasmine is begging Denise for a lock-in. And karaoke. And baskets of chicken and chips. Everyone's now on Rusty Nails.

Did I make a huge mistake not inviting Christopher out with us tonight? Maybe he would have loved this? Maybe it would have been the perfect introduction to everyone at the *Gazette*? I know Mark has reason to believe he's not trustworthy, but I've not seen him be anything other than kind and committed. I guess this is what it's going to be like for the foreseeable future as Editor in Chief, always wondering if I'm doing the right thing, always second-guessing, always reviewing and wondering what I can do better. So maybe, next time, I will invite him out with us. Because the way this staff night out is going, it looks like there'll be many more next times. And I think that once my colleagues get to know Christopher, they're going to really like him, just as much as I do. I steal a glance over to the bar stool where Christopher was sitting earlier. I watch him drain his drink, gather his things and wave his thanks to Denise as he exits through the side door.

Jasmine takes my hand and we both stand up on the seats, clapping and swinging our hips together. The lights go down and the volume goes up. I think the coast is clear and it's safe to presume that Christopher has turned in for the night and we needn't worry about disgracing ourselves any further.

I knock back a Rusty Nail. Sometimes, you've just got to take one for the team.

CHAPTER 6

I wake to the soft, rough tongue of Chaplin licking my ear. How can it already be so bright? I feel like I just closed my eyes ten minutes ago. The sunlight streams through the crack between my wonky home-made curtains and I thank God it's Saturday. I stretch out like a starfish in my bed and decide that straight after I get up to feed Chaplin, I'm going to slip right back in under these soft, warm blankets. With a big cup of tea. Endless cups of sugary tea will be required today. And some cheesy toast with marmite. That's the beauty of living by yourself. You can do whatever you want, whenever you want, for as long as you want. And you can do it all in your pyjamas.

And of course, once I feel human enough, I'll spend the rest of the day tucking into a book from my towering TBR pile which looks like a little paperback city on either side of my bookcase since I ran out of space on the shelves. I tried to have a clear-out a few months back but just ended up rediscovering favourites and, in the end, I threw out nothing. I couldn't bear to. My books were there for me when I had no one else. They didn't force me to open up or pressure me to pull myself together. They calmed me down, kept me sane, helped me clarify my thoughts and most importantly, did so with infinite patience. And sometimes a little solitary reading is all the therapy a person needs. It's one of the many things that annoys my mother about me – she can't understand how I love nothing more than snuggling up all by myself with a novel. She says it's 'closing myself off to the world'. I say it's entering a new one.

When I was a teen, she'd throw her hands up in despair, screeching whilst banging on the table and opening the door, pointing out into the darkness to the lights of Newbridge twinkling in the distance. 'Where the hell did I get you from, Lily! Go out, get drunk, get a tattoo, sneak out to a concert, throw a party, shoplift! For God's sake, live a little, you're only young once, you're supposed to be reckless and crazy at your age. Not bloody hiding behind a book and baking cakes. That's not normal! It is not living!'

But I've become used to my quiet little life and it suits me well. I throw back my duvet, open my windows and breathe in the glorious early autumnal smells, colours and views of rolling hills and trees. I scoop up Chaplin and we pad our way to the kitchen for a lazy breakfast for both of us. I'm weirdly not feeling half as hung-over as I deserve.

My phone rings on the kitchen counter. I glance at the screen and brace myself. Speak of the devil. Here comes the headache after all.

'Morning, darling!' my mother sings into the phone. In her time zone, it's just before 2 a.m. on Friday night. This is her witching hour, when she's still buzzing from a gig and can't wind down. It's too late to drink but too early to do anything else. Except call me. 'Just calling to catch up! Keep you in the loop, you won't believe the week I've had, sweetheart...'

And she's off.

In many ways, once you accept that she's calling to talk *at* you and not *to* you, you stop treating it like a conversation and it's a lot less frustrating. I've learnt to make timely 'ohs' and 'wows', so I can just let her chat away while I get on with other jobs.

'...So I've just moved in to a brand-new apartment, Half Moon Bay. You should see it, Lily – *stunning*! Right this second, I'm standing on the balcony, I've got views of the whole city, there's an indoor pool, an outdoor pool, a shared terrace for parties...'

'Wow... oh, wow... unbelievable...' I reply as I open a tin of chicken liver for Chaplin and slide the jellied meat block into a bowl (just what I need to smell to help my hangover), while I stick on the kettle and toaster for myself.

'The rent is outrageous, but you wouldn't expect anything less for this neighbourhood. And besides, it's not like I'm paying for it all by myself, right?'

'Wo—' I stop in my tracks. 'What do you mean? Are you sharing?'

My mother is not the sharing sort. When she's not being loud, she's asleep and then everybody has to be pin-drop silent or she'll lose her head and start wailing with fatigue like a small child. She is also bad when she's hungry. Or hangry. Which is tricky because she's always on a diet. In her industry, she feels the pressure to look young and skinny and stylish at all times. High-protein, low-carb, high-fat, no-sugar, vegan, Atkins, South Beach, Ketogenic, Paleo, Zone, Dukan, 5:2. She does them on a loop. I can't remember a time in my life when my mum has *not* been on a diet.

I hit the fridge closed with my foot, slump on the couch and bite into the block of red cheddar in my hand.

'Do you listen to me at all, sweetie? I've moved in with Maxwell remember?'

'Maxwell? I thought Maxwell was your therapist?'

'And so much more, baby. So much more,' she purrs.

This is going to be a long call.

'He's the one, Lily. I know you'll think it's premature to say that, but I don't care. I can feel it. He's my angel. My rock. My soulmate.'

'Oh.' My mother has even less faith in the illusory promise of 'The One' than I do.

'I found him through my agent's dog walker's therapist.'

Only living in California makes crazy sentences like this possible.

'You know how much I've tried to find peace, sweetheart! I've tried Xanax, Prozac, Zyprexa, Chinese herbs, hypnosis, leafy greens, fish oil, vitamin B12, St John's wort, group therapy, light therapy, cognitive behavioural therapy, eye movement desensitisation and reprocessing, but none of it really did the trick, you know? But Maxwell… I feel the difference. The energy… He's a self-qualified art therapist, which was not necessarily what I was looking for, but after a lifetime of people nodding and smiling at me and suggesting I try breathing in different gears, the fact that this Adonis in dark-denim cut-offs offered me a hot glue gun and a vision board seemed like it could only be a good thing.'

'Right. Okay, I see…' But I don't. This completely erratic, whirlwind infatuation with a virtual stranger already sounds like it's going to end in tears. I hope not, but this does sound like everything has moved very fast. Too fast.

'This time a month ago, when I first met him, how could I ever have guessed the change he would bring? I didn't know he believed in spirit guides or that he would give me hand-drawn tarot cards as a birthday present. I didn't know we would go night swimming together naked in Lake Tahoe or that he would hold me for hours while I cried as I wrote the words of all my burdens and regrets on rocks and then slung them away, freeing myself from the past and all the heaviness weighing me down. How could I ever have known last night when I was on stage singing in front of five hundred people he would stand up and call out to me, "I love you so fucking much, you have no idea!"'

'Wow.'

'I know. WOW, right? Lily, he's the one. I've found him. You know when you just know?'

Well, no, I don't actually. You might remember the day I got it all wrong? It was quite a scene. You were wearing purple.

I make some high-pitched noises – encouraging ones. I think… I hope. I'm hardly an expert in this area.

'And the timing couldn't be more perfect because I'm working with a new producer, remastering all my greatest hits. She's young, she's cool, she's going to take me to new audiences and I'm thinking to myself – you know what? For once in my life, I'm going to get my happy ending!'

I'm speechless. And I've got a mouthful of cheese.

'So, what have you been up to, darling? I'm guessing same old, same old in Newbridge? You know I've offered to pay half your flight over here. You'd love this place, you could try writing for a paper over here? Or what about a complete change? Be my PA, God knows I need the help, come work for me, honey! Please!'

She's made me this offer before. And I don't want to sound ungrateful, but it is exactly what it says on the tin. I'd be moving over as her PA. I'd be working around the clock, attending to her endless needs – one minute I could be rescheduling a flight, the next I could be giving her a foot massage. So thanks but absolutely no thanks.

'Well, there has been some news actually,' I say.

'Really?' She sounds more than a little surprised.

'Yes, we had a shake-up at work, I'm now Editor in Chief and I've got to write a full-length feature for our print and new online editions. So that's exciting.'

Finished with his breakfast, Chaplin scampers over to me and folds himself in to my lap.

'Oh-kay, not bad! What's the feature? Are you interviewing famous people? I could put you in touch with so many, darling… Arts and culture or inspiration? You just tell me the angle and I'll pull in some favours. You could do me of course – rags to riches kind of thing – small-town girl makes it big stateside. I had some new headshots done recently, so I'm happy to send them through. Actually I'll send you some pics right now…'

A feature on my mother would absolutely be the last thing I'd want to do. For three reasons. Firstly, it would take forever to write and edit because she loves to tell her life story in a rather long-winded way. Secondly, I'd then have to re-write and re-edit the whole damn thing over and over until she was satisfied. And thirdly, it would mean telling everyone she's my mother and be ambushed with all the unwanted attention that would spring from that. 'Thanks, but there's no need, they've already decided. It's a bucket list.'

'I beg your pardon?'

'A bucket list; you know, things you've always wanted to do but you were too scared or didn't have the time or money, that kind of thing. Extraordinary experiences.'

I hear her make her characteristic retching sound, as if the mere idea of something so banal is so distasteful it makes her gag. 'Whose idiotic idea was that? It's so morbid! Trust the puny-minded *Newbridge Gazette* to come up with something as boring and overdone as that. You're too young to be thinking of bucket lists. Hell, I'm too young to be thinking of bucket lists. Tell them no, Lil, tell them where to shove it.'

Okay – here we go. My mother hates Newbridge and everything it represents. She insists that Newbridge stifled her creativity, repressed her independence as an artist and as a young woman and branded her a troublemaker for 'simply living her life her way' i.e. indulging in all varieties of intoxicants, being a bad influence on other less rebellious and experimental peers (whom she now calls The Beige Brigade, living without colour or depth) and getting pregnant with me at the tender age of sixteen. She would have left the second it was legal for her to finish school except she had me to care for. But a decade in, she'd had enough of that (parenting being stifling also, I imagine) and left me to live with my granny to build her career in America. So, Mum hating Newbridge and calling it puny-minded is exactly what I expect to hear from her. But what she sees as small-town banality, I see as security, as community, as the people who were there for me when she chose not to be.

'It's not morbid,' I tell her, with a heavy touch of defensiveness in my voice. Who does she think she is telling me what to do from her loved-up luxury apartment in LA? She's not here, she's not really part of my life now beyond texts and calls, so why should I even listen to what she has to say? 'It's brilliant. It's positive; exploring exciting life goals.' I'm trying to think of how Mags McArthur put it… 'Things that push you out of your comfort zone, so you feel fully alive.'

'Right. So what are you going to do then?'

I scramble for an example. I still can't think of anything that I want to do. How very Beige Brigade. I'm going to have to tell her something that at least sounds exciting. But what? My first three ideas went down like a lead balloon, and I can't risk that happening here with my mum on the phone. It will just confirm all the other notions she has about me living too small, too safe and, well, not really living at all. Well, maybe I am boring and dull and backward, but all the sensational, circus act stuff that other people do just fills me with dread. And I don't think that's really the spirit of a bucket list. Surely, you're supposed to want to fulfil a goal or ambition, not torture yourself.

'Lily? Don't tell me it's swimming with dolphins or I'll puke. They should call it "pass the bucket list". You should tell them you want to do a "Fuck-it" list. All glamourous, high-end things and let them pay for it. At least that sounds promising. For Newbridge, I mean.'

'Skydiving,' I blurt out, louder than I intended and I think even Chaplin flinches when I say it. I wink at him. I'm only feeding her Christopher's idea to get her off my case. Surely, if it's good enough for a high-flying media consultant from London, it's got to be good enough for my mum.

My mother's laugh crackles loud and clear in my ear despite the five and a half thousand miles that separate us. 'Oh, this just gets better and better. You and heights! Jumping out of a plane!

Crashing through the sky nose first! Remember when you were eight, you wet yourself on the rock-climbing wall, you were that scared of falling. Is this supposed to be a comedic piece?' She's wheezing with cynical laughter now. 'Go on, tell me what they really have planned.'

Again, I am bone dry in terms of ideas, I cannot think of one thing I want to do for myself. And she's not making matters any better. Why can't she just support me for once? Why does she always have to undermine me, make me feel I've been foolish or naïve? I've had enough. I'm sorry I even mentioned it now. 'That's it. No joke. I've got to do it for work.'

A sharp intake of breath from my mother passes through the phone line. 'You don't have to do anything, Lily. Is this really how I brought you up? To be pushed around by some small-town big-balls who thinks he's editor of the *New York Times*? Is this from that runt Gareth again? Is some sick sadist making you do this? Whatever you choose to do with this silly list, fine, do it, but only on your own terms. Of course I'd love you to push yourself and live a little, but not if some idiot is exploiting you to shift a few extra copies of his crummy paper. Nobody can make you do...'

'Nobody is making me...' I cut in. I actually thought she may be pleased about this. I actually thought this might be a nice conversation. How on earth can she accuse me of being stuck in my own comfort zone when I endure listening to this crap from her... with a hangover.

But she's not listening. 'We need to get you out of this. Scare them off. Tell them you have a broken rib. It's impossible to verify medically. Inconclusive on an X-Ray. I used it to get out of touring Canada last winter, too cold. Worked a treat.'

'Mum, it's fine. I want to do it.'

'No! You? Never! I don't buy that for one second! You're being a pushover, letting them bully you into this. Skydiving is not your bag. I know you, remember? I know you better than you know yourself. And I know that you would never want to do this of your own accord.'

I need to show her she's wrong. That I'm much stronger than she credits me to be. And if that means skydiving, then so be it.

'Mother, I'm a grown woman. I'm fully capable of standing up for myself. I'm the editor and I want the paper to succeed, so if this is what it takes, then I'm doing it. *Of my own accord.*'

'Well, you better start looking for a new job, because, baby, I really can't see you pulling this one off. It took forever to peel you off that rock-climbing wall. And you were only about four feet off the ground.'

'Yes, but I was only about four foot tall!' I remind her.

'Sweetheart, don't take this the wrong way, but do you think it's a delayed post-traumatic stress reaction to being so hurt and betrayed by Adam? It could be, you know.'

'Mum, don't. It's not. That happened a lifetime ago,' I tell her, rubbing my head and feeling a mother of a migraine coming on.

'Three years is not a lifetime. And that's a major trauma, the rejection, the humiliation, the betrayal, the fallout could take time to surface. Shall I ask Maxwell to have a word? I can see him pulling up right now, hold the line, I'll call him. MAXWELL!! Darling!! Come quick, it's my daughter! She's having a crisis!'

I start to scroll through photos she's sent me, a few nice, arty headshots to begin with and then her and Maxwell by the lakeside smiling (and semi-clothed, thank God), her and Maxwell enjoying a wine on the balcony, the Californian sunset in the background, Maxwell adjusting her mike as she prepares for a show, just like I used to do. Maxwell has no hair on the top of his head but a long, thin, silver braid that hangs down his back. His skin looks like a worn dark-brown leather belt. From these pictures, he never stops smiling. A big, toothy, gleaming white smile. He looks like he could be Hulk Hogan's long-lost vegan brother. I shudder at a full-length shot of him posing, legs spread, arms akimbo in his cut-offs. I think he cut off too much.

My head is starting to throb. I've had enough of my mother now. And I certainly don't want to hear Maxwell's long-distance assessment.

'Mum, I've got to go okay. I'll call you next week. Love you.'

'Don't do it. Leave that paper and move over here with me. Be my PA,' she calls down the phone.

'I'll let you know. Enjoy the new apartment, Mum, give my best wishes to Maxwell too.'

'Fine. I'll pay your full fare, how's that? I'll even give you a day off every week.'

I close the call and lift the phone right up to my face to peer at the last photograph. One I think she's sent me by mistake: a cluster of rocks stacked up against the blazing orange sunset waiting to be hurled into a ditch. I zoom in on one of the largest rocks in the pile. In black felt-tip, in my mother's hand, written out in big, capital letters, is my name.

I zoom in further to double-check. But there it is, no mistake – LILY

I wrote the words of all my burdens and regrets on rocks and then slung them away.

Well, no holding back there. It's crystal clear in fat black letters.

I am a burden. I am one of my mum's great regrets.

I'm surprised to see it, of course, but I suppose I can't claim to be shocked by it. I always knew I was a mistake. An accident. My mother had me as a schoolgirl to some guy she wouldn't speak of. As a baby, I held my mother back from her dreams and as a growing girl it became abundantly clear that I wasn't the go-getting, fun-loving, creative daughter she'd hoped for.

So, she thinks she knows me better than I know myself? She thinks I'm just a dead weight that drags her down and trips her up?

Well, I'll show her.

I rummage in my jeans pocket and pull out Christopher's number. My hand is quivering and I've broken out into a cold sweat that's part fury and part hangover. But I'm determined. I can't leave things as they are. I need a catalyst. I need to act now.

'Hi, it's me, Lily, I hope this is a good time?'

'Yes of course! Everything okay?' he answers immediately, which makes me feel better, even a little happy, as though he has been waiting for my call. Which I know is ridiculous, of course.

'Everything is great,' I lie, surprising myself with the control in my voice. 'In fact, I've been thinking. Let's go with the skydive.'

'But I thought you were scared?'

'Not as scared as us screwing up our first feature, so let's just go for it.'

'Only if you're sure, because last night you seemed very much against the idea and I don't want to push you if you're not one hundred per cent.'

I can't help but blush at his kindness, giving me the chance to pass once again. I can safely say to my mother or anyone else who cares to know that Christopher is certainly not making me do this. Every decision from now on is all mine.

'I am sure, I promise. Less thinking on this the better. I'm decided.'

There. It's done.

Buckley's Bucket List or Lily's Fuck-it List Item No.1: Skydive – shorthand for me shitting my pants at 10,000 feet and showing my mother that she knows nothing about me or what I'm capable of doing.

Bring it on.

CHAPTER 7

'Okay, so let's just dive in, shall we? Who wants to start?' It is Monday morning and my newly invigorated team are all gathered in the meeting room ready to brainstorm ideas to get this newspaper back on track.

Amy begins, 'The chef from the golf course wants to print his sticky toffee pudding recipe, even though I told him we did that dessert last month, but he's insisting. What do I do?'

Then the rest of the team start to bubble over, firing requests like machine-gun bullets.

'For the fashion and style feature on designer wellingtons for the folk festival, do you want all size models?' asks Jasmine.

Mark then pipes up again. 'Also, I was thinking it would be good to do a piece on juice cleanses. Pre-wedding season, everyone's on a diet and all the celebs are doing them and they have amazing powers of rejuvenisation. So, my idea is that I get a juice cleanse and then we can, like, measure my toxins...'

'The local council say we can't have an interview with the mayor until two weeks after the election campaign starts. What do we do?' asks Amy.

'I'm just looking through my piece on psychic animals, would you prefer a parakeet or an iguana?' Jasmine adds in quickly before I get a chance to answer anybody around the table.

'Oh! Breaking news, people! Just in from a very reliable source, a great story out of Newbridge East about a retirement account scandal! Who can we send?' asks Dylan. 'We've got to move quick.'

'Whoa, guys, slow down! I'm sorry, I can't keep up with what any of you are saying!' says Christopher, giving up on taking notes and throwing his pen into the middle of the table.

Right, Christopher is probably used to a lot less chaos in his London office so it's time to bring some order in here before he loses the will to live.

'Okay, tell the golf chef if he wants to make sticky toffee, it better have a twist, because the readers will write in and tell us we're recycling content. Pitch him a fun golf-themed dessert idea – Tee-rimasu, Coconut Golf Balls, Hole in One Donuts. Designer Wellies: Yes, all size models. And all patterns. Press suppliers for a giveaway, win a pair, answers on a postcard, that kind of thing. Toxins? Who said that?' I ask.

Mark raises his hand.

'They can't be measured. And "rejuvenisation" is not a word. Tell the council people that they can't plug their next clinic in our What's On column unless we get the mayor within a week of the campaign kick-off – we want to be first, or they are on their own. Definitely Parakeet. Retirement scandal, that needs you, Dylan.'

Surveying all faces, everyone seems happy and on board. 'Great. I'm out for the rest of the day with Christopher for the skydive, so, if you need anything in my absence, Amy's in charge.'

I scan the table and see the team all scribbling away, pushing out their chairs and getting ready to work.

'Anything else?' I ask.

They all shake their heads. Even Christopher.

'Super, in that case, let's have a great day.'

I look out my office window down onto the street below. A very stylish man in a sky blue blazer is standing outside The Black Boar handing out leaflets to everyone who passes, young and old, with a smile and a cheeky glint for every one of them. I've never seen him before but I bet I can guess. By Mary's description, I'd say he's the new theatre director, out canvassing to attract his new audience. He's doing a great job; already a small crowd have huddled round him and I can just about hear his laughter above the din of morning traffic.

'Amy?' I call back into the office. 'Could you go down to the theatre club and write up a piece about the new director, Julian? They're going upmarket and doing a Shakespearean play for their next production. Be good to give them a boost and let everyone know that it's under new direction.'

'Really!' she squeals. 'I didn't even know there was a theatre in Newbridge. I *love* the theatre. I wanted to be an actress, in fact.'

'Oh, what happened?' I enquire.

'Nothing. That was the problem!'

'Well, who knows, go down there and see what's going on. Full artistic licence. You write the piece, take some pictures and we'll give it a full page.'

I can't help but feel a little ashamed that I've been working here alongside these people every single day but yet I don't really know them at all. I have a hunch as to why that is; I guess I didn't really want them to know me. I didn't want them to know that I was the girl whose husband-to-be waited till we were standing at the altar to tell me he was in love with my best friend. I didn't want to be that girl, even though I was. So I stopped asking questions of others so that they'd ask no questions of me.

Amy tilts her head and squints at me. 'Seriously? You trust me to run this piece on my own?'

I pause a moment, recognising the look on her face, the uncertainty in her voice.

'Amy, you are a brilliant reporter. You are personable, intuitive and more talented than we even realise fully just yet. This team needs you! *I* need you!'

She raises a shy half-smile. 'Thanks, Lily. That means so much. Sometimes, if you don't hear anything good for a while, you question yourself; it's easy to think that maybe you're not doing a good job or you're not up to it.'

I swing round out of my seat and wrap my arm around her elbow. I know exactly what she means. This is how I've felt for the last few years, if I'm being honest with myself, and I know that self-criticism is the hardest criticism of all. It can take a while to build yourself up again. But I'm beginning to, and I want Amy and all my team to feel the same way. When I walked through the doors of the *Gazette* on my first day, I really hadn't a clue about reporting. But JJ Oakes made me believe that I could, so I did. And once you believe, then you unleash the best in yourself. And others.

'Amy, I'm promoting you to acting Assistant Editor. Unfortunately, I can't pay you any more straight away, but I'll see to it that you get more freedom in the content you want to cover and widen your experience in any area you like – marketing, editing, whichever – so you can build your CV and really develop your skills. It's high time we give the stars in this place a chance to shine.'

Amy's eyes widen and her hands fly up to her mouth. 'Lily, this is amazing. I won't let you down.' It's clear to anyone that she's thrilled. And excited. And chomping at the bit to get started.

A light shower of rain patters on the open window by my desk. I stand to close it, knocking the potted plastic plant as I reach for the handle.

Amy rushes to pick it up, relieved that the soil is also moulded plastic, so there's no need to sweep up any mess. 'That was close.' She spins on the spot. 'Do you want me to set it down somewhere else? It's a bit of a nuisance sat there on your desk, bound to fall again and it blocks your lovely view of the town! You can see right up to the church from here.'

I could tell her, that once upon a time, that was the whole point.

But she's right. It is a nuisance. And actually, the ugly plastic pot plant does block my view. Not only of the church but of everything else down there.

'Yes, I think it's served its purpose. I'm done with it. You can drop it into the theatre and see if they can use it as a prop if you like.'

She nods happily and we both stand by the window, watching the droplets of rain land on the glass and enjoying the market scene below, locals and tourists alike, buying bread, walking dogs, sharing umbrellas, waving their hurried hellos as they take shelter under trees and in arched doorways.

I spot Mary, in her pre-loved red bobbled hat, peering through the opening of the tall red postbox. And it reminds me. Of a public service announcement of great urgency that I've neglected to address. I nudge Amy and hold up my finger.

'Oh, and if you don't mind, there's one last thing that needs to be done today. Could you ask graphics to make me two signs, both A3, laminated, large, clear, bold print, one reading POST BOX and the other reading DOG POO ONLY.

She raises her eyebrow at me. 'If you say so.'

'I know. But, trust me, sometimes it's the smallest changes that can make the biggest impact.'

And Amen to that.

CHAPTER 8

I got zero seconds of sleep last night, unable to imagine anything going right, imagining all that can go wrong, and praying that they won't have to scrape my splattered remains off the landing strip. The bits they can find of me that is. My first proper day as Editor in Chief could very well be my last.

Christopher does not hang around. I truly did not expect to be booked in so soon. I thought we may come to check the place out. To do some research, mull over the idea and then probably ditch it in favour of something else after realising that it is all a bit inconvenient: too much fuss with the paperwork and the planes and the parachutes. And the possibility of paralysis. But I can tell by Christopher's optimism that this isn't the case. We're not heading to the Skyfall centre on a reconnaissance mission. He's booked it. I'm pencilled in to go up and come down *today*.

'Lily, are you sure you want to go through with this?'

I dart Christopher a look. 'We're here now, so I think it's a bit late to back out, don't you?'

'Not at all! Of course, you can still back out. I've done this myself countless times. It's addictive! Everyone I know feels apprehensive before their first flight and then they love it – every single one. However, if you're not comfortable, you've got to tell me. Nobody – especially me – wants to push you over the edge…'

'Of a plane? That's exactly what you are doing,' I snap, feeling rattled but instantly regretting it. 'Sorry, I'm just mentally preparing myself.' I try to sound bright and nonchalant, but it's clear from the way Christopher winces that I do a bad job.

We avoid eye contact and I pretend to pick at imaginary pieces of lint on my sleeve. I know I said I would do this and that I was one hundred per cent sure, but that was before I actually got here. I was pissed off with my mum and probably still a little drunk and full of hot-headed bullishness. I didn't really think this through. But now I certainly don't feel even one per cent sure about this. I'm an idiot. A gobby, impulsive, childish, fear-stricken idiot with no one but myself to blame. What the actual fuck have I gotten myself into?

I feel like I'm watching from a distance. Like it's a dream. I can't believe I'm doing this; I think I've shut off the part of my brain that says, *Run! Now! Run for your life.* My knees are like jelly and I can feel the last meal I ate flip in my stomach. I nod and breathe and try to imagine that this is happening to somebody else.

Christopher rubs his neck and motions for one of the instructors to come over. I think he's also getting increasingly nervous about how this is going to go. I guess I did make it sound like I was ready, I was hoping that if I committed, told myself it was fine, that I'd have time to get used to the idea and be prepared by the time I got here. But now, it's pretty obvious I'm not.

A thought shoots through my brain before I can stop it. Maybe this is exactly what Adam thought as the countdown to our wedding day approached. Maybe he also thought he could convince himself to come round, that it would all be good in the end. But that didn't happen did it? It didn't work for him, so why on earth would I expect it to work for me?

Before I have time to dwell any more, a really tall, tanned guy with a hive of blonde dreadlocks woven around his head takes long, sure strides towards us. He introduces himself as John Boy. I don't know whether that's his real name or not, but once more I question why I'm putting myself in the hands of a complete stranger. Maybe it's a skydiver rule. Don't divulge your real name in case something goes wrong, that way they'll never trace you. I'm hating this. This feels all wrong. Not to mention stupid.

'You guys, okay? All set for the jump of your life?' John Boy asks.

I shake my head and feel behind me for the wall. My head is swimming, I need to sit down.

'How natural is it to be nervous?' asks Christopher. After a moment's thought, he adds, 'Like, this nervous?'

They both regard me in a foetal heap on the ground. I typed in 'skydiving fails' into Google last night. I was hoping 'no results found' would come up. It didn't. There were nearly half a million results. Half a million times when something went wrong. And those are only the ones that have been uploaded. What are the true survival rates? Does anyone really know?

John Boy bites his lip and uh-huhs a lot while Christopher fills him in on the feature and the reason I'm here, whilst I just lie on the soft, cool, solid ground.

'So you think it'll be okay?' Christopher asks him.

He sucks his teeth and looks sidelong at Christopher. 'Why do anything if you are aiming for "okay"? It is going to be *absolutely phenomenal!* I shit you not, like nothing she's ever experienced. Believe me, I wouldn't be here if this was an okay way to spend a Monday morning.'

I grab Christopher's ankles. 'This is insane. Tell me I'm not insane thinking that this is insane. If my spine snaps and I become a quadriplegic, I have no one to take care of me. My mother will refuse. She will just text me "I told you so" and literally never see me again.'

'It is insane,' John Boy answers as he squats down to meet my eyes. 'But this isn't even the craziest part. You see, the craziest part is that you are going to strap yourself to me like an infant in a Baby-Bjorn with a parachute, and you are going to put your life in my hands. Right now, Lily, we are the most important people in each other's lives. My whole job is to throw you out of an airplane and not let you die. And I won't let you die, okay? Because I'm a bit of a stickler like that. I'll be with you every step of the way.'

I want to believe him. I want to feel reassured. But I can't ignore the physical reaction of resistance I'm experiencing. I wish I could just say okay, get excited and not over-think this. But if I'm going to entrust my life to this guy, I'll need to know more about him; 'Can I see your qualifications?' would be a start. But just as the words leave my lips, a car pulls up in front of us with another 'excited' kamikaze skydive participant and John Boy turns from me and runs to greet them. So much for being there every step of the way! He's already abandoned me mid-sentence!

Christopher hunches down beside me. He waits to meet my gaze and places his hands on both my shoulders. 'I really appreciate you coming this far, but it's clear that it's too much, so I've got an idea. Why don't I do the skydive for you? No one will know. We'll get some great shots of you in your jumpsuit, here on solid ground, then we'll edit the rest so that there's lots of vague skyscapes and sun shining through the clouds, that kind of thing.'

'Really? You'd do that?' I like this idea. I like him for having this idea.

'Of course! If it spares you from your worst nightmare, then of course.'

I take a moment to study him, now lying flat on his tummy beside me. His face is so close, I can hear him breathe. He steadies himself on his elbows and meets my gaze, his eyes staring earnestly in to mine. In terms of distracting me, this works. I can't stop looking at them – such a beautiful, deep green colour, so unusual, like flecked marbles, a glasslike quality that makes them shine in a way that I've not seen before. But it's even more than that. They are so expressive. Looking at him this way, this close, right now, with nothing but a few blades of grass between us, there's nowhere to hide. Those eyes tell me everything. If he didn't care about me or the paper or if he was running out of patience, he'd have to be an Oscar winner to keep that from coming through, as up close and personal as we are now.

I absolutely don't want to do this. But I also don't want to let him down. I don't want to let myself down. But which is worse? How do I choose the lesser evil of what I don't want?

'But what about the article? How can I write the feature if I don't experience the skydive?'

'I'll help you with it – we could definitely cobble something together,' he tells me.

'I've never backed out of a story before,' I say, starting to pull at the collar of my jumpsuit. God I would love to be back in my bed now, tea, book, onesie. Definitely not here. Not doing this. As much as I'd like to think I could rise to the challenge, maybe I'm not wired that way. Maybe I'm simply unable to adjust, to evolve, to grow. Maybe I'm just going to be me. As I am. Forever. And everything I've got is all I'm ever going to have. From now on. So maybe it's time I stopped deluding myself that I'm ever going to be anything different. I'm not going anywhere, I am not changing, I've landed in my spot in life and will stay put for ever more. Just like the rock with my name on it in some LA ditch.

Is this what I want?

My skin prickles with the realisation. That if this is all I want, then this is the way to get it. By staying still, by saying no, by chickening out. But if I want something different, I'm going to have to *do* something different.

This feels definitive, like something I'm going to remember, that I'm going to refer to when I think about who I am. Just like that rock climb when I was eight; it defined me as 'scared of heights'. Just like my non-wedding day, which defined me as 'jilted', as 'betrayed', as 'unworthy'. Maybe today, *I* can define the moment, define what happens here. I just wish it wasn't as terrifying as a freakin' skydive.

I can feel my eyes pool with tears. I'm so embarrassed for crying, it only makes me want to cry even harder. I cover my face with my hands. *Get a grip Lily!!!*

Christopher gently brushes a stray hair from my cheek and stoops to find my eyes. 'Hey! No need for tears. Oh my, Lily, what have I done? I'm only here a day and already I've made you cry!'

I shake my head. 'No, it's not you. It's just me, I'm sorry, you probably expected someone way more professional…'

'Enough; you are amazing, okay!'

Amazing? Seriously? I'm streaming from my nose and I'm face down in a field. I shake my head. 'That's well meaning, but I don't believe that.'

Christopher wriggles forward on his elbows and takes my hand in his. 'And that is exactly it. I have no idea what happened to make you so unsure of yourself, Lily, but believe me, you are a breath of fresh air and you are brilliant at what you do. I knew that from our first meeting when you got McArthur and Jennings onside. Look at the way you handled that meeting this morning. I couldn't keep up; I'd have totally bombed if you weren't there. I'm going to come clean; I barely slept last night, I was so nervous about meeting the team. I've never really worked so… closely with people before.'

'But you work at headquarters? Surely you work with hundreds of people every day?'

'Yes, but not so intensely, so personally. Generally, I email them, then they email me back and we keep going like that until the job gets done. So, face to face, real time… it's a new thing for me.'

I wipe my eyes and, for a second, the tears seem to stop. Christopher was nervous this morning? About talking to us? I hate to think of him sleepless and anxious. I feel even worse now for not inviting him on Friday night. It is hard to arrive in as an outsider. All of us already know each other. We're all pretty comfortable with how things work and what we want. But everything is new to Christopher. This is something I'm going to have to keep in mind, make sure he feels welcome while he's with us at the *Gazette*, consultant or not.

Just then, I notice John Boy holding the door open for the other tandem skydiver.

She's a nun.

She's an ancient, tiny, sweet-faced, smiling, hunched-over nun.

And here I am flat out on the floor acting like a spoilt brat. Or a drama queen. Or a coward. A dramatic, spoilt coward.

Either way, I'm not acting like anything I'd be proud of. I'm not acting like an Editor in Chief, I'm not acting like the person who fought so passionately to save the paper when face to face with McArthur and Jennings. And that makes me feel like a fraud. Like I've misled him. Like I didn't mean everything I said back there, but I did. So now I need to follow through and put that into action.

I smile up at Christopher. 'Do you really think I can do this?'

'Absolutely! The trick is to have complete faith that you are in safe hands, let go of all control and remember you can trust these guys, they know what they are doing. You can trust me too, Lily, I wouldn't let anything happen to you. I cross my heart and hope to die.' He crosses his chest and then twirls his fingers around each other, making me laugh at the action despite his unfortunate phrasing. 'My sister used to do that when she was about eight.' He takes himself by surprise and half-smiles.

I smile back, remembering that I used to do it too. Back then, it seemed the greatest measure of trust you could give to someone else. And somehow, it actually feels meaningful, right here, right now. It makes me believe him.

I look up and blink slowly at the sign above reception. *Skydiving—Everything will probably be all right!*

'They have a zero percent death rate. I checked,' Christopher assures me.

'But I bet the dead don't review,' I answer back.

'They're the best in the business.' He regards the sign above the door that reads, *If at first you don't succeed, then skydiving is not for you.* 'They just at suck at jokes.'

That's true.

'Really. McArthur let me on this leadership programme by the skin of my teeth. A staff death in the first week would reflect very poorly on my judgement. So, believe me, I've got almost as much to lose if you crash land.' He offers me his hand. 'All you have to do, Lily, is get up and then come down. We'll take care of everything else.'

I take a deep breath and look into his lovely green eyes a second longer than I should.

He raises a half-smile and says, 'Trust me?'

Without my job at the newspaper, I don't have much. Without the feature, I won't have the newspaper. Without Christopher, the paper is almost certainly going to fold. What choice do I really have?

Because I've got to start trusting people again.

Or die trying.

So I nod and slip my hand in his.

The first thing I'm handed is a thirty-page document of waivers, saying that in the not-as-unlikely-as-I-would-like chance we die, they aren't responsible for anything. There is no such thing as risk-free or the perfect equipment or the perfect instructor – just as everything in life, we can only hope for the best and, even so, shit happens.

As I squidge my eyes shut and sign my name over and over, deciding to just 'let go of control', John Boy takes thirty seconds to demonstrate proper form. When I try to imitate him and show him my form, he shrugs and says, 'yeah, close enough,' telling me to sit back down and try to remember to breathe.

I really thought it would all be over by now. Not that I'd spend most of the morning winding myself up before I even leave the Skyfall centre. But some suspicious whispering and nudging and chin-stroking begins. People notice that a lot of dark, thick clouds have rolled into the area. Even I can guess these aren't ideal conditions, because when you're in the sky, you need to see the ground so you know what your route down will be. Not that there's much more to it than falling straight down, right?

I remind myself I've already signed the forms. I'm doing this. I just need to quieten the manic monkey chatter in my head.

Time goes by, but those thick, dark, stubborn clouds remain…

The more experienced jumpers are now packing up, resigned to the fact that the conditions are too bad and it doesn't seem like it's going to happen at all. Maybe it will be possible that I escape this and save face at the same time? But the reality is that I need to do this today. I can't possibly put myself through this again and I need to write this feature, so it can go to print on Friday. If there's no skydive, then there's no feature and McArthur will shut us down before we've even taken off. I'll break the news to the staff that we're done, we lost, the *Newbridge Gazette* is no more. That I was exactly like Gareth in the end, all talk, no action. Just another bullshitty suit who couldn't follow through when things got real. And my mum will tell me in no uncertain terms that she told me so, that I'm not up to this. That she knew all along. And that I'll have little option other than take the job as my mum's PA. And that's not a conversation or a life I ever want to have.

And if I fail here, Christopher will go back to wherever he came from, which I don't want to happen just yet. There's something about him that makes me hopeful. Excited. Like something has woken up inside me. I want him to see me. I want to show him what I can do.

What can I say, but I like him being around. And it's more than him just being attractive. If he was a complete twat, I'd not even see his good looks. I'd discount him straight away, because I've been there, done that with gorgeous guys with ugly attitudes. But Christopher, I can tell he's not a twat. At least my experience has taught me that. A real twat would not have been patient with me back there – he'd have sighed and rolled his eyes and stropped off, pretending to be on an important call. Or he'd have hissed and shrugged and told me I was fired. But he didn't do that. He even offered to do it for me. And that makes him 1000 per cent better than both my previous boss and my previous fiancé. Dare I say, he's one of the nice ones. And that makes him different. Special. And really, really nice to be around.

But that's *not* to say I'm interested. Firstly, he's a colleague, so out of bounds for a million obvious reasons, and secondly, for all I know, he's probably already got a girlfriend. Even if it's that blonde that screamed at him in public that first day in the car park, more than likely he's attached to someone from his London life so that is the end of that.

We sit quietly for a few minutes, gazing up at the swirling, grey sky. Just when I begin to feel awkward about the silence between us, he asks if I'd like some tea and I accept the offer gratefully. When he returns – with chocolate biscuits – we relax a little more easily and begin to chat while we hang around to find out whether the jump will go ahead. I learn that he's staying in an Airbnb in the centre of Newbridge, just a studio flat for the four weeks he's here. He likes it; it's basic, but really, he's here to work and McArthur is still sending him work from head office, so she sees to it that he doesn't get much spare time, so it serves its purpose and means he can walk to the office in a few minutes.

We talk for ages, and then, just like that, the clouds scatter and the sun pierces through and shines down on us. Could this be a good omen?

He nudges me. 'You okay still? You look a bit pensive, or like you're about to be sick.'

I take a deep breath and decide that, today, failure is not an option. Today, I will fly. 'Mostly pensive. But a little sick,' I tell him.

'You know, the first time I did one of these, my instructor told me that when it feels most scary to jump, that's exactly the right time. Because if you don't, you've let your fear own you. And if you do that, you'll end up letting it rule you again and again and then you'll never be the strongest person you can be.'

'You think all skydiving instructors are failed philosophers and comedians?' I ask.

He shrugs. 'Maybe. But it is true. I think it works on every level. And it's not killed me yet.'

Soon the sky brightens completely and sunshine streams through. John Boy announces that it's okay, we can do it, not the best conditions, but still, a partly cloudy day instead of a fully cloudy day. But not everyone can jump. There was a small window, and although some people would indeed get to skydive today, the rest would have to come back another time. In a way, I'm now hoping I do get to jump today which is something I never believed I'd hear myself say, even if only in the privacy of my own thoughts.

They announce the names of the first group to go up, which includes me and the eighty-six-year-old nun, who I discover is doing this to raise money for her convent roof. So if she can muster up the gumption to do this for a good cause, surely I can too. It's now or never.

I step forward, trying to remember to breathe the slow deep breaths John Boy advised. And I'm not even off the ground yet. Christopher starts taking photos and it dawns on me that not only am I doing this, I'm doing this for the whole world to see… in the paper, online and for Mum in Half Moon Bay. I am here not as the shy wallflower daughter my mother thinks I am, but as a determined, fearless skydiver. It's time to be that person. And even if that feels completely unnatural, I'm going to fake it till I make it. So, dressed in a hideous bright orange jumpsuit, I dutifully paste on a smile and act like I'm excited to be here… Then the main instructor gives me an extra rip cord.

'What's this for?' I ask.

'So you can pull it in case something happens to John Boy mid-jump. If he faints or has a heart attack, that kind of thing, and you need to release the parachute yourself.'

My stomach heaves. If I'm not allowed to die up there, then neither is he. If John Boy has a heart attack on me, I will be *furious*. I will kill him myself.

Christopher snaps my photo.

I tell him that I hate his guts. And that if I don't make it, he'd better make sure someone feeds Chaplin.

We board an airplane so small, it looks like it came from Toys R Us. And this is a brand-new avenue of fear. I won't be coming down in this plane, I'll be falling hard and fast through the atmosphere, and that's all I can think about. A nightmare I can't wake up from.

But I am not telling my mum I walked away. So I take a deep breath and take my next steps forward.

The plane's seats have been removed, so it's just a hollowed-out space, where we huddle in our straps and helmets like apocalypse survivors. The little nun gives me two thumbs up, her face beaming. She's looking out the window and smiling serenely. And that's when it hits me.

Maybe she's okay about dying because she's satisfied with the life she's led? Is that why I'm so not okay with it? Is that why all I feel is a huge amount of anger and frustration with myself, because I'm sitting here wondering what's going to flash before my eyes in my final few seconds? Memories of making lemon curd tartlets with my grandmother? A rare tender moment with my mother as we sang together? Time by myself reading and writing and imagining… Imagining that my wedding day was going to be the best of my life, when it turned out to be the worst? Imagining that a best friend like Hannah would never hurt me? Imagining that, one day, I'd have a life that would be rich and full and fearless?

I have been waiting for life to begin. Always believing that when one thing fell into place, that everything else would follow. But it's not worked like that so far, so why do I still believe it to be true?

Maybe what I should be focusing on is how my life feels right now. Not in the future, not when the paper is in a better place, not when my mother says she's proud of me, not when I meet someone or change my hair or read a new book that will transform my life. All the time I'm spending imagining is robbing me of experiencing my life as it actually is. It takes me away from now. It takes me away from the life I'm living. Or leading. Or maybe sleep-walking through.

Lost in thought, I now realise we've taken off and we're rising. One of the guys opens the sliding door on the side of the plane, revealing the hatch that we will be leaping from. We are incredibly high in the air, above clouds, in a very cold grey stratosphere over the earth. This must be the place.

Then John Boy tells me we're only halfway up.

Halfway?

So much for my calculations.

I watch my altimeter slowly go up – 5,000 feet, 7,000 feet, 9,000 feet, 11,000 feet, and then finally to 13,000 feet. That's a little over two miles!

The plane circles the area. I think we're close. I think it's time.

Very suddenly, the door slides fully open and freezing cold air rushes in. The nun and her tandem partner begin to inch their way towards the opening and, just like that, they topple out into the vast, white wilderness. It is surreal seeing somebody drop out of the door and disappear into the sky, but not anywhere near as surreal as knowing I'm going do the same in about fifteen seconds.

My heart is thumping, and my mind is racing as a million and one thoughts go through my head. Palms sweaty, my vision tunnels, and all I can hear is the loud sound of the propellers along with that tiny voice inside screaming *holy shit* as John Boy and I creep towards the plane door. It's our turn now. There's nobody left here but us.

Soon, I am at the opening of the airplane. I curl my legs over the side and against the belly of the plane, as instructed, my toes hanging over into the abyss, but I can only manage to prise one eye open.

I cross my arms over my chest. 'I can't do this. I can't move,' I say, my voice rasping and tight. Even I did not expect to be this scared. This is a whole new level! My body has taken over and I can't release my hands. They are clenched tight and rock solid, my skin stretched white over my knuckles. It's like my body is telling me no! In the same way that you can't hold your breath past a certain point or keep your head under water. It's survival instinct.

I think of the botched skydive YouTube videos I shouldn't have watched last night... I can't... I just can't... I can't help it. The fear has gripped me. I'm not in charge of my own body, my own words. I just know I cannot do this. This is crazy. I tried to trick and distract myself with life-affirming hype and that may have been enough to get me up here, but it's not enough to get me to the end of this. I just cannot freakin' move from this spot.

John Boy is tilting himself outside of the hatch, ready to lunge forward. 'You don't have to do anything, just let go... let go of everything, all your fear, all your thoughts, just relax and leave it all to me. I'll do it for both of us. Just let go.'

I shake my head and shut my eyes. 'I mean, I really can't do this. I'm too scared... I'm too...'

'Yes you can, Lily! Don't you dare bail on me.'

I hear the words echo over and over.

Don't you dare bail on me!

I remember the last time very similar words were said. I had Adam's hand in mine and I begged him over and over, *don't you dare bail on me. Please, don't, not now, not here, not ever…*

But that was before I knew that actually there was no going back. There was no going forward. There was only free fall. Adam was in love with Hannah. He wasn't in love with me. This was not pre-wedding jitters or cold feet. This was him telling me that we were finished. Done. Broken. Unfixable.

Then I had no more choices. No more ways to go or places to turn. I let go of Adam's hand and I stopped begging. I walked out of the church. Down the aisle I should have walked as a married woman. A tear-stained bride heading past the packed pews, breaking out in the wrong direction.

And if in that moment, I could have thrown myself out of this moving plane, I would have done it. My body wouldn't have resisted. It would have been far easier, much less scary than catching the eye of confused guests, of a concerned vicar, of my disoriented grandmother and downward-gazing mother.

John Boy squeezes my hand. 'Lily, I bet you've done scarier things than this…'

Oh yes, that's certainly true. I have done scarier things than this.

'And believe me, on the other side of your fear, the other side of those clouds, is pure freedom, elation and nothing you've ever felt before. It's not falling – it's flying.'

I look at him. I want to see the other side. I want to feel the other side of fear.

I nod. 'Okay.'

'That's my girl. You ready to fly, Lily?'

I am. I am finally ready.

'Ready, set…' And we launch into the wind.

In one graceful swoop, we are free-falling 13,000 feet in one giant leap of faith, adrenaline and excitement. There is only one way to go now and we've got to roll with it.

The earth gets very close, very quickly, and if my fully conscious skydiving partner doesn't pull the parachute soon, we will splat. This is what John Boy calls the 'fun' part. I open my mouth to scream but nothing comes out because it feels like my throat has been sealed tight. And the wind-rush is so powerful, I can't shut my mouth closed! I'm a human wind tunnel hurtling against the earth. Sweet Jesus, I actually deserve to splat. This shouldn't be legal.

Finally, after the longest minute of my life, John Boy pulls the chute. There's a light tug and then we are floating. The biggest difference now is how quiet it is; with the rush of the wind gone, it seems like the most peaceful, serene experience ever, gently gliding through the air.

'Is this the other side?' I shout to John Boy and he nods, smiling with his eyes. And I agree. It feels like the other side of something all right. A better, brighter side.

This is the moment when I properly appreciate that we're still alive, that it's done, that the whole thing actually becomes un-fucking-believable. These few minutes after free fall, when the parachute opens and we soar through the sky, looking down at the most spectacular views, the rolling hills, the river, the town, the animals. John Boy was right, this is flying. Perhaps this is what makes us appreciate life so much. In that moment when you realise how fragile but miraculous your life is, you want to live it to the fullest. I am terrified, no doubt about that, but I know that I've been through worse and survived, that there must be something in me that is bigger than bailing out, stronger than that, despite my fear, pushing me further than I thought I could go.

I thought I'd feel like I was plummeting to the ground, but I don't. I don't really even get the sensation of falling. The world is so far away, and the wind resistance is pushing up against us, holding us, it feels like we're just floating in place.

We land smoothly and softly on the grass. John Boy high-fives me. 'You could be good at this! I think you'll be back.'

I shake my head and throw my arms around him. It seems the right thing to do, like he rescued me up there, maybe even before we left the plane.

Christopher runs towards me, camera in one hand and a bottle of bubbly in the other. I pop the cork and let the shower of bubbles spray all over us, and I take a sip from the neck and hand it to John Boy, laughing from the pit of my stomach. Now that I'm on terra firma, I feel on top of the world.

It feels like a lifetime since I was on solid ground; Christopher assures me it's been twenty-three minutes.

It's only Monday, and this is already shaping up to be a hell of a week.

Christopher puts down his camera and gives me a huge hug, 'You did it! Trust me now?'

I hold my face in my hands and nod. 'Yes! I do! I can't believe that just happened!'

And then we're both laughing so hard I've got to bite the side of my hand. And somewhere in between breaths, he catches my eye and tells me that I'm amazing. Hearing that for the second time in one day, now that's a record.

He promised that everything was going to be just fine. And sure enough, it was. Maybe that belief he has in me is catching.

Lily-1, Fear-0.

CHAPTER 9

I've been up since 5 a.m. Can't sleep. Can't stay under the duvet any longer… too much to do. Too much to feel, too much life, too much energy, too much gratitude for the big, sprawling day of opportunity ahead of me.

My eyes spring open and I jump out of bed, leaving Chaplin asleep as I dust off my old bike and go for a cycle as the sun comes up. *Glorious.* I watch the fan of warm, light oranges and pinks creep up from the horizon. The sun slowly lifts its head, beating back the cold grey shadows until they fade to a perfect, clear blue sky. And I think to myself, I've been up there.

Back home, I take a long, hot shower, using all my best toiletries that smell wonderful – rhubarb and rose – and I'm lathered in luxuriant bubbles. Then I blow-dry my hair properly in sections with a round brush and not in my usual upside-down shake and blast frenzy. I put on my make-up at my little vanity table as I sing along to the radio and finally snip off the tags and slip on a new blue dress that I have held off wearing, waiting for some unidentified future occasion to justify its purchase. But today is as good an occasion as any. It feels that it is the beginning of something new. And that's the funny thing about beginnings, you often don't realise that they've already started.

I make fresh coffee as I fling open my windows and let the early morning sunshine breathe its buttery warmth into my little kitchen. Breakfast is a delicious, nutritious one of eggs and toasted bread with fresh cherry tomatoes.

And then I do something that I've actually wanted to do for a long, long time. Maybe, something that wouldn't qualify as a very exciting bucket list item but, none the less, something I long to do more often, more regularly, something that really makes me happy. I take out my light blue Moleskine notebook, sit in the morning sunlight with Chaplin in my lap and I write.

I pour out everything that is in my head, loving the feel of my hand brushing against the soft, silken, cream-coloured pages and watching in quiet fascination how the once blank space fills with dancing ink and cursive flounces. A bit like the skydive, I'm often fearful before I do this. That's what keeps me away from it, the paralysing nerves that convince me that I'll sit down and no words will come, that I'll stare into the abyss of the empty page with nothing to say, no mark to make, the mute, vacant face of failure staring back at me.

The last few submissions to Gareth hadn't exactly bolstered my confidence. I wanted to break into longer features, so I'd drafted some and sent them to him, but his feedback was that they were too long, too detailed, too personal/emotional/girly. The last one I'd sent I got no feedback at all, which I guess meant he couldn't be bothered to even read it. This crushed me altogether and I felt silly for even trying. Like I was kidding myself that I could ever write beyond car-boot sales and classifieds.

But this morning, whether it's still the adrenaline coursing through my veins from yesterday's skydive or the real beginning of a new me, I'm not yet sure, but I feel brave. More than brave, I feel the fear, my hand quivering, my breath stuck in my throat, but I sit with it anyway.

And guess what? I start writing, and words come, and the world doesn't end. And by the time I've finished, I've written eight pages. And it feels good. Really damn good.

I'm starting to appreciate how lucky I am. There are so many situations that I could have been born in to that would never have allowed me to live my life the way I do. What if my chance on this earth was as a cavewoman being dragged around by my hair, or a medieval concubine, or a slave riddled with leprosy, or an unloved daughter traded for livestock?

Unloved daughter. Well, maybe my new outlook doesn't change everything. True, my mum is a complete narcissistic pain in the backside, but she's living her own life, far away, without a chance in hell of ever returning to the low-lights of Newbridge, so even that cloud has a silver lining.

And the main point is, I will survive. More than survive. More than just show up. It is time I lived my life without the snooze button. I've got lots to be excited about. A lot to live for and look forward to. I get to do a bucket list without being at the end of my life. That's a win-win.

So, with my new-found appreciation for my serendipitous existence, I make a pledge to myself that, from now on, I'll make the most of my time here on this planet. I'm going to embrace opportunities and give things a try, approach things with hope, be a person that knows I didn't waste any of my chances. And if I ever do slip into a state of existential apathy ever again, I'm going to take myself back up to 13,000 feet and throw myself out face first. And that should see me right.

But no need for that this morning. This morning is the first morning in as long as I can remember that I feel like I've stolen away a perfect day before it was even supposed to start. And I'm going to make sure the feeling continues. I'm going to walk into the newsroom. Editorial check! STRUT into the newsroom. I'm not going to lie or downplay how I'm feeling. I'm pretty bloody proud of myself. Okay, significant downplay there, the truth being I feel *unbelievable*.

I texted my mum last night and she hasn't replied. This is a great sign. It means she's completely stumped by the news that I went through with it and that I'm ecstatic about it. And that makes me feel every shade of wonderful, that I've already challenged her view of me as the mortified eight-year-old stuck up a climbing wall. Maybe I'm challenging my own view of myself and what I'm all about. And that's exciting because who knows what new doors this may open. For the first time in a long time, I'm excited; there's a world of possibility to explore.

I check the time, delighted to see that I've got an hour and a half before I set out to work. As if he can hear my thoughts, Chaplin meows and rubs his tail against my bare ankle. I snap a quick photo of him and text it to Mr Clark's phone, just so he knows that he's getting on fine and being well looked after. I haven't heard back from him yet, but when he does feel better, I'm sure he'll be in touch and I'll arrange a visit. Chaplin in tow.

I open up the pantry and find I'm stocked up with eggs, flour and sugar and a few remaining jars of my grandmother's lemon curd that I made weeks ago. Mary likes it, so when I make it, I always pass her a few jars as a small token of my gratitude for all her leads.

Chaplin begins to purr.

'Oh, so you think so too? Well, it's settled then, as we've got some people to thank. If we get cracking now, we've just enough time to rustle up some tartlets and start spreading the love.'

CHAPTER 10

'What the hell?'

I arrive in the office to a standing ovation. A home-made banner hangs from two coat racks reading 'Congratulations!'

I stand in utter confusion and disbelief, slowly placing my bag and Tupperware box of lemon tarts on the nearest desk. It is only 8.30. Why is everyone here? Why is anyone here? This place is usually dead for another hour or so at least.

But these guys are very much alive. Amy wolf-whistles me with two fingers stuck either side of her mouth. Jasmine and Dylan are whooping and clapping and howling, 'Go Lily!'

Even Mark salutes me with one finger.

'What is actually going on here?' I ask them. Why are they so excited? They all knew I was doing the skydive, so why this? Have I missed something?

Amy tiptoe-runs in her too-high heels to me, taking both my hands in hers. 'When Christopher came back to the office yesterday afternoon, he asked us to help pick the best photos for the campaign… Oh my goodness, Lily, I heard you mention that you were frightened, but the look on your face! You looked like you were going to the gallows and that was before you were even kitted out. You were deathly white and then all shades of greenish grey. You must have been absolutely crapping yourself, girl…' She grabs the back of my head and presses me into her ample bosom. 'But still you did it! Like a true professional, an inspirational leader! And even more than that, you did it for us!'

I attempt to shake my head in disbelief but can't whilst wedged in Amy's chest. I pull back for air. And that's when I see it. Dylan and Mark step apart and roll out a life-size, colour poster of me mid-air, in my wind-blown orange jumpsuit, my face stretched in a smile wider than I've ever seen, my two thumbs up, a rainbow parachute filling the background with eye-popping colour against the electric blue sky. This is an amazing picture; it looks like it belongs in a gallery or an award-winners collection. I can't believe that person there is me.

'Who? What? When did…?'

I hear the door click open behind me; it's Christopher, with a tray of coffees.

'Lily! What do you think? The tagline will read, the *Newbridge Gazette*— Wait a second…' He hands Jasmine the coffees and stretches out the top of the poster. 'The *Newbridge Gazette* – before you make up your mind, open it.'

I am speechless. It's perfect! 'You did this? So soon?'

He shrugs. 'Least I could do after what you put yourself through. You've really raised the bar now.'

'And the tagline? You came up with that too?'

'I thought the idea of opening your mind would work well with the parachute image, and this is my favourite shot. I mean, you look like you're having the time of your life! So, it just came together. With the help of these guys, of course. Dylan sorted the graphics, Jasmine got us a great deal on the express printing and Mark hooked in a huge account with Escapades Travel and Tourism, which is insane, so ad sales will see a massive upturn which should make McArthur and Jennings very pleased. We set up a *Gazette* Local Projects charity link for donations and sponsorships – I thought it would be good if we use anything we raise to support the nun with her roof fund? We should be able to get a couple of quid for her and I got a great shot of her landing too. So great team effort all round.'

I mouth 'thank you' to each of them one by one. We're doing it. It's happening. This paper is going to fight for its life.

Christopher turns to Amy. 'And it was Amy's idea to let you know how much we appreciate you putting yourself out there yesterday. Think it sent a very strong message to each of us about how much this place means to you and how important it is we get it back on its feet.'

I can see a shy half-smile of satisfaction cross Christopher's lips as we guzzle down our fresh coffees. I break open my tub of lemon tartlets and we all dig in to a staff breakfast party.

Once we're sugared-up and caffeinated, everyone settles down to work. Christopher sidles in beside me, lowering his voice so as not to disturb the others. 'Everyone's so excited Lily, you've really made a great start and as they say, a great start is half the battle. So, once you get a chance to write up your feature, send it over to me and I'll take care of the layout and photographs. If we aim for midday? Does that work for you?'

I open my bag and slide out my blue Moleskine. 'Draft already done. Once I started writing I couldn't stop. I'll trim, polish, type it up and have it over to you in the next hour.'

He reaches out and runs a finger along my notebook. 'You write longhand?' he asks, his gaze settling on mine.

'Yes, I guess it's habit from interviews with people, trying to scribble notes and keep eye contact and stay personal at the same time. Funny how people don't mind a pen and paper, but take out a Dictaphone or a laptop and they clam up altogether. So, I always carry a notebook.'

'Me too.' He smiles, and I blush.

'Of course, in the pub, that's what you were working on. I'm still really sorry about that...'

He waves a hand in the air. 'I'm really sorry for suggesting something that was so far out of your comfort zone. I mean it,

Lily, if I knew how scared you were, I never would have suggested it. It really is over and above—'

'No, I'm glad you did – I loved it,' I tell him.

'Really?'

'Yes! So, thank you for suggesting it, and helping me. I feel great, better than ever. You're the expert on bucket lists and what McArthur wants, so whatever you have in mind next, I'll do it, I promise. No meltdowns, no fuss.'

Christopher reaches into his pocket for his notebook – a new one I notice, red Moleskine this time – and flicks through some pages, sliding the pencil from behind his ear. I must have soaked the old one beyond salvation, despite what he says. He stops on a page, scribbles down something that looks like a drunken geometric shape and then ticks it. 'Okay, in that case, I've got a few ideas that will really strike a chord with our target audience. I'll get back to you at the team meeting after lunch?'

I nod as he takes a bite of his tartlet.

'These are delicious by the way.'

'They're to say thanks for… you know.' I take a strand of hair. 'For all your support. With the paper.'

He smiles. 'Worth every bite. Now – go write! The future of the *Newbridge Gazette* is in your hands! Twenty-two per cent remember!'

The future.

Yep, I like the sound of that.

And as soon as I sit down, I start to type.

Buckley's Bucket List
No. 1 – The Skydive

I am not a daredevil. I am not an adrenaline junkie. In fact, I wouldn't even call myself mildly athletic, seeing as the last time I ran was for a taxi home on Friday night after a few too many at The Black Boar. I've generally been known to tuck away in my little cottage with a good book and go to the library and wander through the labyrinths of shelves or make a cup of tea and spend a lazy day gazing at a computer screen. Even on my days off.

So, you can imagine my response when skydiving was suggested as the first item for Buckley's Bucket List.

I was horrified! Not only did I not want to do it, but I believed I couldn't do it. That I was physically, psychologically and emotionally UNABLE to see this through. I wanted to bail.

And that's when I started to get my breakthrough, to realise what bucket lists are actually for. And why skydiving was the perfect choice for me.

When it comes to skydiving, I believe there are three kinds of people.

The first kind hears the word 'skydiving' and thinks: 'The Best. Idea. Ever!' These are people who enjoy rock climbing and ultra-marathons, snowboarding, bungee-jumping and push the limits of their bodies and minds for fun. For them, life is a relentless adventure, with all their experiences flickering by in jump cuts as they endlessly quest for the next big rush. Or so I imagine. I know these people exist, but they don't know that I do. I am absolutely not one of these people.

The second kind of person thinks skydiving sounds stupid and horrifying. This person is likely to say something like, 'Why on earth would you jump out of a perfectly good airplane?' The idea of falling from such a great height is entirely alien and goes against all instincts to stay alive. It's a pointless and unnecessary risk. Why do that when you could have a great meal, watch a brilliant movie or spend time taking a leisurely stroll? On safe, solid ground! There is no force on earth that will make them change their mind and fling themselves out of a plane. I can relate to this person. I absolutely get it.

And then there's the third kind of person. This person has a profound instinctual fear of skydiving but also knows deep down that if they could find a way to break through that fear, they could really enjoy it. Or it will go some way to help them learn about themselves in a completely new light. Hopefully. That is, if they are alive at the end. If you'd asked me before this week which person I was, I would have answered the second kind, but it seems that when push comes to shove, quite literally, I am in fact the third kind of person.

I showed up at the Skyfall open to the idea that I might not go through with it but as a reporter, news is my life. I'm always on the hunt for the next story, the next breakthrough. I keep moving. So, in work mode, I do the next thing I'm told to do, and the next, right up until I am in the door of the plane, looking over the most eye-watering sight: the bluest of skies and the arch of our planet. And then, heart pounding and shaking, I remember that fear doesn't own me, I am more than the monkey voices in my head telling me I can't, and I keep moving until I have leaped from the plane and I am flying through the clouds.

And oh, the flying. I could jabber on for ages about the thrill of flying. It is nothing like falling, or roller coasters, or anything else I have ever done. In the moment you leave the airplane, not only does the monkey voice stop, it becomes meaningless. Free fall is the most perfect release and the most perfect form of 'nowness' I have ever encountered. My instructor tried to initiate some conversations with me, but after I could only murmur a breathy 'Oh wow... oh, wow...' he gave up and encouraged me to keep on looking at Mother Nature.

We pierced through the cloud and emerged into a landscape that unrolled every which way around us. With gushes of wind pressing against me and such majestic sights below, I couldn't speak, whoop, yell, think; I just soared towards the earth without a single thought. That may be the most exciting and extraordinary part of skydiving: all the BS fades away and you are overcome by beauty.

We landed smoothly, lifting our legs to touch down on our butts. And then? I won't deny it, I tied my jumpsuit around my waist and fist-pumped the air. Everything felt HD, everyone was my best friend, the world was new, beautiful, refreshed. Or maybe, just me.

The prospect of being afraid and jumping anyway is something that may seem impossible but, when it is faced head-on, it is for many the purest form of joy and an incredible sense of achievement. And I've already found that it doesn't wear off straight away. Right now, I feel like I can do anything, and I want to take on the world.

I can't wait to share more details of my new adventures each week on this Bucket List, and even more importantly, I can't wait to hear from you. So what have you done that's changed your life or your perspective? Comment below and see you back here next Friday.

I sit back from the screen and re-read what I've written. The first draft of my first feature. But now I've reached the end, I can't help but doubt myself. Despite the progress I've made these last few days, there's still that niggling fear that I can't shake away as I prepare to show Christopher my writing. I hope it's good enough. I hope Christopher likes it. I hope he doesn't think I'm rambling and amateur and scatty compared to the standard of the London press. Maybe I should just ask one of the others to give it a once-over first? Jasmine is across the floor on a call. I could wait till she's hung up, it'd be good to get a second opinion before I forward it to him—

There's a rap on the door and when I turn around to answer it, I see it's Mary, duster in one hand and Post-it note of leads in the other.

I wave her in and pass her a tartlet.

'Lovely! Just like your gran used to make them, Lily,' she tells me.

This delights me. I love being compared to my grandmother.

'You look like you've got news for me,' I say, gesturing to Mary's Post-it as she takes a seat.

She leans in, lowering her voice and cupping her mouth as if sharing something top secret. 'Word has it that if Johnson becomes mayor he's going to close the library.'

I gasp my disbelief. 'But he can't do that! People use it every day! What will they do instead?' Newbridge is not a very wealthy town. The library has always been not only a main source of books for entertainment but also for education. I did all my study there, during school and afterwards when I tried to better myself with some online courses. That library is a lifeline; without it, we'd have even less chances than we do already.

'Well not enough of them use it and he needs to be seen to be running a tight budget,' she says.

'That's horrendous. We'll have to stop him, let people know what he's got planned!'

'Not yet.' Mary holds up her hand. 'Too early to go to print till we've got the full story. Once I've gathered all the evidence we need, then I'll be back and we'll make our move. What do you say, Lily?'

'I'm behind you all the way, Mary. You just tell me when.' Mary may not be an investigative journalist in title but she is in every other way. Timing is of the essence with politicians, so once she tells me to make a move I'll be ready to take action. What that action is yet, I'm not quite sure.

She nods approvingly and takes a deep breath. 'All quiet besides. Auditions went well at the theatre. Full cast for this new play. My granddaughter is involved – she's a horse or something – so I said I'd lend a hand with costumes.'

Mary sits up from her chair. 'Right, I'd better get on my way. Oh yes, I hear you've got Mr Clark's cat?'

How the hell!

'Well, you may be interested to know that he's having brain surgery this morning. They discovered a tumour when they were examining his head after his fall. Lucky thing he got the fright he did or they'd never have found it and he could be dead by now.'

'That's unbelievable! I'll go visit him tomorrow,' I say.

She shakes her head. 'He's been transferred to a specialist ward, won't be back till next week. I'll let you know when he's up for visitors. Not that he'll have many. Quiet sort he is. Good with animals; people not so much. I'll see you soon.'

I glance out as she leaves, and I see that Jasmine's still on the phone. I look back at the draft feature on my screen. I've tried my best. If Christopher doesn't like it, I can just redo it. Hardly the end of the world. The longer I leave it, overthinking and second-guessing, the less time I'll have to rewrite it if it's not what he's after. As he's been assigned as our consultant, McArthur trusts his judgement to turn this paper around, and so he has the final say as to whether this goes to print or gets fed through the shredder.

I type in his email and hover over the send button. Too long? Too detailed? Too personal? Too emotional?

Feel the fear and do it anyway. I press send.

I refresh my inbox every twenty seconds thereafter, because I want to know what Christopher thinks of my draft ASAP; I can't think of anything else until I know how it is received. I'm excited and slightly nervous at the same time, in that hell of waiting for his feedback – you know, that tiny I'm going to die of panic every time my email pings and then the disappointment when it's just another depressing offer from a new dating website or a mailing list I've already unsubscribed from or someone wanting you to accept five million quid for free, just hand over your bank details and it's a done deal!

I am supposed to be doing so many other things. I am supposed to leave the office. I am supposed to leave this seat. But I don't, because I am unable to do any other work, because I can't think about anything else, because I'm WAITING.

Soon an hour has passed and I am now one hundred per cent entirely and completely sure that he's trying to decide how to sack me. Or worse, how to tell me I can't write.

As I've already raided my secret chocolate stash, I turn to the final lemon tartlet, my third of the day, and move the tell-tale sweet wrappers around my desk in an effort to tidy up and distract myself. And then ping!

I scramble back to my screen. It's him. It's in. Message from Christopher. I pause a moment. Please be okay. Please don't hate it. Don't think it's crap. Because that'll mean you think I'm crap and everything will then change around here. And I really don't want it to because I'm loving every second. I'm hopeful. I'm excited. And I want to stay feeling this way. My phone starts to vibrate with messages, reminding me that I'm at work and I can't afford the time to sit here and overthink this. I'm going to have to look now, to face the music one way or another, just in case I've got to dash out and pick up on something else and then I'll be torturing myself about this all day long. I bite down on my lip and click it open –squinting through semi-closed eyes to read the first line.

This is incredible, Lily – beyond my wildest expectations. Just want to make sure you're okay sharing so much with the

readers? Personally, I think it is wonderful. I only wish I had
your bravery. I'll definitely be reading every week with quality
features like this. If you're sure you're happy with it, I'll schedule
publication time for bright and early Friday morning. And then
we'll go from there. I love it, really great job.
  Kindest regards,
  Chris

I let out a little sigh. Yes, it is personal, but that's how I want it
to be. I didn't want to it to read like another characterless column.
And yes, I'm sharing my honest feelings with readers, but I want
it that way too. Because at least I know it's real, it's the truth.
Not some pretentious bravado or phoney facade. I can, hand on
heart, say that everything I wrote in the feature is true.

I re-read Christopher's email one more time.

Yep, it's says it there in black and white. He likes it. He loves
it. He's got a really good degree and an MBA and he's been
nominated for all sorts of awards and I can't help but feel proud
that my little effort, home-grown from my Moleskine and the
guidance of JJ Oakes, has managed to impress him. That I've
done a decent job. It means a lot to me.

Jasmine pops her head around the door. 'You look like you've
just got some good news! What's happened?'

I beam at her. 'You know, nothing. And everything.'

Which sums it up pretty well.

CHAPTER 11

We sit round the table in Christopher's office for our 2 p.m. planning meeting. 'Hell Raiser. Who's heard of it, done it or wants to do it?' he begins.

Amy and I shrug our shoulders. Dylan and Jasmine high-five. Mark starts laughing and shakes his head.

'Okay, that's good. Three out of five of you know what I'm talking about and that matches general stats, meaning we'll engage with those in the know and pique the interest of those who don't.'

It is on the tip of my tongue to ask him what he is talking about when he hands me a glossy file of photographs of very muddy, sweaty, muscly, bedraggled-looking people, looking like they are screaming inside.

'Lily, as you're the one that's going to be doing it, probably best you have a flick through and get a feel for what it's all about. Basically, Hell Raiser is a hardcore adult obstacle course that pits brave souls against 5K of muddy terrain and five impossible-seeming obstacles. It's not a race and it's not a competition. It's a challenge. Team members range in age from twenty-two to forty, with different levels of fitness and from all walks of life.'

I open to the first glossy page where there is a list of events with names such as Halfpipe to Hell, Barbaric Barbwire Crawl, Devil's Enema…

'Devil's Enema?' I blurt out.

Mark catches my eye. 'Last time they held it in Newbridge, about two years ago, I volunteered to help out. Grown men on their knees, weeping in the mud.' He raises an eyebrow at Christopher. 'Are you actually trying to kill her? There's no way I'd suggest this as suitable for someone like Lily. And before you say anything, I'm not being negative, just realistic.'

I nod. Mark's right; I don't even like getting out of the bath without heating up my pyjamas *and* my slippers on the radiator. I glance back down at the brochure. 'Hellfire's Sniper Alley? You are trying to kill me.' My finger races through the descriptions; swim through ice water, crawl in the dirt under a low canopy of barbed wire, wade through electrified cables and run at a near-vertical half-pipe slathered in mud. 'Bloody hell, why would anyone want to do something so horrendous?'

Mark grabs the tuft of his beard in his fist, his other hand running over his forehead. 'I appreciate what you're trying to do here, Christopher, I really do. And from those skydive photos, Lily, it's clear you're busting your back trying to make a great feature and capture those new readers, but this is a different league. It isn't just physically hard, it's mentally hard. I'm not sold on this idea.'

Christopher listens patiently to everything Mark says before speaking. 'Okay, I hear you.' He stands from the table, flips over a new piece of chart paper and begins explaining with shapes and words and arrows and numbers in black felt-tip. 'The reason I'm pitching this to you all is this; a lot of research has been done about the generation now in their twenties and thirties who are more connected globally but have fewer daily interactions at a local level. Headlines suggest loneliness and depression are running at record levels, even among groups that appear by other measures to be outwardly successful.' He trades his black marker for a red one, draws a big zero and continues. 'A recent paper characterises this generation as "nones", on the basis that when asked to tick boxes about political or religious or other social organisations or clubs to which they belong, "none" is the box many check.' He marks a big 'x' in the middle of the flipchart. 'Yet the human need for community, for belonging, has not gone away. People still aspire to feel part of something bigger than themselves. And the question arises – how do we address that need in new ways?' He trades markers again and draws a big green question mark.

I take a sip of water and wait. I want to hear more. Because I relate to everything he's saying. I am a 'none'. Looking around the table, I suspect we all are, but nobody is going to admit it and Christopher is on the brink of losing them.

Mark coughs into his fist. Amy picks at the turquoise jewels stuck onto her acrylic nails. Jasmine and Dylan are having eye-sex. Christopher needs some back-up.

I press both my hands down on the table. 'No wonder no one else has covered it; it looks absolutely terrifying! But it's for that very reason that we need to go for it. We have our foot in the door with this new readership. Look at the Escapades deal we got off the back of the last feature and it hasn't even run yet! Who knows where this could lead us next. I'm in. I think it is exactly what we need.'

Jasmine peels her eyes away from Dylan and looks up at me. 'Good on you, Lily. I like that we're doing new stuff. I like that we're trying to stand out and be different and that we're not just doing the same stuff every other small-town paper is doing. It's exciting.'

I clap my hands together. 'Exactly! That is progress, right there. We're moving in the right direction, we are the right people in the right place at the right time. So, let's hear this idea out, let's give it a chance.'

Each of the team straightens up in their seats and looks back towards the flipchart. Amy starts making notes, the rest follow suit.

Christopher fixes his glasses, flashes me a smile and continues. 'One of the things that people, especially young people, increasingly gather around is the idea of well-being. They have seen the junk food and workaholic lives of their parents' generations and many of them rebel against it. The trend towards fitness and health has grown consistently over the last decade. We're spending more time thinking about how we can live happier, healthier lives. We look for dramatic experiences that might enhance them. That's why the Hell Raiser event in Newbridge this weekend is already nearly sold out. This demographic of Newbridge wants this. And we want *them*.'

There's silence around the table. Only this morning I told Christopher that I trusted him to come up with my new task and I'm convinced by his pitch. I'm fascinated by his grasp and insights on people and society and our place in the world. But even if I want to do this, for me, for the paper, for him, I actually don't know if I can, physically. I can't just strap myself to the back of an expert on this one and let the equipment do the work. I will have to do this thing myself. And no matter how keen I am, I won't have a pair of bulging biceps ready in time.

Dylan holds up his iPad and starts a slideshow of images from the website's gallery. It doesn't look like a running track, that's for sure. It looks like an industrial obstacle course in the middle of a field. Completely different from anything I've ever seen before. But just as Christopher said, there do seem to be all shapes and sizes of people, and they all seem to be grinning and laughing and having the time of their lives while sliding down mud tracks.

Amy clears her throat. 'What about being fit enough? Like, aren't there people training for his kind of thing for months?'

Christopher sits back down at the table. 'Six-packs and zero body fat are great for some, but they are not a Hell Raiser requirement. Fitness can only get you so far, this is really about mental endurance. Remember, it's a challenge not a race. I've seen musclemen get intimidated by the ice swim and I've seen groups of friends push each other over the wall by their butt cheeks. It's what you make it.'

Dylan passes his iPad around. 'Me and Jasmine are already signed up. We got free tickets because they're using the field by

Jasmine's dad's house. The organisers are cool, I'm sure they'd sort you out if you told them you're going to write it up in the paper. They'd be thrilled with the publicity.'

'So you two are definitely going to do it? No chickening out?'

'Yeah, why not? It's more Jasmine's thing but I want to do it with her, be around to help her if she gets stuck.' A wry smile dances on his lips. 'Or vice versa.'

Jasmine winks at him and blows him a kiss. 'Oh my god, I have just had the best idea. Why don't we do this as a team? That way Lily can still do her feature and we can get behind her. Amy, you're up for that right?'

Amy bites down on her bottom lip, her eyes lighting up. 'How much FUN would that be, all of us in it together. Yes! Team *Gazette*!' She turns to me. 'Can we? Say yes. Yes, yes, yes!'

I turn to Mark. 'What do you think?'

He stretches back in his chair, elbows high above his head. 'Only seventy five per cent of entrants finish.'

Christopher holds his hands up in the air. 'Only a quarter don't. And teams always finish. No man left behind is a powerful motivator.'

'Or woman!' Amy adds, puffing out her chest whilst trying to flex her non-existent muscles.

Mark strokes his beard again. 'I have to say it was one of the most positive events that I've been to. It's friendly. People help each other out and it truly takes teamwork to get through the obstacles. Especially tough challenges like running the Half-Pipe to Hell. It's practically impossible to do without catching someone's hand and being hauled up.'

I think Christopher has managed to change Mark's mind. I think he's changed my mind.

Mark swings forward on his chair and a cheeky grin appears on his face. 'And that beer at the end. There's nothing like it and that was when I was just a volunteer! Imagine the satisfaction if you've just put your body through miles of mud and you're aching all over, nothing could possibly top the first sip of ice-cold beer at the finish line. Forget the sports massages and back patting that follows a marathon. If there's one thing Hell Raisers know how to do, it's how to have a well-earned drink at the end. There's an idea – maybe I could chase down the local breweries for some ad space?'

Dylan rubs his hands together. 'Genius. Get the craft beer guys on board. They might even drop in some courtesy crates of pale ale to keep us hydrated.'

Mark wipes his lips. 'Now you're talking. Okay, Hell Raisers, I'm in. Hands up who else?'

And, one by one, all hands around the table are raised high.

Even mine.

CHAPTER 12

There must be a full moon or some other bizarre cosmic behaviour on the horizon because the freakiest thing has just happened. My mother has texted me.

Well done on your skydive! Just read your article this morning on my phone! The photos are amazing, you look so happy, my baby doll. Ah to kiss that face! Missing you too much. Recording all day, so can't chat. Wish me luck. New producer is evil. No taste. Too many ideas. Indecisive then bullish. I've got her down for Oppositional Defiance Disorder. I say white. She says blue. Wish she'd take a skydive without a parachute. Love you love you love you xx

See? Freaky.

Then Christopher arrives at my desk and draws a box of chocolates from behind his back.

'It's official. Head Office have had their 11 a.m. progress meeting and I'm just off a call from McArthur herself. She's asked me to pass on her congratulations.' He hands me the box of very posh handmade chocolates. 'Cliché, I know, but you're the creative one, right? I noticed your little chocolate stash, so thought you might like them. They're my personal favourite.'

'Thank you! That's too kind.' I raise an eyebrow. 'Come on, then. Don't leave me hanging. Hit me with some numbers. Was it good enough? We really need a five per cent reader increase this week. I mean, five per cent would be awesome, but I don't want to get my hopes up. In the first week that's probably too ambitious, right?' I know I'm jabbering on. It's a nervous habit. So I stop and pause and take a really deep breath. Trying to silence the teeming chatter in my mind. If I hear anything less than five per cent, I know I'm going to be devastated, despite McArthur's congratulations. And these chocolates.

I cross my fingers. And stare him down.

'Please say five per cent. I have been praying for five per cent.'

He laughs and clears his throat. 'Brace yourself. The *Newbridge Gazette* hit... 3,200 new readers this week. Sales up nine per cent. Escapades have signed up for another ad run, doubling the usual weekly profit from commercial sales alone.'

'Nine per cent? That is AMAZING!'

'And your feature was shared, liked and retweeted two hundred and eighty-two times within hours of going live. That's a great start, Lily. You should be really proud of yourself.' He hands me his phone. 'Have a look at some of the comments people have written on the main site.'

I forgot that people could or would comment. I guess that's the big difference between traditional print press and our new online version: readers can feed back instantly – good or bad.

I swallow before I look. I actually don't think I could take it if there were some nasty comments in there.

But it's like Christopher has read my mind; he nudges me gently. 'Seriously, take a look. Nothing but good stuff, I promise.'

I take the phone from him and lean against the edge of the desk, scrolling through the twenty or so comments from names I don't recognise; these are real readers, not encouraging boosts from Jasmine or Dylan.

i read this over and over & really love it sooo much. thanx for sharing your experience with us <3. I live across from the centre but was always too chicken, booking now! #bucketlist

Goin skydiving next week and this article helped me a lot. I'm terrified of heights but my best friend is getting married and this is what she wants to do with her wedding party. Was going to bail, but now I'm going for it. Thanks! #motivated #feelthefearanddoitanyway

I plan to read this 2 more times before I jump this Saturday for charity... DAAAAAMN, I hope I don't forget you Lily!!! #skydiveforbreastcancer

I just can't believe it. I wrote this article and people have read it and it's moved them enough to write back to me! Just when I thought I couldn't love my job at the *Gazette* any more, this whole new avenue has opened up; a connection to strangers, colleagues, the wider community. It's so much more than I've ever felt before. So much more than I ever expected. After withdrawing into my own little world for the past few years, it's as if I'm waking up from a long, deep sleep. And it's glorious. I'm overwhelmed that people are reaching out and taking notice. They don't think it's weird or mad or bad. They like it and that makes my heart feel ready to fly straight out of my chest.

Christopher has already opened the chocolates and offers me one. 'Jasmine told me that she popped in to the hairdresser just now to make an appointment and she overheard them discussing the skydive piece. Asking each other what they would put on their bucket list. She said it was the first time she wasn't embarrassed telling strangers that she worked at the *Gazette*. Well done, Lily, looks like Buckley's Bucket List is doing its job. And some.'

'The skydive was your idea. And the tagline, and the photos, so thank you, Christopher. What a team, eh? We'll break the news when everyone's back in the office after lunch. I can't wait to see their faces. This is the best news this paper has had in a long time.'

I high-five Christopher and pop a heart-shaped chocolate into my mouth. And then bam. What is happening in my mouth eclipses every other sense in my whole body. This is, literally, sensational. My brain can't focus on anything else except the silken chocolate on my tongue. It makes me stop breathing, it's so good. I perch it still on my tongue as if it's hot, I don't want to waste one second of this little chocolate bomb, covered in finely chopped hazelnuts and really smooth dark Belgian chocolate. I let it melt ever so slightly until creamy caramel oozes from its centre. Christopher stands in silence as I savour and finally swallow this cocoa gold, making little noises of appreciation along the way. I lean against my desk once it's all over, giving myself a moment to recompose.

'I thought I was addicted to chocolate, but that was before I tried *that*. How am I supposed go back to a standard whole nut bar now?'

He hands me the box. 'They're yours, so no need for standard stash for a while. If you pace yourself.'

Hmm. Those chocolates have zero chance of survival in my office. They won't see next publication day.

His phone rings out in his pocket and he excuses himself to take the call.

I close my office door, pull down the blinds, kick off my heels and pop one more chocolate in my mouth.

And I breathe out a deep, throaty, exhausted yowl of relief.

Week one and we're on track for success. Everything is going well so far: the team, the new direction, Christopher – and the sales are picking up. We've got three weeks left to make up the numbers and bring us to twenty-two per cent. Then we're home free, just as McArthur promised. I'll tell Mary; she's a one-woman media machine. By tomorrow morning everyone in Newbridge will know that the *Gazette* is back with a vengeance.

Now all I've got to do is drag myself through Hell Raiser.

CHAPTER 13

I am standing in a wet, wind-swept field, in the middle of nowhere, somewhere near Jasmine's dad's farmhouse, with 854 other rain-drenched lunatics. There's no other word for people who would give up their perfectly quiet and cosy weekends lounging around the house to do this. It's not normal behaviour. Certainly not at this time of the morning. In this weather. The misty hills stand in front of us, nothing but fog and a few cows behind us. A random scattering of concrete barricades and old broken farm equipment makes the place look post-apocalyptic, like some evil overlord has bombed the crap out of the Newbridge countryside and all that remains are bits of rope and wire, dirty water ponds and industrial skips. What a mad idea. Place a few bits of wood and ragged netting among well-watered mounds of muck and the crazy people of the nation will come flocking.

It is freezing and I'm shivering already. I've not eaten, and I can see my breath in the air, it's so cold. I'm dressed in our *Gazette* team kit of black leggings and red rash tops. My hands are blueish white and waxy, despite rubbing them together with enough friction to start a small fire. I remind myself that all I've done so far is make it here on time. Which admittedly is more than can be said for the rest of the team. I can't see anyone, anywhere. Have they come to their senses and decided that they've got better things to do with their weekends? Did they end up in a lock-in at The Black Boar last night? If so, they've got no chance of making it here. I can hardly blame them, after all they've probably got much more going on with their lives than me. But it would have been nice to do this together. Though really I'm the Editor in Chief, this is my job, my bucket list, and I'm the only one who can do this, so I might as well go through with it. If nothing else, I've got that beer at the finish line to look forward to. That's of course assuming I make it to the finish line.

I register with an official whose neck is wider than his skull. Again, I find myself signing a waiver to say that I'm cool with destroying my quality of life for the sake of a few good photos.

To be honest, getting up at 5 a.m. and standing around waiting on my own is hellish enough. It's like a dystopian film set, and I feel like some weirdo mutant extra, not sure why I'm really here because I certainly don't belong. I shuffle on the spot, hoping someone will tell me it's much easier than it looks and all will be well. Oh, and a bacon sandwich and a hot milky coffee, two sugars would be nice.

As I look around and take it all in, I can properly appreciate how heavily filtered those glossy leaflets were that Christopher brought in for us. This isn't an adult obstacle course with some cute little devils and a 'hell' theme of fire and pitch forks. This is a real-life shitshow. In every sense of the word. There aren't even any food stalls. Actually, I can't see any Portaloos either. But I see ambulances. Lots of ambulances. Great.

I pull my sunglasses down over my eyes. Not because it's sunny – it's dark and wet and windy – but because I want to hide my horror and lack of enthusiasm for this and just hide generally. Mark was right on this one, if it was up to me, I'd definitely be with the quarter that don't finish. Probably because without an article to write, I wouldn't have started in the first place.

At 6 a.m., a claxon sounds for the first call of Hell Raisers. I make my lonely way over to the Gates of Hell, a precarious arch made of dented, rusty oil barrels.

'Lily! Lily, we're here!' Christopher jumps up and gives me a wave. I spot all the others there too, Mark, Amy, Dylan and Jasmine. Every single one is kitted out and waving their hellos. The relief is like an adrenalin shot and suddenly, I can't wait to get over there, to join them and get to grips with whatever it is we've committed to.

I jump up and wave back and start running properly to where they are, unable to stop grinning despite the cold wind in my face. Yes! I just knew they wouldn't let me down! Even this may be bearable if we take this on as a team and I've got Christopher by my side.

Music starts blasting from the speakers, all the other Lycra lunatics flock towards the entrance, pumped and raring to go. I pick up my pace to a proper run, in order not to lose sight of my team in the crowds.

I can tell they are excited, even Amy is stretching and smiling and taking selfies, so I figure it's best to paste on my best smile too and suck it up, take one for the team as it were. After all, they are doing this for me, for us, to help me write the feature that will hopefully keep us in our jobs. This is their day off and they've sacrificed their time and sanity to show up here with little clue how mutilated we may be by the end. So I slide off my sunglasses and I find a smile of gratitude. Because whatever happens, we're in this together and we won't be abandoning each other or leaving anyone behind. Who knows, we may even be able to look back at this in time and laugh... I'm guessing not for a long time, but it's possible. If we get that twenty-two per cent, then anything is possible. I steal a glance at Christopher as he concentrates on setting his watch. This is the first time I've seen him out of work-wear. Even at the skydive, he wore a shirt and trousers. But today he looks completely different. There's no two ways about it, he is hot. Strong, tanned, athletic. His tight redrash vest shows off every ripple in his arms and chest. I can't even bring myself to be caught checking out his legs in those cycling shorts. He is gorgeous. Even in this hell hole, he looks like he belongs on a film set.

'Welcome Hell Raisers!' a deep disembodied male voice booms through the loud speakers. A hush descends. 'To survive, you must conquer all the elements thrown at you, whether that is the temperamental weather conditions, the gruelling natural environment or the torturous man-made obstacles. Or maybe you've come to battle your own demons... mwah-aha-ha-ha... So, are you ready to give it some Hell? If you're ready to give it some Hell, then let me hear you say HELL YEAH!'

'HELL YEAH!!!' the crowd answers, yelling, surging and waving fists in the air. Buoyed by the fact that my team have shown up and the sight of Christopher in his kit, I run on the spot and start warming up in earnest, joining in with the battle cry at the top of my lungs. All of us do the same. I think it means we've now made some kind of pact with the other lunatics. Why not? We're here now; we may as well give it everything we've got.

The mega-phone starts up again. 'Well then, put your hand on your heart and hear me out: As a Hell Raiser – I am here to do my best. Only I know what my best is. I am not here to judge or be judged but to participate and have fun. I support my fellow Hell Raisers at all times. Teamwork and compassion before my course time; I do not whinge, because I am a bad-ass. When I fall, I get back up and I don't look back.'

Everyone is smiling now. Psyching themselves up, patting each other on the back. There's no doubt that you really get a sense of being a part of something. Even I've got butterflies. Even though I'm not sure whether that's excitement or nerves.

Mark hands us each a GoPro to strap around our heads. 'We're going to add some video footage to the feature this time. See if it increases reach. And the craft beer guys want to record the moment we take that first sip at the end.'

This is the first I've heard of this. Probably on purpose. Easier to ask for forgiveness than permission, as they say. But I can't pretend that I'm particularly keen on having the world potentially witness my epic failure. Now there's not just going to be pictures but videos with full sound and movement. And the video camera doesn't lie! It'll spill the whole ugly truth. I won't be able to write up that it was amazing, scenic and fun and that I found it a breeze and I enjoyed every second because people will see me swear and fall and God forbid, maybe even bawl like a baby! But what choice do I have but to go along with it now? It's too late to object to filming if Mark's already sealed the deal with the beer people.

'Fine. But *no* filming my ass,' I say. 'I don't want footage of me from behind.'

'I don't mind which way you film me,' says Amy, giving Mark a wink.

Even in this extreme cold, Mark's cheeks flare red. It's hilarious. I have never seen him lost for words before and it works wonders for team morale as we all stifle giggles and look into the distance.

But the moment of hilarity is short-lived as the second and final claxon sounds, meaning it's nearly time to start. Jasmine, Dylan, Amy, Mark, Christopher and me huddle, GoPros touching in the middle.

'Everyone okay?' Christopher asks.

We nod.

'Then let's do this.'

The first challenge is called Hell and High Water – one team member piggybacks the other through the mud. Relatively easy, you'd think, especially because Jasmine has jumped on Dylan's back, Amy on to Mark, but that leaves me with Christopher.

I try to warn him. 'I'm much heavier than I look. Cheese does that… And chocolate also plays a part. Have you got any history of slipped discs or lower back pain?'

He shakes his head.

'You will,' I tell him.

But, unfazed, he squats down. 'You're not heavy. You're perfect, so just shut up and climb on. Hurry up, because I don't like losing.'

Perfect. I heard that right? Or do I have mud in my ears already. I try to think of other words that rhyme with perfect that I may have misheard. But I can't think of any. So maybe that's what he actually said. And, for a split second, I understand exactly how Mr Clark must have felt when he first saw those lottery numbers come up. And then he checked them. And then he checked them again and then he promptly passed out. Because, some things are beyond your wildest expectations. Even if you do buy a ticket. Even if you do harbour little dreams of 'what if'.

Perfect. Wow. That's certainly beyond my wildest expectation.

He nudges me and I realise I've been daydreaming. Jasmine, Dylan, Mark and Amy are already nearly out the other side! So I do as I'm told, climbing on top of him and wrapping my legs around his waist. And then we are off, cheek-deep in beetle-infested icy brown water.

He is impressively strong. Not just because he can hold my body weight without grunting or turning purple or keeling over, but because we speed past some of the other teams, even the ones carrying lighter-looking people than me, which makes me feel fantastic, so I start to whoop and shout and feel like this wasn't such a bad idea after all. Maybe the whole thing will be like this, suitable challenges for the fitties and shortcuts for the slackers like me. Good. I like it when things turn out that way.

By the time we reach the other side, we're completely drenched with mud and unspecified sloppy dirt and I'm thrilled because it's actually keeping me warm. Well, less cold. We gather as a team, buoyed by our initial success in completing the first stage and steering ourselves towards the second. Maybe it is much easier than it looks after all!

But, of course, it isn't. The next half hour is much tougher. We belly-crawl under barbed wire, we climb up vertical walls while trying to hang on to wet rope. We jump through huge tractor tyres while being power-hosed with even more icy water. But we stick together. Despite being the clumsiest team by far. Every time there's an opportunity to fall from a beam or trip over a mere rock, Dylan and I are on the ground.

From 3k on, I am cursing Christopher. It's not normal to have to work this hard just to save your job! Surely, with his genius, he could come up with a better, safer and more comfortable way to make the paper succeed, right? And I'm really freezing. No doubt this is going to bring on a cold, if not pneumonia. And I hate this GoPro. I'm doing a *lot* of unlady-like coughing, hocking and – how do I put this – projectile nose-blowing sans tissue as the mud and sludge keeps going up my nostrils. Poor Dylan got an eyeful of my mucky behaviour at one point. No doubt his GoPro got an eyeful of it as well. There's nowhere to hide with those bloody things. Maybe it would have been better for them to film my ass after all, at least that way they wouldn't be able to see my face smeared in all sorts of mucky nastiness.

Two hours in, we enter Hell Fire, also known as Sniper Alley, which says it all really and again confirms that whoever came up with this event is a total masochist. Pellets shoot at you from every angle. And, unfortunately for me, Jasmine and Amy, who are in front of me, keep stopping and screaming instead of ducking and running. Every time they do this, I ram into them and get shot in the ass. I am now the proud owner of around eight raised welts on my left bum cheek. But I don't cry, and I don't stop. Mostly because I want this to end as soon as possible. I'm actually quite proud of the way I absorbed those shots though. They're my 'medals'. Proof that I've suffered for my art.

Despite the welts, and the mud, and the screaming, the best bit of this whole thing is doing it as a team, laughing as we watch each other fall over and slip up and slide backwards and help each other back up again. I couldn't do this alone and it wouldn't be nearly as rewarding as helping and being helped by your fellow team Hell Raisers and also by complete strangers. I love the way everyone rallies around and lifts each other up just out of kindness, pushing, pulling and propelling us forwards. They may all be burly lunatics, but they're big-hearted, generous lunatics and it feels like we're all one big lunatic family, which isn't so far from what I'm used to. If I wasn't here doing this, I would be home alone with Chaplin and wouldn't get to experience this camaraderie that is only possible from being in a do or die situation like this, together.

I huff and puff up the rocky hill trail and, suddenly, I see a sign reading that we are approaching the 5K mark. Does that mean the finish line is in sight? That it's all over and we really made it? That we survived? The elation I feel is unlike anything I've ever experienced. I scramble to the hilltop, only to learn that we're nowhere near done. I should have known that was just a way to distract us from the fresh hell around the corner.

We enter Hell's Bells.

It is the coldest, dirtiest swim of my life. Both my calf muscles seize up and my brain forgets everything it's ever learned, including, briefly, how to breathe. After the first crossing of the river to ring a bell, I stand to the side shivering. I'm supposed to do two more crossings but I've reached my limit. I accept that I'm beaten. I don't need to do everything. What I've done is more than sufficient to write the article. This is a challenge and I have challenged myself. The rest is just vanity and unnecessary risk.

I watch the rest of my team complete the three crossings before Christopher pulls himself out of the water and runs towards me.

'What's up? Are you all right? I can swim it with you if that's easier?'

And I suddenly think to myself, Amy and Jasmine are also first-timers and they're pushing themselves to do this, so, as Editor in Chief, I can't be the only one to quit. It's bad form. It's a poor example. It's selfish.

I take a deep breath and straighten up.

'Just cramp. I'm okay, I'm in,' I tell him, and we slip in from the bank together.

I manage to swim across and back, ring the bell to the sound of their supportive cheers and, although it is truly horrible, I am ecstatic that I did it.

And then, with my team around me, I lead them off to the next challenge, determined to show them that I can do this. We turn a sharp corner and, unbelievably, we are at the last hurdle! Somehow along the way, I forgot that this hell would finally end! I'm delighted. We've nearly done it! This is the last thing in the way of me and that beer and then complete and unrestricted comfort for the rest of my days. From now on, I'll probably opt to live in Uggs and all my outdoor clothes will now also be made of fleece. I start fantasising about a roaring fireplace and hot chocolates and cushions and fresh linen and soft, dry hair and not having sharp pebbles in my squelching trainers, but before any of that can come true, there's the not-so-small matter of Half-Pipe to Hell. A wall that looks like a huge wooden tsunami wave. The idea being you run at it and then somehow run up it far enough so someone on the top can grab your hand and pull you up. Mark's already up there, having made the ascent whilst I dreamt about food and warmth. Christopher is limbering up, Dylan and Jasmine are talking strategy and Amy has taken off her T-shirt and ripped it in two to use as a rope.

Even if I start running at it from a mile away, I know I have no chance of surmounting that wall. Um, gravity, people? So

I just decide to go for it anyway. Why not? It's the last hurdle and everything else has gone okay so I'm feeling fairly confident that I can tick this one off too and call it a day. Even if I merely attempt this final one, it means I've tried everything and I can hold my head high when I cross that finish line knowing I'm not a quitter. I'll be a proper Hell Raiser!

I wait for a clearing and then propel myself forward at my fastest speed. I scramble up to about halfway, then feel the grab of hands on my back and bum as I receive a twelve-man boost to push me up the final few feet.

I reach out my hand and Mark extends both his hands and his full strength to pull me up. But he is actually *too* strong, as he hoists me up and then loses his balance as he over-reaches, at the same moment as the twelve-strong team behind me disband and fall away and we both barrel back down the wall. Headfirst, I hurtle towards the ground at a very sharp angle, twisting out my elbow to take the brunt of the impact. Unfortunately, the impact is more impactful than I expect, and it crushes me. Not physically, but mentally. I break my Hell Raiser promise to not be a crybaby and I cry out, in a colourful rainbow of expletives. Mark keeps apologising, Christopher is trying to calm me down, other Hell Raisers look shocked to see me holding my elbow like a broken branch.

It hurts. It really *hurts*!

Amy runs to my aid and understands exactly what I need. To hide. To get out of sight. To not be the humiliating centre of attention. As my arm isn't working, my hands have been excruciatingly numb for the last 2K and my body feels like it has been passed through the paper-shredder, I limp across the finish line, where a volunteer steward wraps me in two space blankets.

I start laughing. But it's a bit manic, even to my ears.

Amy wraps her arm around me. 'Let me take you to the ambulance. I think you need someone to look over your arm.'

'No, I'm fine. Honestly, I just need to get dressed and—'

'They have hot chocolate,' she says.

I hook my good arm into hers as we make a beeline for the ambulance.

I lie down on the stretcher and close my eyes. It feels so good to be lying down, my bones feel like they are defrosting and I'm just so happy to be safe and horizontal.

Amy sits by my side and explains what happened to a first aider. As I drift to sleep I hear the first aider ask us to wait for the nurse. Lovely, take your time. I just want to lie here. Some extra-strength painkillers and I'll be blissed out...

But then I hear a voice that snaps my eyes wide open.

'Elbow injury and possible concussion?'

A voice that feels like a slap across my face.

'No problem, I'll take a look right now.'

I take a deep breath. There's no mistake. No doubt. And no escape.

It's Hannah.

I've known that voice since I was ten years old. The sound of it used to make my heart sing; sleepovers, long phone calls, urgent chats over lunch and lazy lunches over wine.

I open my eyes slowly. She's kneeling next to me. Her face inches from mine.

It really is Hannah. So familiar yet so strange.

'Lily, it's you,' she says, her voice now small and awkward. Her face reddens and she swallows.

I look at the ceiling of the ambulance.

'Yep.'

'Quite the surprise. Right, well, let's see what we've got here. Can I take a look at your arm?'

I wait a long moment. I don't want Hannah to be anywhere near me. I can feel my heart pounding in my chest and I feel so light-headed. Partly the pain in my arm but mainly rage. Pure, unadulterated fury.

Amy places the back of her hand on my forehead. 'She's burning up. Is there anything you can give her?'

I'm at the mercy of this stranger who used to be my best friend. This woman who ruined my relationship, my wedding day and a subsequent chunk of my life that I'm just now starting to feel is healing. She chose Adam over me, and Adam chose her over me, and my heart was doubly broken because of that.

And despite all of the obstacles I've faced today, this is by far the hardest. This is hell.

'Your arm? Can I take a look?' she asks again gently, uncertainty in her voice.

Amy strokes my forehead. 'Just let her look at it quickly, Lily. Once you get the all-clear we can get out of here. And then I'll definitely get you that hot chocolate, I promise.'

I shut my eyes. I can't lose my rag here in front of Amy. I'm her boss. Everything that happened between me and Hannah happened a lifetime ago and Amy doesn't need to know about all of that. I try to control my breathing, try to calm myself down. To her this looks like a very straightforward interaction between patient and nurse. I've got to keep it that way.

I nod and lift my arm slightly. It really does hurt and feels leaden, but I don't want to prolong this any more than it needs it to be. Hopefully Hannah will have the good sense to give my arm a cursory glance, tell me that I'm fine and let me out of here. Surely she doesn't want to be here any more than I do?

She examines it slowly, carefully, thoroughly, cleaning me down with an antiseptic swab before wrapping up my elbow in gauze, before finally saying, 'All done. I recommend a tetanus shot and a follow-up with your doctor to x-ray for a possible fracture.'

'Fine,' I say and can feel Amy wince at my barbed, ungrateful response.

'She's just tired,' Amy tries to explain away my rudeness to Hannah. 'Lily's not usually this bad-tempered! We'll take care of her from here, don't you worry.'

'I'm glad she's got such great friends,' says Hannah, her voice stammering slightly.

Amy turns back to me. 'I'll just drive my car around this way, so you don't have to walk much. I'll be back in five, okay? I'll try to get you a hot chocolate for the ride home and we'll have you home and dry and all cleaned up in no time.'

I nod my thanks. I wish I could walk out with her now, but I know I don't have the strength.

Amy leaves the ambulance and then it's just me and Hannah. Alone. She can't leave as I'm in her care. I can't leave because I can hardly stand. I hope she just chooses to ignore me, busy herself with some paperwork, stay quiet and spare me any awkward pleasantries.

'Just so you know, he did the same to me,' she says straight away.

Oh well, so much for that. Hannah never found silence easy. That hasn't changed then. I blink slowly and keep staring at the ceiling as if I haven't heard her.

'Adam. He cheated on me too. Someone from his work. We didn't even last six months. So, I guess what goes around comes around.'

Again, I keep staring. I don't want to revisit this; it was painful enough the first time. We were friends, but we're not now, we'll never be again, how could we be after what happened? What does she want from me? Sympathy? Pity? A sense of outrage on her behalf? That's not going to happen. Because I can't give her that. I don't have it to give.

'Lily, I want you to know that I'm sorry. So many times I've wanted to call you or show up at your house and say that I was a bitch and an idiot and there isn't a day that goes by that I don't want to go back, slap myself across the face and tell myself that my best friend is the last person in the world that deserved to be hurt this way… by me.' She leans in to me, trying to meet my eyes, pleading, her voice now broken with tears. 'I so wish there was a way I could make everything all right. I miss you *so* much. I don't know what I was thinking. You can tell your mother she was right about everything…'

My mother? Why is she bringing mum into this?

I flinch. I want to ask her what she means, but I bite my tongue because I don't want to talk to her, I don't want to get into this, it's over with. It's done. I've wasted enough time on this part of my life, I can't let it creep back in and rob me of now.

'Lily? There you are.' The ambulance door swings open and Christopher appears in the doorway. I've never been so happy and relieved to see anyone in my life.

I stretch out my arms to him and he rushes in to me, scooping me up gently under my knees and around my shoulders. I don't resist. I just want to get out of here. I can't get away from this place and these memories quick enough.

'The car's just outside. Let me carry you.' He turns to Hannah, 'If you're happy to let her go?'

Hannah nods her permission as I bury my head in Christopher's chest. All I can think about is that last Hell Raiser pledge. That I am a bad-ass. That when I fall, I get back up and, most importantly, I don't look back.

So I let Christopher carry me out of the ambulance and I don't look back. Like a moth to the flame, I just go. I just let him take me and I don't resist. I can't help but melt with the heat of him, the solid, strong warmth from his chest, the tightness of his hold on me. I let my good arm reach up to his neck and my fingers curl around his skin, in to his hair. Even in the midst of all this chaos, the pain, the cold, the shock of Hannah, I can't help but feel my heart soar, because I am in his arms and it feels phenomenal. My stomach flips and I close my eyes, to settle myself, to calm down. I'm glad I can blame the cold for the quiver in my fingertips and the incessant swallowing I'm doing because I can hardly catch my breath.

I often wondered if I would ever get close to a man again after what happened. And I wondered what it would be like – the same? Different? Worse, due to all my hang-ups and fears? But I've just realised something. I haven't forgotten what it feels like to be this close to a man I find attractive. Because I've never felt this way: I've never quivered at a mere touch, I've never felt this physically lit up by Adam or anyone else. This isn't reliving a distant memory. This is all brand new. And I like it.

I settle into the front seat of Amy's car and she starts the engine, and I'm homeward bound with Dylan, Mark, Jasmine and Christopher. My team, the people I can trust, the people who won't leave me behind.

My team.

My friends.

Buckley's Bucket List
No. 2 – Hell Raiser!

There's something exhilarating about facing all your fears in one day. Of course, I was scared. Can I run the distance? Am I strong enough to get across rings and monkey bars? Am I going to have a panic attack in the underground tunnels? Am I going to be able to run up a half pipe and trust that someone will catch me (hello control issues!!)? Can I handle thrashing around in ice water? Will I get shocked? Will I hurt myself? Will I chicken out?

The old me would have let these questions get the best of me and I would have made up an excuse to get out of the race entirely. The new me took this as a challenge and used these fears to push me to do something out of my comfort zone… That's where the magic happens, you know! Something mysterious and inexplicable that made me rethink some things I already thought I understood. Certain ideas I held true about myself and about others seemed to take on new angles, become more complex. Or maybe I'm just delirious because I'm on super-strength painkillers. I'll keep you posted!

I could not have made it without my teammates. They were crucial to my success. They helped me over walls, through waist-deep mud, ice-cold waters and miles of treachery. Being with my work colleagues was great; it made me push myself to keep up and give it everything I had.

During this challenge, there was no time to think about fears. Only time to jump in, without hesitation, and OVERCOME. I did hurt myself, mainly because I experienced a bout of recklessness due to brain-rust and hurled myself against an obstacle without thinking straight. Luckily, it was nothing but a scratch, some swelling and a touch of melodrama on my part, and I was rewarded with a tetanus shot in my poor sore bum and the best battle scars of all six of us.

We were mud-caked, bruised, wet, cranky and mentally confused, but there were also tears of accomplishment mixed with pride. Someone has already marked it on the office calendar for next year. Give me some time to recover and, you never know, I might just do it all over again. Because all those things I thought were so scary weren't so scary after all. I left my fears at that finish line and, I'll tell you this, I won't be going back to get them. The only thing I'll be going back for is my ice-cold beer, which I managed to miss out on in my final fall from grace.

If you'd like to watch some footage of us making mucky fools of ourselves, click the link below! Thank you so much for your comments and support. We appreciate every single one of you, and remember, we're in this together! Till next week, Lily xx

CHAPTER 14

Here we are, another week down at the new and improved Newbridge Gazette. The Hell Raiser article went to print this morning and it's already causing quite a storm. The accompanying video footage has been received really well and turned out to be a brilliant way to engage even more readers near and far. According to Dylan, my headlong Half Pipe is a real hit. I can't bring myself to watch it. It's bad enough to review it in memory. But the feel-good Friday excitement is certainly catching and that's my main focus for today.

Even Jennings is smiling as he claps Christopher on the shoulder. 'Eighteen and a half per cent in two weeks. You're nearly there! We've got to hand it to you, guys. We didn't really believe you'd be able to make it, but it's happening. You guys are making it happen!

'Your digital vision is thriving, we have new income streams opening every day – businesses, corporate and independent – keen to advertise long-term with us and a visible boost to our profile in national media rankings, which has never happened before.'

Tapping her pen on the desk, McArthur clears her throat. 'Christopher. You have a very bright future with us, young man, once the *Gazette* is back on solid ground, we can talk. And I have a feeling you're going to like what we have to say.'

Christopher nods along graciously and then winks at me.

McArthur picks up his cue and turns my way. 'And you, Lily Buckley, Editor in Chief. You've managed to pull this office back from the brink of extinction. And with a very lean team. I'm really impressed. But that's enough basking in glory for now, there's still work to be done. Not only do we need to make that twenty-two per cent target as agreed with our shareholders, we need to show them that our growth is sustainable. No plateau, no dips. So, this next column has got to be good. In fact, it's got to be the best yet.' She nods to Jennings.

'Don't worry; we've done the brain work for you this time. We've already got your next activity all planned out,' adds Jennings with a grin.

This is worrying. I have a hunch that Jennings and I will differ greatly on what constitutes a fun, entertaining or ethical way to spend my time.

'You've done that already? Planned the next activity without us?' I ask. I want to tell him that we don't need to have the brain work done for us. We like the brain work.

McArthur passes me a thick file across the table. 'The Shankley Hotel. It's good for the community, showcases the history of the area, capitalises on sites of local interest.'

Before it even registers with me what she wants me to do or what's involved, I hear Christopher cough into his hand. 'You are *kidding*...' he says, head shaking. 'That's never been on the list, Mags, I would *never* suggest that, it's too much. I said right from the beginning that I wouldn't ask Lily to do anything that I wasn't prepared to do myself.'

'That's exactly the response we want from our readers. It's dramatic; a radical step for the *Gazette*, show them how we're breaking new ground,' McArthur says with two raised eyebrows. 'That's what we're here for and that's why this is perfect. To quote you back to yourself Christopher, "before you make up your mind, you should open it".' She turns back to me. 'You're familiar with The Shankley, right?'

I nod, opening the bulging file of brochures, newspaper clippings and printouts of reviews and testimonies. I start flicking through, scanning each page quickly and buying time to gather my thoughts. When I arrived in Newbridge as a ten-year-old, one of the first things that Hannah and the other local school kids did was pull me into a corner at break time and ask if I'd ever heard of The Shankley Hotel.

Not knowing what they meant at first, I shook my head and they gleefully lowered their voices, checked over their shoulders and proceeded with the story. This was a Newbridge initiation. A test. If you winced or cried or shook or ran scared once you heard the history of the haunted hotel on the hill, that was it, you were deemed weak and cowardly, delegated to a lesser social group forever more, never picked for sports teams or sleepovers, proms or parties.

But I was lucky on this. Mainly, because I could never resist a good story. As an only child to a work-around-the-clock single mother, I spent most of my childhood entertaining myself quietly and that's why reading and writing became so important to me. It could be done anywhere at any time, soundlessly and secretly, and it always held an adventure. I've spent the most wonderful times with dragons and witches and monsters and warriors and wizards, zombies and goddesses, fairies and werewolves, murderous ghouls, creepy clowns and chainsaw-wielding freaks. I've been to bed with them all.

So, the undead of any variety isn't something that scares me one bit. In fact, I'm really excited. My granny and I used to walk the grounds sometimes when I was a teenager. But we could never get inside. The house itself was locked up for years and then only opened on request for special paying guests. And the prices back then were extortionate. Way beyond our budget although she often said she'd treat us sometime. Sadly that time never came. I never imagined I'd be one of those guests one day. My granny would be so excited. She'd be the first to read this article, even if I wasn't the one writing it.

'Fantastic idea!' I tell McArthur. 'I can't wait. In fact, if I had been able to think up my own bucket list, this would be top of it. Thank you. This is the first one I actually *want* to do.'

Jennings shifts in his seat and begins to do a stiff shimmy while he sings the *Ghostbusters* theme tune. This idea has certainly piqued his interest and put him in a good mood.

McArthur joins him. 'Excellent, Lily! I knew you'd love it!'

Christopher turns to me in utter confusion. 'Are you serious? You're going to say yes to this?'

Smiling, I show him the photo on the front of the file. 'Of course! This is the stuff of legend! They only open to the public for a few weeks each year and that's if you even get on the waiting list.' I find a price list and tap my finger underneath. 'Look here, it costs an absolute fortune for the tour, far more than I could afford myself, so I'm definitely up for this. It'll be fun.'

Jennings clicks his fingers, two clicks then a pause. McArthur gives him a playful nudge. '*Addams Family?*' He winks back at her.

Christopher is shaking his head, slowly turning the file pages in disbelief. 'Fun? This is not my definition of fun. And I don't think it will work. I think the majority of readers will turn off to this and feel as I do, uncomfortable…'

I turn to him and see discomfort in his face, a concern that I've never seen before. He's been working so hard, we all have, and maybe, he's finally reached his limit? The burnout point of anxiety and overreaction that comes with exhaustion? Or maybe he genuinely thinks we're going down the wrong route and that this is not the right choice of focus for our feature and we could damage the great following we've worked so hard to build up?

It's so confusing! I trust Christopher's judgement completely; he's kept his word on everything so far. But I really want to do this and McArthur and Jennings are the real experts, with decades of experience behind them.

'Nonsense,' McArthur says. 'This is the perfect feature. The Shankley Hotel is what put Newbridge on the map. Folk around here have heard the stories surrounding this old building all their lives. We've run it by the marketing department and they agree; it's a great hook, so we're going with it, that's decided.'

'But what if something… happens?' asks Christopher.

'Let's hope it does! The worst thing that can happen is that nothing happens, then there'll be nothing to write about.'

'Correction.' Jennings holds up his finger. 'If nothing happens, then you can dispel the myth of The Shankley Hotel. That's an interesting angle, putting the ghost to bed. Either way, it opens up the discussion? Is it haunted or is it not?'

'Oh, it's haunted all right,' says Christopher. 'My friends told me stories about that place all my school life. It's infamous up and down the country but I never realised until now that it was so close to here.' He pulls his chair towards mine and lowers his voice. 'Lily, believe me, once you research this property and get the full story, you'll feel differently. You won't be so eager to even pass the gate, never mind step inside it.'

'You're booked to stay overnight,' McArthur says, without looking up.

'Overnight? For fuck's sake.' Christopher pulls at his collar. 'Seriously, I have a really bad feeling on this. People have lived and died there. And it's ancient and dark and it'll be crumbling and rat-infested and completely unsafe. And that's during the day. Only morbid weirdos would stay in a place like that. Have you thought about the spiders?'

'Spiders don't bother me,' I tell him truthfully. 'They're small and silent and utterly harmless, what's there to be scared of?

'Oh really? And you're completely cool with evil spirits and eerie noises and slamming doors? You're just going to turn in for the night and sleep through it all? Have some sweet dreams and wake up fresh as a daisy? What if you feel something, Lily? Like an icy finger on your skin or heavy breathing in your ear.' He shivers at the thought and swats at his own neck.

I've never seen Christopher frightened. This is a complete role reversal. Every task so far it's been me who has to be talked round and then talked down. Never would I expect someone as smart and sophisticated and rational as Christopher to be spooked out by something like this. It's just a heady mix of myth and superstition. It's not real – everyone knows this, right?

'Ghosts don't exist, Christopher. This is just a gimmick. It's just fun. Like a gothic adventure to make you jump and set the scene for telling ghost stories.' I'm sure I can get him on board, make him see the fun side. 'It's going to be amazing. Candles lit, great old building, all those decadent antique rooms. I bet the staff have some stories to tell. Imagine if it's a full moon. It will feel as if you're a character in a real story, in one of those incredible literary houses like Wuthering Heights or Ravenclaw House or Northanger Abbey...'

This is a dream come true. I want to do this right now, why have I never thought of this myself?

Christopher squeezes his eyes shut. 'It is going to smell. It is going to smell so, so bad.' He picks up the file, pointing at the front page. 'It looks like something out of a horror film. Devoid of any colour and fun and innocence, just full of violence and death. Why on earth would you want to have anything to do with this place?'

I start to appreciate that despite anything I say, Christopher's fears are real – to him. I wonder what's behind this. Did he have some kind of experience himself? In this scientific age, it's astonishing that people can still be convinced that the paranormal are a real and present danger? This is a completely new side of Christopher that I've never expected. I'm intrigued. Completely intrigued. Not now, but sometime, when the time's right, I'm going to ask him all about this – the who, the what, the when and the why behind his fear of ghosts. I've got to. What kind of reporter would I be if I let this pass without digging deeper?

He scans the small-font description under the photograph. 'Hidden rooms, a creepy basement and what used to be a billiards room where paranormal investigators have captured countless unexplained incidents and activities. See here! There've been rumours of murders and scandals throughout the history of the hotel, giving it a rich background for creepy activity.'

McArthur sits back in her seat; her glasses slide down her nose and she studies Christopher a moment. 'Looks like you have some fears to face yourself,' she tells him in a slow, low tone. 'I've not seen this side to you before; negative, obstructive, defeatist. It's not exactly leadership material.'

'I just don't like dead or creepy things. And I think some stuff – stuff that we can't fully understand – just deserves to be left well alone,' he tells her, running a hand through his hair.

'Well, as you said, we don't want Lily doing anything that you wouldn't be prepared to do yourself. So, I think it's best for everyone that you go along with her.' She turns to Jennings. 'Book another room. Christopher is going too.'

Christopher's mouth hangs open, but McArthur claps her hands together as if to say that the matter is closed.

'A challenge, Christopher! Challenges and curveballs, that's business. That's the real world. Sometimes we don't know or like what comes our way, but we've got to get over ourselves, find a way to suck it up and push on through. Lily's already demonstrated she can operate outside her comfort zone, so I think it's only fair we ask you to do the same. This is going to be a hot ticket article, kind of thing that gets people talking, just might stabilise our current position. Personally, I love it. And I'm interested myself in how you're going to get on.'

Jennings leans into McArthur and they begin to whisper and collude between themselves.

Christopher pulls both hands down his face. I need to reassure him that it's going be fine! That I've got this, that, finally, I can be the one that spurs him on and makes sure we get to the end. But I don't want to say any of that in front of Jennings and McArthur – I don't want them homing in on any perceived weaknesses. But I really don't want Christopher to sit there, suffering in silence.

Aha! I whip out my notepad and start writing.

Hey you! I've got your back. We are going to sail through this one. I promise. You leave it all to me and, who knows, you may even change your mind! Trust me?

I slide my hand out of my lap and under the table. I find his knee and squeeze it. He shoots a look straight at me and I scooch my note in front of him, as if we're swapping notes in class right under the teacher's nose. I then pop my hand in my pocket and take out a silver foiled chocolate noisette. The last one from the box he gave me. I slide that over too.

He tilts his head at me, blows out his cheeks and mouths 'thank you'. And I nearly forget that we're not the only two in the room.

Until I hear McArthur slap down her gold-ringed knuckles on the table, leaning forward and giving us a very hard stare. 'Don't get too cosy, you two. You may have nearly achieved your twenty-two per cent, but can you sustain it? We'll know this time next week, if you haven't been scared witless that is.'

I look down at the reservation. Master Bedroom at The Shankley Hotel for Lily Buckley c/o The *Newbridge Gazette*. For tonight.

Friday 13th.

I place my thumb over the date before Christopher can see it.

Because by the way he is not breathing, I think he's already frightened the living crap out of himself.

CHAPTER 15

I take the narrow, twisting dirt road towards The Shankley Hotel. I regret taking this old short cut now as brambles and branches scrape at the windscreen and along the doors from both sides. With every mile, the sky seems to close in and darken with storm, the odd clear patch of clear light swallowed up with heavy clouds so that now it's even harder for me to see where I'm going, and it's not even twilight yet. I hear another low sigh from Christopher in the passenger seat beside me. I steal a glance at him. He's not himself at all today and it is no secret as to why.

'You look tired.' I tell him gently. 'Why don't you close your eyes a while and I can wake you when we get there?'

'I don't know how I let myself be talked into this,' says Christopher, pinching his lips. 'I might never get over it... I had nightmares well into my teens after watching *The Shining*, yet somehow I let McArthur – who loves making people suffer – railroad me into spending the night in a haunted hellhole. So much for strong leadership, it appears I'm a pushover.'

'Nonsense,' I tell him. 'You're not a pushover at all. You're doing it for the greater good! And trust me, as a local I know there's a lot of other people in this town who would refuse to even venture to The Shankley Hotel. My mother included. I didn't even tell her I was coming.'

'Really? You're just saying that to make me feel better,' he says, a faint smile on his lips.

'I'm telling the truth! Cross my heart and hope to die. Now push back your seat and get some rest. A little nap will do you the world of good.'

Thankfully, he does exactly as I suggest because the way he's going, I don't think Christopher is going get a wink of sleep tonight.

The Shankley Hotel made headlines in 1936, when a pair of photographers working for a *Country Life* supplement took a picture of what appeared to be the ghost of a woman on the staircase. Legend claims that the 'White Lady' (named for the colour of her bridal dress) is Lady Dorothy Shankley, a bride who, in a fit of passion, killed her groom-to-be hours before their wedding as she discovered his infidelity with her handmaid. Well, Dorothy, pull up a chair! Although I chose to let Adam live, there's a part of me that empathises with poor Dorothy. Crimes of passion are real. I believe it is entirely possible to see red and lose your mind and all control in a fit of blind rage. We know she did it, but I wonder if she was really in full possession of all her faculties. I guess a night at The Shankley will help us find out.

I can't remember the last time I was this excited. I've packed a bag of essential supplies: my Moleskine notebook, new fountain pens, a torch, a range of chocolatey snacks, candles and matches just for ambiance and a few of my favourite spine-chilling classics. I can't think of a more perfect place to wrap up and read them than in this great crumbling, creaking historic house, with the wind rattling the windows and mysterious shadows casting shapes on the walls. I know it looks impressive in the fading light of day, but it is going to be so atmospheric and eerie once it goes dark.

But Christopher is awake and sighing again and his clear unease is making me question if this is a good idea after all. His instincts have been spot on so far. Maybe its McArthur that's got it wrong this time? Maybe this is a step too far and we're on our way to losing the readership we've fought so hard to win over. What if they think that this is silly or stupid or superstitious? Or just plain boring? There's a lot at stake. This article doesn't have to be as good as the others, it needs to be better. A decline this week and we won't have the time or momentum to turn things around before our target deadline. Maybe that's why Christopher is really freaking out. Because he feels that this feature is the beginning of the end for us.

'You okay?' I ask.

'Great,' he answers, staring out the rain-dashed car window.

We lapse into silence again. I'm not going to push him. We're on our way as directed by the big bosses so we'll just have to make it work. Normally, I would put on the radio, make small talk about the weather, the paper, the news around town, favourite lunches of all time, but today I'm not so sure. I steal glances of Christopher in the car mirror about ten times, trying to send reassuring subliminal support or even just trying to catch his eye. This is a new dynamic for us, me supporting him. And I have to say, by the increasing sense of anxiety in this car, I'm not doing very well.

I want to pull over, drive in to a lay-by and get him to spill the beans. Turn to him and ask: *What are you thinking? Tell me what's wrong. Let me in!*

I glance over once more and I see that he has closed his eyes.

'Christopher? Is everything all right?' I chance again.

But he just nods, pulls his hoodie up and turns towards the window. 'I'm fine. Just tired. Wake me up when we get there.'

Maybe he is just tired. We have been working non-stop. Perhaps he needs some time alone to think, some space. Why am I prodding and poking him with questions and answers? He's perfectly entitled to feel the way he does without a full-on

Spanish Inquisition from me. Yes, I decide to shut up and ask no more questions. Leave him alone and let him sleep if he wants to. Even if it is only half three in the afternoon.

On the drive up the hill, I keep reminding myself that ghosts don't exist. They can't exist. Like unicorns or Holy Grails or aliens. They just don't. If they did, they'd all have their own Instagram accounts by now. My biggest concern is that nothing remarkable is going to happen and I might still be doing this sort of journalistic nonsense in ten years' time. When I started, I guess I thought I'd be writing contemporary, bold and agenda-setting features by now. I couldn't be further from the glamour of that right now, with my car stuck in the wrong gear, my wheels and windscreen caked in mud and my colleague huddled up in the front seat, gently murmuring protestations to himself in half-sleep. But since writing these features, I feel like I'm much closer to that career goal. I'm writing from the heart. I'm experiencing new things; I'm learning and growing. And to be absolutely honest, if I can make it so that I can feel that way here at home, right here in Newbridge, then I'm on my way to having everything I need. And that's more than I dared to dream for a very long time.

It dawns on me as we walk into The Shankley, just after 4 p.m. on a windy, rainy Friday afternoon, that it doesn't matter if it is actually haunted or not. The fact is, this house is an old murder site where someone's life ended violently. And I've committed to spending an entire night in it. Book-geek and professional fantasies aside, I wonder whether it is right for a twenty-nine-year-old woman to spend her Friday nights hunting for spooks with a gift-shop torch? Is it any wonder that I'm single?

Mr Dean, the manager, meets us at the door and takes our bags, beginning our education in the hotel of horror. Christopher looks like all the blood has drained from his body. A telephone rings on the front desk and he nearly jumps out of his skin.

'How are you?' I ask him in a low but firm whisper while Mr Dean takes the call. 'Be honest.'

'I really wish I pushed for swimming with dolphins now.' And he disappears into the men's room.

Twenty minutes later, he's still in there.

'Christopher, are you all right?' I gently knock on the toilet door.

'Yep,' a small, forced voice assures me.

I'm not convinced.

'The twilight tour is about to begin and I don't want to leave you in there all by yourself,' I tell him.

'I'm fine, really, just go,' he mumbles through the door.

'I'm hardly going to leave you like this. I'm skipping the tour, so just come out and we'll take a walk outside in the fresh air or get a cup of tea and a bite to eat maybe? How does that sound?' I very much doubt that Christopher is hungry, but I just need to coax him out, so I can make sure he's okay.

'You can't skip the tour,' he tells me.

'Of course I can.'

I hear the bolt shift back, the doorknob twists and the heavy wooden door creaks open. Christopher is grey and looks like he's not slept in weeks despite the fact he dozed all the way here.

'I think it's best I drive you back home, Christopher. This isn't for you.'

I know what it's like to be facing your fears, how physically and emotionally exhausting it can be.

It takes all his energy to raise his hand and shake his head. 'I'll be fine.'

'You won't. I can do this one by myself, honestly. Remember: "I ain't afraid of no ghosts".' I say this in a terrible cartoony American accent, just trying to make things light, make him feel that it's really no big deal if he withdraws from this one.

'McArthur,' he whispers.

'What about her?' I ask.

'She's testing me. This could make all the difference between graduating the leadership programme with real prospects or just scraping through. I've worked too hard to lose it on this, especially so close to the end. I've got to stay. I'm a grown man. I can handle this. And I'm certainly not letting you stay here by yourself. Absolutely not.'

Mr Dean rings the bell to commence the tour.

Right, if this is crucial for Christopher's career, then I've got to help him, just as he has helped me.

'I hear you. This is exactly how I felt during the skydive and the Hell Raiser, but we got through it together, and this will be no different. Believe me, if I can do it, then so can you. We're just going to check in, stay over and go home, as we would in any hotel. And this *is* just a hotel, remember. Just four stone walls and a leaky roof. That's it. Nothing more. I'll go on the tour. You go wait in the car.'

He surveys the walls and looks up to the ceiling, seeming a little brighter, a little more detached. 'Okay. That sounds like a plan. You go on the tour. I'll wait in the car. I brought wine. Even some mini-bottles of brandy just in case. So, if I just have a drink, listen to some music get my head down for another hour or so, I might be all right. Just go on the tour and come and get me when you're done? Deal?'

I wink at him. 'Deal... but one thing...'

'Yeah?' he asks uncertainly.

'You better leave some wine for me.'

The tour of The Shankley Hotel is just as intriguing as I imagined it would be. Starting in the parlour, our tour guide launches into the history of the Shankley family – the wealth, the societal expectations, the betrayal, the murder – and me and the dozen or so other guests hang on to every macabre word.

Mr Dean explains to us that he can communicate with the spirits, which are apparently releasing different energies in each room. Right this second. Some are angry, others are sad, he tells us, as his eyes roll backwards in his head, his eyelids fluttering like his face is being slowly electrocuted. How on earth am I going to write an article for the general public on this craziness? But I remind myself that I'm here with an open mind, so I force myself to shut up and keep listening.

Mr Dean then points to a fiercely flickering candle surrounded by still ones and alerts us to the fact that it's 'just a spirit passing through'. There are no windows open, but still, I'm cynical. But judging by the gasps and wheezes of the others in our group, I'm the only one who is.

We follow him up the stairs to the top floor: the former staff quarters. Bare iron beds, wooden floorboards, white-washed walls. We wander around with torches, trying our best to 'feel' something in the dark, dank corners. The candle-lit rooms are packed with antique ornaments and freakish, broken-eyed dolls. I don't have any of the physical reactions Mr Dean claims people experience, such as dizziness, nausea or difficulty breathing. But he is adamant that many visitors report having strange experiences, be it a ghostly slap or a sudden chill. Particularly if they stay in the master bedroom.

My bedroom for the night.

Forgetting momentarily that he's not here, I turn to nudge Christopher, as even I'm starting to feel a little queasy at the idea, but I startle an elderly Japanese tourist instead.

I really wish Christopher was here. Since we started the whole relaunch of the *Gazette*, he's been by my side every step of the way. And now that he's not, I miss him.

I apologise to the wheezing Japanese gentleman and look at the clock. The tour should be finishing up soon, and I want to go check on Christopher. See if he's all right. Just see him really.

As Mr Dean describes the details of the groom's murder, he also passes around a binder of laminated photos guests have taken while staying at the hotel. One picture was taken by a woman staying in the murder room a few years back. In the middle of the night, she spotted something on her partner's side of the bed, so she jumped up and quickly snapped this photo. A faint ethereal figure in a wedding gown – just a trick of the light or a vengeful ghost-bride trapped in time?

Majority opinion was the latter.

And this was the exact bed I would be sleeping in later. Great. Christopher's reservations are not so irrational now. I'm starting to get it. This doesn't feel like a staged themed experience any more. Even I feel like I'd rather stay at the Travelodge down the road. Order pizza to the room and watch a movie in a soft, clean bed with a mound of cushions. Minibar, en suite, spectre-free.

As if this isn't all unsettling enough, there are several vintage Ouija boards on display in the hallway – one of which our guide strongly cautions us against using. Believe me, I don't need to be told twice. Feelings more than a little swayed by Christopher's wobble, I'm beginning to think that if restless spirits do exist, then we really shouldn't be disturbing them. Maybe we should let lie the things we don't yet understand. Especially if we can't see any good that may come of it.

After the tour, I take a moment to compose myself before I go out to the car to meet Christopher. The reason being, despite all my earlier protestations, I'm a bit freaked out. But under no circumstances can I let Christopher know this. I breathe in deeply, grounding myself. I've got to keep it real. I've got to remember that there's no such thing as ghosts, that Mr Dean is an expert in creating an atmosphere and amplifying the tension and he's just sucked me in with his ghoulish voice and exaggerated stories and contrived effects so get over it, see it for what it is and hold it together for Christopher. I can't show him that I'm somewhat spooked now too, and I'm definitely not going to mention that I'm staying in the murder room.

Okay. I fetch a still pale Christopher from the car and we haul our bags up to our adjoining rooms.

Back in the foyer, Christopher is jerking his head left to right, memorising all fire exits and possible escape routes when Mr Dean reappears, this time just with fire safety info and housekeeping, which relieves me. I'm really glad Christopher missed the tour; it even gave me the shivers. I leave out almost all details and tell him it was just a 'historical talk'. A wave of relief passes over his face.

Mr Dean claps for our full attention and points out the escape route, noting he leaves the lights on because visitors often flee in the middle of the night.

'I figure they'd have to be pretty frightening spirits for someone to throw away the £295 it cost for the tour, bed and breakfast,' says a tall blonde girl to her friend in a poor attempt at a whisper.

Christopher nudges me nervously, I smile at him and roll my eyes as if it's all just silly nonsense and I hook my arm into his. I'm so glad he's here. I'm so glad to have someone to share this with. I became so used to living and working all by myself, I convinced myself that others would just hold me back or let me down. But now that Christopher is by my side, I feel like everything is so much more interesting when it's shared. My heart clenches in my chest whenever he smiles at something I say. Even when he needed space today in the car, I loved being part of what we had. Actually, I'm really flattered that he felt comfortable enough to be himself, not the ever-confident, unflappable consultant that McArthur is grooming him to become.

I lean into his ear and whisper, 'The tour is over, so now all we've got to do is bed down for the night.'

He pats his bag. 'Cheers, Lily. You've been a lifesaver today. I wouldn't have done this without you. Couldn't have. Nearly there, eh?'

We head upstairs and I bid goodnight to Christopher outside his room, assuring him there is nothing here but myths and make-believe – even if I'm rethinking this myself a little now – and I retire to my master bedroom to get some much-needed rest…

But that isn't to be.

I must have nodded off, because the fire alarm tears me out of a deep sleep. Then three loud blasts ring through the house. And then the screaming starts. It's piercing and relentless – so much so, I need to press my palms against my ears. I race out into the hallway to evacuate, waiting for Christopher. But I'm the only one here. Did I imagine a fire alarm? That's disturbing, because it means I've just had a full-on auditory hallucination. Or perhaps it was real, but nobody actually believes there's a fire.

Thankfully, the screaming stops and soon Mr Dean, still fully dressed despite the early hours, rounds the corner with a flickering candle and two shivering, breathless teenage girls. No doubt in my mind that they were source of the operatic shrieking. He ushers me back to my room. 'No fire. Happens all the time. False alarm. Please, go back to sleep. No one is in danger.'

I take him at his word. Firstly, there's no one else in the hallway or fleeing down the fire escape, and secondly, I can't smell any burning or smoke. And it means I'm not out of my mind and Dorothy Shankley isn't playing tricks on me. I can't believe I'm even entertaining that as a possibility. But hey, twelve hours in The Shankley Hotel does make you question stuff about what's real and what's not, about what you thought you held true. I'm finding that out rapidly.

Mr Dean guides me back into my room with his candlelight, shutting the door behind me and I climb back into bed.

But now I'm wide awake and my bed feels freezing. How is that? It should still be warm, considering I bundled out of it less than five minutes ago?

As I try to rationalise this and warm my feet at the same time, suddenly I hear a loud, urgent rapping on my door. I locked my door, right? I can't remember if I did or not! Holy crap! What is this place doing to me? I hear a sudden gust of wind blast against my window and I'm not going to lie. I scream. I scream and I scream and I scream. The door flings open and I jump out of my bed, screaming harder than I ever have in my whole life, and bolt backwards against the window, yowling every swear word I know.

Then, with the flick of a switch, the chandelier snaps in to life and I'm blinded with an assault of cold, bright light.

Shielding my face with both arms and squinting at the door, I see a figure. I see it move on the spot. But it isn't the White Lady standing in my doorway half-dressed with a cricket bat in hand.

It's Christopher.

Oh my God, I can feel my heart throbbing in my throat. I want to kill him and kiss him at the same time. He places a finger to his lips, gently pushing the door closed behind him. We both stand and wait, breathless, listening.

'There's someone outside the room,' Christopher whispers as he tiptoes carefully towards me, his voice more uncertain than I have ever heard it.

AAAAAAAAGGGGGGGHHHHHHHHHH!!!!!!

More screaming! And we both jump. I grab Christopher's shoulders, clinging to him and ducking my head in to his chest. More hideous, piercing, high-pitched shrieking comes from down the hall. We hear the opening and shutting of doors, pounding feet down the stairs, a bounding across the floorboards.

Already confused and more than a little alarmed at the chaos in the corridor, I start to hear a frantic beeping through the wall of my bedroom. I take Christopher by the wrist and we head out into the hallway to investigate. We run into one of the teenage girls staying in the adjacent room. The beeping is coming from a 'ghost detector' app she's downloaded on her iPhone. While basic logic tells me that an app clearly can't detect supernatural occurrences, I can't get over the fact that the 'detector' calms down whenever she goes back into her room – where no murders happened – and increasingly gets louder, faster and more agitated as she gets closer to my room. When we venture into my room, the app gets *very* excited. Especially over the spot where the ghost was supposed to reside.

Where my pillows happen to be.

I convince her to delete the app, especially if it's going to incite more of her blood-curdling shrieking, or mine and try to get some sleep. By which I mean, let us get some sleep. I'm heading back down the hallway to my bedroom. Hopefully for the final time tonight. And this time I will certainly be locking my door, that's for sure.

I check my phone, and see it's just after 2 a.m.

Christopher escorts me to my room, stands at the doorway and points wordlessly at the four-poster bed, where all the 'activity' seemed to hover. 'Really?'

'I know,' I say. 'But it's only a couple of hours till the sun comes up and once it's light, we'll just get in my car and drive far, far away from here.'

He swallows and trails his hand down the back of his neck. 'Mind if I stay in here with you? On the ground, of course, I'll grab my bag, just in case it disappears overnight,' he says. 'I don't want to stay alone in my room.'

I nod, inwardly delighted and relieved. The more time I spend with Christopher, the more I'm realising how much I want to spend time with him. And how I miss him when he's not around.

Plus, I have to admit I could do with the company right now. This whole evening has got me surprisingly worked up and I don't want to be alone either.

'You can't possibly sleep on the floor, Christopher, it's freezing. This bed is huge, more than enough room for the two of us.' I pat the bedspread, just as the fire alarm sounds again, but fortunately it cuts halfway through. Christopher tip toes across the hall to get his things. There's no chance of a decent night's sleep now, but I'm utterly exhausted. I want sleep so bad. Not just because my eyes are starting to sting but because I want to drift away in a dream and forget that we are still here.

'If you're sure?' Christopher asks as he stands by the end of my bed, travel bag in tow.

'I am. Now lock the door and turn off the main light, I'll keep the nightlight on. Just get in and let's try to get some shut-eye.'

The light goes down. I feel the weight of him climb into the bed beside me. He stays on top of the covers, and I feel him wriggle and settle, pulling his own blanket up to his chin to try to stay warm.

This will work. There's nothing weird here. Just two colleagues adapting to the situation. If I was here with Amy or Jasmine, this wouldn't even be considered inappropriate or unusual. So why shouldn't it be fine just because we're a man and woman? We're grown-ups. We can do this without making it a big deal. Right?

I've been snoozing for less than thirty minutes when I wake up to what feels like a gush of air on my feet. Praying that my frightened, fatigued mind is playing tricks on me, I try to drift back off to a happier place, but a few moments later, I hear Christopher tossing and turning, making distressed noises, as if he's having a very vivid nightmare.

I shake him awake, and his wide eyes are full of fear until he realises where he is and who I am.

'I felt a weight on my chest,' he says, still gasping for breath. 'It was wet and cold.' He looks at me, and I know we're both thinking the same thing. Neither of us is getting back to sleep. 'I can't do this sober.' Christopher turns on the lamp by his side of the bed and reaches down for his rucksack. 'Which is a positive, because it means I can do it, just not without the filter of intoxication. Baby steps.' He pulls out a half-finished bottle of wine and twists the cork to re-open it.

'We'll leave as soon as the sun comes up, I promise,' I say, watching his hand tremble slightly as he pours the wine into two plastic cups. He's really freaked out and I'm desperate to know why, but after the way he was in the car earlier, distant and closed, I know I'll have to choose my questions carefully. 'I wonder if people are born with an innate belief in the paranormal or whether it happens because they experience something in their own lives?'

At least this way, he can decide whether to shrug and say he doesn't know or to open up. The choice is his, but I'd love to find out. I want to find out all about Christopher. What he thinks, why he thinks it, what he wants from life, what's important to him, what he hopes for.

He shuts his eyes and takes a big swig of wine. 'For me personally, it was a bad experience. I know you think it's a gimmick, but I swear my grandmother's house was haunted.'

'What happened?' I ask him, relaxing into the cushions and eager to hear more, eager to just watch him speak, watch the way he runs his fingers through his hair and pauses before he meets my gaze.

'We moved into her place to care for her as she got older. The house was large and old, in a state of disrepair.' He speaks slowly, distractedly, as though his mind is grappling with some abstract problem. 'Local gossip said it boasted three "presences": a woman who stalked the ground floor, an elderly doctor forever racing up the stairs searching for a dying grandson and, in its upper reaches, the victim of an argument that had spilled over into murder.

There was even what appeared to be a bloodstain that could not be removed, which had since been covered with carpet.'

I take a deep breath and look around our room. 'Was it a house like this one?'

He nods. 'Almost identical.'

I sit up in the bed, pulling the covers under my chin.

'You must think I'm crazy,' he says, green eyes flickering in the half-light.

I shake my head. I'm intrigued. 'Not at all, go on,' I urge him. 'What else? I can tell by the look on your face there's more.'

He smiles. 'You really do want to know, don't you. Lily, you picked the perfect career for yourself, you know that?'

I smile back and nudge him gently. 'Come on, I'm hooked. Tell me everything.'

He clears his throat and I watch as he stretches out his arms and relaxes back into the cushions next to me.

'There was something so sinister about the place, a personality, a sense that we were intruding, like it was already occupied. It never felt quite empty. Doors would shut of their own volition, footsteps would sound on the staircase when everyone was in bed. I always felt like I was being watched. Even if I was in the bath!' He shakes his head. 'I can't believe I'm telling you this. Please stop me if I'm boring you.'

'Boring me? Never!' I clink my plastic cup against his.

He takes another sip and indulges me.

'Every few weeks, when the house kicked off, it kicked off in epic style. Some nights at 4 a.m., someone – some*thing* – would tear up the stairs, rattling the doorknobs, then forcing open the old, antique doors, all of which required proper turning and thrusting, until it reached my room, entering in a furious, door-slamming blast. This may sound like nothing, but I cannot tell you how regularly this happened. And how much it shook me.' He blinks his eyes at me. 'One night, I roared at it, told it to "leave us alone and shut the fuck up" and it did, briefly, before recommencing with still more drama. There was a silver lining to this episode: my little sister, then nine, still alludes to my big-brother bravery with the line: "Christopher can send ghosts back to where they came from."'

'She sounds like she really looks up to you.' I say. 'How lovely to have a sibling to look out for. To look out for you. How lovely to have a relationship that begins as an infant and grows right through your whole life. I always wished for a brother or sister,' I tell him. 'I think it's a very special bond.'

We pause a moment and then he gives me a wry smile. 'She was terrified by the rapping on the windows, and the way the dogs would always growl, hackles raised, teeth bared, at a certain spot in the kitchen where the old larder was. Back then, we didn't use the G-word. In fact, we were encouraged not to use any word at all – not to acknowledge any rumblings, certainly not to discuss it. And so the house tried harder, with what, I imagine, would be referred to as classic poltergeist activity. We would return home to find the taps turned on full force, requiring wrenching back into inaction. The new electric oven would have its rings switched to red hot. After the third time it happened, we had it disconnected. But it still happened again.'

I'm starting to understand a little more how much our past influences our present. How protective we are of exposing the secret fears we carry in our hearts. I can't help but feel incredibly honoured that he's sharing his deepest fears with me. How courageous of him to trust me with that, his greatest vulnerability, his most hidden weakness. I'm humbled by it.

'How did you stay there? That's not just frightening, it sounds dangerous.'

'Yes, well, I wanted to leave, believe me. It was the first year of my life I actually counted the days to get back to boarding school. Then things got worse. One night, the disused fireplace in my room sounded as if it was caving in. I put my pillow over my ears, telling myself it must be a trapped bird, but the next morning, I investigated. Behind the fireplace, crammed up the chimney, were Victorian newspapers recording the murder that had happened in the house.

'At breakfast, drinking tea in the kitchen, it just came out; the whole family finally admitted that something was happening. We tried to laugh and tease each other, but, my God, it was a relief. It transpired that even our dog would always shy at the gate, and I've heard that pets still do, padding the ground in fear.'

'Did they sell up and move far, far away? I think that's what I'd have to do.'

He shakes his head. 'It's a family house so not something we wanted to walk away from. Eventually, things settled. Over time, a year or two, events gradually petered out.'

I pour more wine, two big measures this time.

'You should write all that down. You're one heck of a storyteller.'

'Thanks. But I think I'll leave the writing to the writers.'

'You don't fool me. I've seen you scribbling away in your notepad. That's a writerly thing to do. If you weren't a writer, you'd be sat at the bar playing games on your phone.'

'Well, that's very kind of you to say. I did like the idea once upon a time. I even suggested to my father that I study English Literature at university, but he scowled at the prospect. As I imagined he would.'

'Why would he scowl at that? That's amazing, to study English at uni, right?'

'Not as amazing as studying something more profitable, such as Business.'

'I see. Well, I guess it's nice to have a dad that cares so much about you. And your future.'

'I've never told anyone that before,' says Christopher, rubbing his cheeks. 'Any of it – about my grandmother's house or about

my sister or about my dad… or even that I fancied myself as a
writer once upon a time.'

'Not even a friend or a partner?' I query.

He shakes his head. 'My male friends don't tend to discuss
stuff like this to be fair. We tend to keep it simple: sport and
share prices, that kind of thing. And I'm not often sitting up in
bed with them drinking wine and having deep and meaningfuls.'

Fair enough.

'And I guess the closest partner I've had was Victoria. But that
was really just a work romance that went on too long.'

'Oh, I see…?'

I don't know why it bothers me to think of Christopher
working closely with someone else. But it does. I smile and try
to hide any awkwardness my face might betray.

'She's back at the London office, but we're not together any
more,' he adds.

'I'm sorry.' I tell him, wanting to sound sincere but not entirely
convinced on how well that comes across.

'Don't be. It wasn't working. For me. She's very… controlling.
We should have ended things a long time ago, but, well, I kept
putting it off, hoping it would get better, hoping for something,
anything, to change. But we were wrong for each other, we wanted
completely different things… it's messy. And even though we
agreed a clean break, it doesn't always feel like it. She wants to
get back together, give it another go.'

'Do you think you will?' I really hope he says no. I mentally
cross my fingers.

He purses his lips and shakes his head. 'I'd rather spend another
night in here. Much less terrifying. The thing with Victoria is
that she can be great; charming, beautiful, funny, driven. But
the rest of the time…'

I raise my eyebrow, unsure of what he's going to say. I've seen
her, just that once in the car park, and she is beautiful. If she works

at the London office, then she must be really smart and sophisticated and successful too. On paper, these two should be perfect.

'... she's impossible. There were signs I tried to ignore, whenever she got jealous or got drunk, she would lose her temper and lash out, throw shoes, cutlery, whatever she could get her hands on, and I realised, I couldn't be with her any more. So I took this leadership job, I moved out, set up here and tried to start afresh.'

I smile. I know how he feels. 'Good plan.'

'She doesn't think so,' he raises his finger. 'She followed me up here, confronted me in the car park on what she knew was my first day, demanded that we got back together, and when I said no, she threatened to ruin my chance at promotion. Told me that nobody walks out on her just like that, that she'd see to it.'

'Sounds like she didn't take it too well.' Which is the nicest way I can find of saying that she sounds a little psycho. 'Hope she's not a modern-day Dorothy Shankley.' I try to lighten the mood.

'Ha! No, it's not really about me. She just doesn't like not getting her way. I'm sure she's moved on to someone much more eligible already.' He looks down awkwardly. 'That's why my glasses were broken that first morning. She snatched them from my face and flung them on the ground. Let's just say, she doesn't take very well to being told "no".'

'Oh, my goodness! That's awful, Christopher.'

'Yeah, great start to a new job! "Late and tardy," as McArthur said. Thanks for fixing them up for me though. That was really kind. A glimmer of kindness from a stranger when you've been screamed at by someone who says they love you can go a long way.' Christopher continues after a moment's pause. 'I'm just glad I saw the light before I married her. I could have just walked blindly in to that, not questioning if it was really what I wanted at all, just bowing to pressure.'

No truer word said. I know exactly what he means. Rather than looking at how rubbish my wedding day was, I now see that it was the moment I got my life back. Abruptly and painfully, yes, but none the less, a life that is much better than being married to Adam now with him constantly cheating on me. And after what Hannah confessed to me in that ambulance about Adam's continued infidelity, it kind of comforts me. Makes me realise that the reason it didn't, *couldn't*, work was not because of me, but because of him.

'How about you? Are you with someone?' Christopher asks me, snapping me out of probably the biggest realisation of my life to date.

I shake my head. 'Nope, guess I just haven't met the right one yet. I thought I did once, but now I'm relieved it didn't happen, I dodged a bullet too.'

He smiles at me and we wait a moment, the flickering candlelight between us. No screaming, no scratching, no wind whistling. Just us. It's blissful.

'It's funny, when I was growing up, there was this song we used to sing in the playground, "Lily and so and so, sitting in a tree, k-i-s-s-i-n-g, first comes love, then comes marriage, then comes baby in a baby carriage." And I'm like, okay, that's it! That's how you do life. That's how you do a relationship. Love, marriage, baby carriage. Easy, got it. And then I grew up, met Adam and my life turned out to be… Love, live together, engagement, engagement party, hen party, wedding dress fitting, jilted at the altar, ex-fiancé shacks up with best friend, honeymoon by myself, long, confused dry spell convinced I would never, ever fall for anyone again… you get the picture. It's slightly more complicated than I'd expected. But for the first time, I'm starting to feel lucky that my wedding didn't go through. Lucky that I'm not married to him. Not making excuses for his not answering the phone or working late at the office. The problem with all that is that you blame yourself, even though you are not the one doing anything wrong. If I'm completely honest with myself, I had an inkling that he was cheating on me, but I shut it out. He was breaking my heart and I just let him. I was in denial because I didn't want to start all over again. Put all my energy into fixing the unfixable. He promised to change, but he never did.' I smile. 'Yes. For once in my life, I'm glad that I didn't buy into the fairy tale only to lose the happy ending. Because there would have been no happy ending. I see now that it would never have lasted. So, it ended, and I'm relieved it did.'

He lifts the empty wine bottle and shakes it. 'I should have brought another bottle. I didn't plan for us to be up chatting like this into the small hours. It's nice.' Christopher drains the glass. 'If we survive this, will you let me take you out for a drink? Fresh start?'

I remember the little bottles of brandy he said he's brought with him. 'Or we could just have another drink now? If you don't mind sharing your brandy. I mean, I don't think either of us are going to get much sleep at this stage, do you?'

Christopher taps his fingers together and dips into to his travel bag. 'Lily Buckley you have some great ideas. Anyone told you that you are a genius?'

'Not lately.' I laugh. In fact, no one, ever.

Despite the teeming rain outside and the fact neither of us have had hardly any sleep, we talk. I notice that he tries to keep the conversation light now, far from anything that could make things feel more awkward or intense. He tells me about his plans after Newbridge, that hopefully he'll have a chance with a bigger company, how much he'd love to travel, get out of London and work abroad.

And as I listen to him talk of this and that, I can tell he's trying to give me the space he thinks I need, thinks I want. But as I watch him, listen to him, I realise that keeping a distance from him is the furthest thing from my mind.

He sits up on the bed opposite me and our fingers brush as he hands me a miniature bottle of brandy. He raises his in a toast. 'To high, strong spirits for broken, lost souls.'

I take a drink and feel it slide down my throat. It's actually the perfect warming sting to counteract the chill in this big old creaking house. I swallow and set it on my nightstand. Christopher does the same.

Everything about him makes me restless with longing. The shape of his lips, the softness of his dark hair, those green-amber eyes now looking completely different in the flickering candlelight. Those eyes that always seem to reflect what I'm thinking and feeling. Sitting here beside him, within touching distance, I feel the pull of the person he is. And I just want more.

He runs his fingers through his hair, pulling it back from his face. And then CRACK! The storm unleashes its full fury, thunder crashes outside the window and a long streaking lightning bolt electrifies the room. We both jump into the space between us, my hand flies to his arm, grabbing it as I try to catch my breath. The wind gusts, bending the tree branches as they scrape along the brickwork. We stay absolutely still as we listen out beyond the creaking and crashing circling us for anything more sinister, my fingers curled around his forearm. Then, just as we start to blink and breathe again, another deep, thunderous rumble breaks, and we throw ourselves against each other.

And then it's me and him huddled thigh to thigh on my bed. His face so close to mine. Smiling, and parting his lips ever so slightly, he brushes his hand down my cheek and I can see in his eyes that he's as nervous and excited and wary and certain, as I am.

He leans in and raises my hand to kiss it. Then I slide backwards towards the headboard and settle against the pillow and we lie there, staring at each other, sharing this unspoken energy that fills the space between us. Nothing creepy or sinister about this. Nope. This energy is very much alive. And very warm, and very welcome.

'Lily.'

I see the roll of his throat as he pauses to catch his breath, to find the words. 'I really like you. As in, really like you very much,' he says, brushing his thumb over mine.

I feel his warmth, the heat from his body, I inhale his scent and I know that I'll probably regret this in the morning, but right now, the morning feels so, so far away. Everything feels far away. Except him. I thread my fingers through his, leading him towards me.

'Are you sure you...?'

I place my finger on his lips and whisper back. 'I am...'

And it's the most naked truth I've spoken in a very long time.

CHAPTER 16

I smell toast. My eyes flick open and the clarity of what happened last night, all that happened last night, smashes down on me with the force of an ice-cold shower. An arm curls around my waist. Christopher breathing into my shoulder. I hear his deep low murmurings that tell me he's still asleep.

But I am wide awake.

I am fully naked.

And I'm not the only one.

What, *what* have I done?

I press my fingers into my eyes as I realise that the smell of toast means that breakfast is being served and it's soon going to be time to get up and face the cold, bright light of day and try to order the thoughts in my head.

Christopher. Yes, this really happened. A flashing image from last night... his lips trailing down my chest to my belly button. Oh, my God! How am I going to face him in the office? How am I going to face him now?

Oh, shit, another image: my arms thrown back behind my head, his hand in the small of my back. And there was that too – my face pressed against his, my fingers wrapped around his wrists. What was I thinking? What got into me? It was like nothing I've ever done before, it was so different, it was so... un-me. It was... Heat flushes into my cheeks... What the hell does he think of me now?

He will be as confused as I am. He is my boss. I've only known him a few weeks. He must think I do this kind of thing all the time… or at least regularly. Or, worse still, he'll realise that I don't do this kind of thing *at all*.

My head starts to pound at the same rate as my heart. I feel my body stiffen. I can't wake him up, I can't let him see me this way… Bedhead like a banshee and panda-eyed, lips swollen from all that kissing… but mostly I can't mentally face him now with the inevitable awkwardness that will ensue as he realises he has made a *huge* mistake. All this is real. Real and naked. What am I supposed to do now?

Well, one thing is for sure, I cannot stay for breakfast. Another image flashes up in my mind… Sweet Lord, we did that too? Who *was* I last night? I mean, what was I on? What happened to me? I've never been like that before, not with Adam, not before Adam. Not since Adam. Not until last night. With Christopher.

Shit. Shit. Shit. Shit.

I need to get out of this bed. Unhook his arm from my waist. Make a break for it.

Slowly and ever so gently, I slip out from under the covers and snatch up my clothes from the ground, tiptoeing my way to the bathroom, cat-burglar style.

I push open the door to the bathroom, then turn around and lock it shut.

I'm relieved I managed that. At least if I do have to talk to him now, I'll have some clothes on, I'll have a chance to think of my next move and prepare for his, which will undoubtedly be an excuse to get going, to leave me and this haunted house far behind. Imagine Christopher waking up to find me bent over and scrambling around on the floor for my bra.

Thank God I woke up first. I breathe in through my nose, out through my mouth, wash my hands, throw cold water on my face, repeat the breathing.

He's probably in there right now staring at the ceiling trying to strategise an escape plan. Bet he's thinking what the hell happened? Why the hell did he let that happen? We're colleagues. He's a high-achieving well-educated city boy. I've seen his ex, Victoria, guys like him go for girls like her. Not girls like me. From small, back-end-of-nowhere towns with silly middle names and no academic achievements.

This is a classic rebound fail, he's fresh from a break-up and got in over his head. I'm under no illusion that last night will be classified as a big mistake on his part; a silly, drunken mistake. If Victoria was an office mistake, I'm a worse one.

But at least no one else was here to witness it. At least we can keep this under wraps between us. We can just bury it, pretend it never happened.

I'm calmer now.

I'll just go back out there and tell Christopher that I'm not feeling well. I'll leave and whatever went on between us last night will remain here, our secret, we'll gloss over it so well that soon we'll wonder if it ever happened at all. What happens in The Shankley Hotel, stays at The Shankley Hotel – with all the other so-called skeletons in the closet.

A gentle rap on the other side, startles me. Taking a deep breath, I unlock the door, but I don't pull it open.

'Lily? Are you in there?'

Christopher gently pushes the door from the other side, so I step back.

'Hey there, good morning,' he says as he steps inside the bathroom with me, bed sheet wrapped around his waist, his hair ruffled, rubbing his eyes. He stretches out his arms wide above him, running his hands across his cheeks, squinting towards me. His eyes crinkle and narrow; those eyes, they're part of the reason we wound up here in the first place. 'How are you?' he asks.

I nod. 'Good. Fine. Great.' So much for saying I was sick and had to shoot off.

He smiles, and I melt.

'You?'

'I'm fantastic thanks.'

'Really?' Why does he look so calm? so relaxed? Doesn't he remember? Surely he realises that this is a complete disaster, for both of us.

He laughs, then slides one hand up my arm, under my chin and steps towards me, tilting my head upwards. His other hand feathers my shoulder as he moves my hair away from my neck.

My breath catches. I get flashes of last night again. His smooth, warm skin on mine. His hot, soft mouth on my mouth.

Squeezing my eyes shut, his fingers trace across my chest, over my heart and a shudder runs over my whole body.

His lips meet my skin.

When I open my eyes again, they lock with his.

'I thought...' I whisper, trailing off, unsure what to think now.

He kisses me under my ear. It is heavenly, I have no breath.

'You thought what?' he whispers back, kissing into my hairline. So soft, so deliberate.

'I thought you may not want... that you might regret...'

He brings his mouth to my ear again. 'I think you think too much. Let's not think.'

And I do just that, I abandon all thought and walk backwards towards the bedroom, pulling his hands forward, not able to wait, not able to believe that we are here, together, like this again.

And that I actually never want to leave this place.

We just about make last orders for breakfast, where all the other guests can talk about is the rogue fire alarm and the hysterical screaming of the girl in the room next to mine. Overhearing us, the chef who was making our fry-up comes into the dining room.

'What time did you say the fire alarm went off?' he asks.

When we tell him, he pauses and starts to look a little stressed out.

'Well, this is an old house, so the wiring isn't perfect,' he says. 'But I would be lying to you if I said this same thing doesn't happen once every couple of weeks, always around the same time of night. I thought this was going to be an easy job, but I'm not sure how much more I can take.' And with that, his face blanches of colour and he rushes out of the dining room. I wonder if he plans on coming back.

On our way out, Mr Dean explains how many people who visit the house later contact them to say they believe they've taken a spirit home. This time yesterday I'd have laughed at such an absurd suggestion, but after listening to Christopher's story, I'm not so sure.

'Now that you've had this experience, you might go home and notice things you didn't before – maybe a photo that keeps falling or a sentimental item that turns up out of the blue,' he says, casting a side-long glance at Christopher and I. 'But don't worry, when people call us and say they've taken one home, I say "send it back to us in the mail, we need it for business."'

Whether or not that's true or he is just trying to scare us even more, I'm ready to go and feel I've learnt a lot about Dorothy Shankley and her bitter haunting. And quite a lot about myself and Christopher too. So, we zip up our coats, put our bags in the car, and drive home, without looking back. Because suddenly I can't help but look forward.

Despite the ghoulish happenings and strange goings-on, I'm feeling on an absolute high, so excited, so hopeful. Last night was incredible; the first night in over three years that I've not spent by myself. And it wasn't with just anyone, but Christopher, a gorgeous man that I like. A man I like more by the minute. A man that's kind and sensitive and honest and with a smile that makes me melt.

And, if I'm honest with myself, trusting myself, trusting a guy again, is a major bucket list item for me. Because, deep down, I never really believed it would happen.

Until now.

Buckley's Bucket List
No. 3 – The Shankley Hotel

Given the spooky nature of an October night in a 300-year-old hotel – and not just any night, but Friday 13th – even a comfortable canopy bed and crackling fire in the hearth may not be enough to help guests get a restful night's sleep – especially since the spirits within are often restless. There are plenty of spine-chilling stories from those who have resided in The Shankley Hotel, where invited (and apparently uninvited) guests roam the rooms and hallways. When I first wrote this story's tagline, it read 'Sleeping at The Shankley Hotel', but I corrected myself, as there was not much of the former.

A new poll tells us that fifty-five per cent of Britons believe in the supernatural and one in ten think they have a supernatural gift. The findings make sense. Why wouldn't people want to believe in ghosts? Doesn't the thought that the 'bump in the night' is more than just the central heating playing up give us all a little thrill? It means that the great adventure of life doesn't end with death. You've got many more years ahead of you of floating about invisible and unhindered. No more long queues at airport check-in for this weightless soul...

Although a sceptic myself, I'm a curious and respectful one, forever on the lookout for things that can't be explained by science. I always retained a healthy belief that all things are possible. And that was the attitude that I took to our ghost hunt challenge. So, it was with a determinedly open mind that I agreed to stay overnight with my colleague Christopher at The Shankley Hotel.

There were some 'incidences'. A fire alarm that went off for no reason. Lots of screaming (some of it, admittedly, from me). A howling storm outside which made the whole house creak and sway. Flickering candles in sealed rooms, along with unexplained shivers at the back of our necks, frozen feet and vivid nightmares all featured during our stay. The next morning at breakfast, one of a group of American ghost watchers who also spent the night, said things got weird as soon as she turned off her lights. 'There was this feeling of sickness that came over us. Doors opened on their own and the toilet kept flushing of its own accord.' Other members of the group reported flying objects and bone-chilling sensations including nausea and the feeling that their hair was being touched. 'You always got the sense something was standing behind you.'

Were these the antics of ghouls and ghosts or were they figments of our imagination, realised in the context of our expectation? It's anyone's guess. One thing is for sure, though, if you have a nervy, jumpy predisposition, expect to jump. A lot.

So, do I believe in ghosts? I don't know. I believe in atmospheres engendered by people who are long gone; in auras retained in places where folk have been deeply affected; that profound emotions hang around, caught in corners of buildings, trapped in rooms and objects and even people. I can enter one house and immediately feel welcome before meeting its occupants; in another home, the back of my neck tingles with unexplained unease.

But there is something I did sense back there. Something that's left a lasting impression on me.

I stayed in the Master Bedroom, where a raging Dorothy Shankley axed her cheating groom-to-be, after much hurt and heartbreak had occurred. And I did feel something. In fact, I was bowled over by the overwhelming energy of painful feelings, of a restless, unresolved past. Desperation. Loneliness. Anguish. Sadness. Anger. Frustration. This may be what's so palpable at The Shankley and what scares people so much, a resonance with the trapped Dorothy in her torturous limbo, her inability to let go, her inability to move on. And until she does so, I guess she'll be imprisoned in this hotel, in her own suffering, in this ethereal no-man's land, forever.

But rather than be scared of her, it makes me feel sorry for her. Because I experienced something a little similar to Dorothy in my own life at one point. So in a way, I understand the kind of despair and fury that drove her do what she did. Thankfully, I didn't have an axe to hand. And maybe that made all the difference. Because we can't control how others treat us, sometimes we don't get what we deserve, but it's how we respond that really defines us. And after spending some time in Dorothy's room, I've decided that the best way for me to respond to my own situation is to let go of what's past and embrace the future.

Unfortunately it's not so easy for Dorothy. I want to tell her to forgive them, forget them – the groom, the handmaid… not because they deserve forgiveness, but because she deserves peace. The hurt they caused her is nothing compared to the hurt she's causing herself. And that's no way to live… or die. Instead, Dorothy, think how much fun you could have!

While I can't say I left Newbridge's most haunted hotel keen to ditch my journalism career for ghost hunting,

I definitely have a more open mind. I suspected all the stories we'd been fed about visitors hearing footsteps and feeling hands on their shoulders had influenced our perception of our surroundings. Maybe the human mind seeks patterns to make sense of ambiguous information. But how can we ever really know?

If you enjoy being shook up for kicks, or just want to experience a truly unique night away, steeped in the history of Newbridge, I'd advise you to check in to The Shankley. You can decide for yourself if that fear is of real or imaginary ghosts.

As I prefer hanging out with humans, I'm unlikely to return. But what I did learn is that I ain't afraid of no ghosts. In fact, I think I managed to lay one or two to rest.

Till next week! Lily xx

Do you believe Lady Dorothy haunts The Shankley Hotel? Vote on our readers' poll below to enter our draw to receive... a weekend away at The Shankley Hotel, courtesy of Mr Dean and his team. BTW, they serve a cracking breakfast :)

CHAPTER 17

'You look lovely.'

I check over my shoulder just to be sure. Nobody else is in sight. So unless Christopher has got a notable ophthalmic mis-alignment (cross-eyed, as my granny would've said), he appears to be smiling directly at me.

'Likewise. You scrub up well.'

I'm understating. What I want to say is you are positively big-screen gorgeous.

I can't help but look over my shoulder once more, just to make sure I haven't traipsed into someone else's dream date. Into someone else's *life*. I haven't.

'Shall we?' he asks.

I nod. I really want to keep this relationship under wraps. Firstly, this is breaking my rule about 'getting involved' with work colleagues. I know what we're doing is perfectly legal, two adults who like each other out for a meal, perfectly civilised, but I still don't feel comfortable about anyone knowing yet. I definitely like him. As in DEFINITELY. But, once bitten, twice shy. The *Gazette* was my refuge after my last heartbreak. I don't know how I'd cope with another, in plain view of people I've got to see every day.

I dart my eyes up and down the street behind us and figure the coast is clear, so I slip my arm in to Christopher's elbow and we walk in to the Golden Wok restaurant he's booked for our first date. I feel as high as I was on that skydive. Except that this time, I may be falling faster.

Inside, Christopher leads us across the restaurant and pulls out my chair at the reserved, candle-lit round table for two in the corner.

'What do you think?' he asks as he opens the wine list.

Paper lanterns, fans, dragons and huge, bulging-eyed fish adorn the walls, decked out in enough lace and chintz to supply several brothels.

'I've never been here before, but it looks great.' I don't want to tell him that I've never been here before because this restaurant has a reputation for being one of the worst restaurants in the area. I remember Hannah ordering a takeaway of spring rolls with sweet chilli sauce only to get a soggy pastry tube with a single sad beansprout inside and a side of strawberry jam. So nope, this is a first for me.

I study the wine menu too. It lists two kinds. Red and white. That's it.

'Recommendation from Mark – he appears to know all about the best places to go,' says Christopher.

Maybe Mark was teasing? Or keeping his cards close to his chest regarding dating venues, so they don't end up in the same place? I really can't see Mark bringing girls in here to impress them.

Christopher surveys the dining room and eyes the bar. 'Clearly he likes very quiet restaurants with dark corners that serve draught beer and have an early-bird menu. He said that the sweet and sour pork and the satay chicken are the best in town.'

I don't know if that's as impressive as Christopher may think it is, seeing as this is the *only* Chinese in town. Mark's idea of a well-balanced meal is a protein shake followed by dehydrated cow hide. But then again, maybe I've got it all wrong and this restaurant is a hidden gem. We're here to find out.

'Sweet and sour pork it is then,' I say, closing my menu.

Christopher bites down on his lip. 'I didn't mean to suggest. Please, Lily, order anything you want… there's duck, noodles…'

I shrug. 'Best sweet and sour in town sounds great to me.' I take his hand across the table and squeeze it gently 'Confession time; I'm not just here for the food.'

He winks at me and gently squeezes my hand.

'And I'll have the satay then.' He smiles, shutting the menu. 'You know, the more I learn about Newbridge and all it has to offer, the more I like it. More importantly, I want to kick myself at how much of an arrogant city-boy bastard I was, believing that there was little to no life outside of London.'

I raise my eyebrow. I can't picture Christopher as a stuck-up suit. Yes, he wears a suit, and yes, he's really well spoken. But I've never believed him to be cocky.

'But that happens right?' he continues. 'You get blinkered, you live in a city, so you believe that everything outside of it is somehow a scaled-down or diluted version of what you have on your doorstep every day. But that's such a false logic, such a shallow view. In the short while I've been here, I've got to know the team far better than I knew any of my previous colleagues despite being there for years.'

'Why do you think that is?' I ask.

He blows out his cheeks. 'Mixture of things. The office was so big and hectic we rarely had a chance to stop and get to know each other. But a lot of the fault is mine, I spent… correction, I *allowed* Victoria to take over. I got lazy and just let her run my life basically. By the end, I didn't even bother to ask what I was doing on a Friday night, knowing she'd already have made all the plans.'

'It was a major break-up then.' I can't help but feel uncomfortable every time Victoria's name comes up. I know he said it's over but he also said that she wants him back. Who could blame her? And I have a strong feeling that Victoria finds ways to get what she wants. I know better than anyone that it's hard to move on, even when you really want to.

'Major break*through*. I lost myself back there somehow. And now that I can see that, now I've had some space to be on my own, new setting, new people... I feel a lot better, much happier. I just want to make sure I never go back.'

That makes two of us. I'm here with this gorgeous man and I want everything to be perfect. No thoughts of the past. Only of the future.

I can't believe this. The paper is on the up, Christopher is a miracle, and everything is just falling perfectly in to place.

I really need a drink.

I try to catch the waiter's eye, but actually, I can't even catch a waiter. There doesn't seem to be anyone around who works here. There are no other customers so they can't be too busy to serve us. Did Mark really say that this was one of his favourite restaurants?

I unfold my napkin and smooth it on my lap to distract myself. That waiter will be here any moment, surely...

Christopher must be just as thirsty as me as he loosens his collar. We hear shouting in a different language and turn to see a very angry waiter bellowing in to the phone whilst slamming his fist against the counter.

'No! You are the dick cheese! Fuck you!' he calls out in English.

Christopher raises an eyebrow and tips his head slightly towards the door. 'You want to go?'

'Go lick your mother's balls,' shouts the waiter.

I shake my head and smile at him. 'Newbridge's finest.'

Christopher laughs. 'Remind me never to trust Mark's judgement ever again.'

Finally, the waiter arrives at our table, unsurprisingly, without a smile. I try to keep my eyes on the menu as he scratches under his armpit. We order, and he grunts his understanding and shouts the order (without writing it down) to a terrified-looking waitress behind the bar.

She then walks over to the kitchen door and shouts it through.

We hear the final echo from somewhere inside the clanging and steam.

However crazy this ordering system is, a bottle of red and a basket of prawn crackers arrive on the table.

Christopher pours and raises his glass to a toast. 'To surviving Buckley's Bucket list: the skydive, the Hell Raiser and, I'd never thought I'd say this, but my favourite, The Shankley.'

I clink his glass. 'And hopefully surviving the Golden Wok.'

With that, the waiter returns, slamming down a sizzling tray of neon orange pork. It looks and smells radioactive. I'm not sure pork is supposed to look like this. I'm not even sure it's pork.

'I'm sure it'll be delicious,' I offer.

But then Christopher's satay arrives… and I burst out laughing.

Christopher smiles as he lowers his nose to the plate to inspect further. 'Yep, smells just like it looks.'

It looks like a steaming mound of peanut butter poo.

'Do you think Mark did this on purpose?' he asks.

I look at my watch. 'It's nine o'clock. He'll be next door in The Black Boar now. Pint in hand. We could get this in a doggy bag and drop it in to him, seeing as it's his favourite?'

Christopher drums his fingers excitedly against the table and calls for the bill, which comes with a grimace and a handful of fortune cookies.

'You first,' he prompts.

I unwrap mine and hold it up to read it. 'Your head is too small for your body.' I burst out laughing and pretend to measure my head against my body. 'Confucius must have been having a very bad day when he wrote that one.'

'Take another one. That one's rubbish,' Christopher says.

I open a second one. 'First love is the triumph of imagination over intelligence. Second love is the triumph of hope over experience.'

We both stop a moment to ponder this, as if it's real-life philosophical advice, straight from the after-dinner snack gods.

'I do like this one better than the shrunken head one,' I tell him, folding over the strip of fortune paper and sliding it into my wallet. 'Think I'll need to re-read it sometime I've had less wine.'

Christopher opens his. 'Every exit is a gateway to something new,' he reads. 'In that case, let's exit.'

And sure enough, ten minutes later, we're sitting at the counter of a packed-out Black Boar with two drinks in hand and two packets of crisps, while we wait for Mark to finish singing 'Ring of Fire' on karaoke (prophetic, much?) so we can deliver his favourite steaming brown takeaway. It takes every ounce of self-restraint not to kiss Christopher, not to hold his hand or wrap myself around him. But this is a rule I am keeping – no one at the *Gazette* can know about this. This is really new for me, and we're moving very fast.

We work closely, we share the same friends, we haven't known each other very long but yet I'm feeling a lot for him. I'm thinking about him all the time. I've got to tread carefully here before I lose control of myself altogether.

By the time the last orders bell rings, we've had a very fun night out. Including our own little rendition of 'Don't Go Breaking My Heart', Christopher pulling off a rather surprising falsetto which made him Kiki Dee.

'One for the road?' he asks.

'Or coffee at mine?'

We get our coats.

CHAPTER 18

The sun streams through the window of my bedroom. I nudge the sleeping warmth nestled into my back. 'I'll go in first. It won't be so obvious that way,' I tell him.

Christopher rolls back and opens one eye. 'I don't care if it's obvious.' He smiles at me.

I shake my head. 'No, no, no! They can't know; honestly. We've still got to work together! We can't have any distractions, no suspicious mutterings or fuelling of the gossip mill. There's too much at stake. Especially with McArthur coming in for the progress meeting next week. Everything is riding on that meeting, all the hard work we've put in. The *Newbridge Gazette* isn't out of the woods yet. Let's keep our eyes on the prize for now, okay?'

He stretches and yawns theatrically. 'Your call. If it makes you more comfortable to keep me as your guilty little secret.'

'It does. And it's not just me. It could have a negative impact on your leadership programme too. McArthur probably wouldn't look favourably on you cavorting so closely with the staff.' I think back to our very first meeting, her socking her fist in to her palm saying some behaviour 'belonged in the bedroom, not the boardroom'. I wince a little as I realise she meant Christopher and Victoria. That he's been in this position before, from bedroom to boardroom.

I sit up and shake out my hair. 'I know for a fact that she doesn't approve of this kind of unprofessionalism.'

He traces a finger on my shoulder. 'The unprofessionalism is the best bit.' His hand drifts up to my chin. 'And I just want to stay here. Do we have to go in?'

'Yes! And no funny looks. No looking at all, in fact. I caught you at the pub last night. You need to help me not make it even harder! We've got to keep everything normal.'

'It is hard. When you're standing there, so close. What about Mark? He saw us together last night. Surely, he'll suspect something. Maybe we should just come clean?'

I shake my head. 'He was plastered. I mean, he ate every bite of that satay with a plastic teaspoon, so I'm not too worried about his levels of perception.'

Christopher kisses my forehead. 'When work settles down, let me take you away for a long weekend. London maybe or better yet, a short flight abroad? Barcelona or Berlin? Anywhere away from Newbridge, away from the paper, away from everything. Just me and you and no prying eyes. How would you like that?'

I find something to like in everything he just said, hinting as it does to a shared future. Sometime beyond the now, something more to look forward to

'I'd love it. But don't ask Mark for recommendations.' I smile. 'It's getting late. Just about time for coffee?'

'As in…'

'As in hot caffeine in a mug.'

Chaplin starts to meow, calling for his breakfast. I throw off the duvet.

'Hot caffeine, yes please. I'm going to need it. I've got to sort out a new place to stay after today. McArthur had just booked me in week by week and now the landlord needs the place back for holidaymakers.'

I don't want us to leave this conversation. I want to know if there's something here. Something beyond an office fling. Something beyond casual. Something worth hoping for. I hope there is. I take a deep breath and decide to just go for it. Ask him straight.

'So... does that mean you're planning on staying in New-bridge?'

'Staying as long as I'm needed, I guess,' he says vaguely.

'As in... long-term? Staying at the *Gazette*, staying around town permanently?' I want to say staying around me, but I daren't. I open the curtains and let the sunshine flood in. He rubs his eyes with the back of his hand, still adjusting to the light.

'I never really considered this as a permanent move... I mean, I can see why people love it here so much, it's got everything – great pubs, restaurants, beautiful scenery, friendly people, big enough to be lively but small enough not to feel invisible. But I don't think I could ever settle down here. Maybe when I retire or something, but...' He holds up both hands. 'It's not exactly buzzing with opportunity, is it? It's just a stepping stone.'

And that's when I realise what this is. What I am. A stepping stone.

'But you're the same right?' he asks. 'That's why you took the promotion, to upskill, drive forward?'

I just smile and nod. This isn't the time to tell him I just realised that we're never going to make this work. That we're both at the *Gazette* for two completely different reasons. I'm there because I want to stay. He's there because he wants to move on. I don't know why this comes as such a surprise to me. A guy like him could never settle in a place like this. It's too quiet, too remote, too dull. This is all just a bit of fun for him – a change of scene, nothing serious, nothing permanent. Just like our relationship.

I realise I ran into this exactly the same way I ran into the Half-Pipe to Hell. Unthinking, reckless, heart over head.

And it's going to hurt, just the same. If I let it.

Which I can't. It was lovely. It was nearly perfect. It almost felt possible. I guess sometimes love is wrenched from you unexpectedly and sometimes it just slips away without ever really having its moment.

I pick up Chaplin and nuzzle him. *Looks like it's back to me and you again, kiddo.*

'Come on, you get showered and changed and I'll make breakfast. I'm leaving here in fifteen minutes.'

And just like that, it's almost as if nothing's changed, I'm back behind the wheel of my car, driving to work, waving my good mornings and sipping my coffee before I get to my desk. But even though it looks like I'm together and completely composed – make-up on, hair up, broad smile – deep down, I know the truth. It's my default and it's called autopilot with a chronically broken heart. When will I ever learn?

CHAPTER 19

Jasmine meets me at the elevator. 'I just got the email. Marked Urgent! Exactly the same as the one I got when Gareth freaked out. McArthur is coming tomorrow morning and she's bringing people. Fourteen of them.'

Shareholders. It's got to be. The time is passing so fast, I can barely keep up. It feels as if I'm living in double-time. Christopher has stayed at mine almost every night since our 'sleep-over' at The Shankley. For the first time in ever such a long time, I actually can't wait to clock off and leave the office, because there's so much I want to do: cycle, write, cook dinner, snuggle Chaplin, have a glass of wine by the fire with Christopher. I have a life! And I'm loving every second of it. As long as I manage to forget that it will come crashing to an end when he leaves. I understand it's not forever but I can't help myself. How can I possibly turn away from this when he is in touching distance of me every day. Setting every moment alive with longing and possibility. I'm crazy for him. And I'm doing pretty well at blocking out anything that'll interfere with that.

But I really hope this email doesn't spell the beginning of our end. That our time is up.

'You are kidding. We're not expecting her until the end of the week!'

She certainly likes to pounce on us when we're not expecting her. Maybe she thinks it's the best way to catch us off guard and expose us, no time for cover-ups.

Jasmine shows me her Excel checklist. 'Don't you worry, Lily, I've already arranged for the Conference Room to be set up. I've ordered pastries, tea and coffee, all that jazz. We're ready for her. This whole place is unrecognisable since you took over. She's going to see that immediately.'

I raise an eyebrow. I know we're doing well. When The Shankley Hotel article went live it took us to a new level. It was read and received all over the country and became a major discussion point on a national morning radio show. As a result, Mr Dean has extended their season now they have so many bookings, and a Ghost Hunting Society has asked if they can get a marriage licence to perform weddings there (Do you really want to upset Dorothy in that way?) and they've been contacted by a TV company who produce a show called *Old Haunts*, bringing a great buzz to the area and the office.

So, three weeks and three bucket list tasks and three features down, we've come a long way, but we're not done yet. There's still one feature to go before the end of the month and our final review. And now an impromptu meeting with 'people'.

'I've never presented to shareholders,' I tell Jasmine. 'This sounds like it's make or break.'

She nudges me. 'You're going to smash it. You're ready for this, Lily, don't doubt yourself.'

Jasmine is right. We are ready. We are so ready.

At my desk, I open my top drawer and lift out my large green portfolio that contains everything I suspect they'll need to know about how we've been doing; graphs, sales figures, rankings, progress charts. If it can be considered evidence that the *Newbridge Gazette* is fighting its way back to glory, then I've got it in this folder to prove it beyond any doubt. Backed up with Christopher's tech whizz to show individual region-by-region sales breakdowns, as well as digital expansion plans and future trajectories, we should knock their socks off and send them back to headquarters with huge smiles on their faces.

They came to close us down, they set us a challenge and I'm proud to say we rose to it.

Jasmine covers the handset of the call she's taking and waves a hand over to me. 'McArthur's just asked me to order in a case of champagne! Looking good!'

McArthur doesn't waste time. She's already had Jennings go through the books. She's already made up her mind and evaluated the situation. She must have, she's ordered champagne!

Professionally, tomorrow is going to be one of the best days ever; for our office and for me.

Looks like we're back, dear *Gazette*, and better than ever. But victory for the *Gazette* means that Christopher's work here is done. So I guess that means we're done too.

I sit at my desk and try to distract myself with work. Maybe I'll give Mr Clark a call? See if he's feeling better. Yes, that's exactly what I should do. Maybe I can even justify a few hours out of the office, where I can just drive around, be by myself, have a little cry and avoid Christopher altogether. It was a terrible idea getting involved with a work colleague for every reason I knew before this thing started.

Somehow, telling myself *told me so* doesn't feel quite as satisfying as I'd hoped.

I rummage in my wallet for Mr Clark's number, but a little slip of flimsy paper falls out instead.

'First love is the triumph of imagination over intelligence. Second love is the triumph of hope over experience.'

I wonder why it doesn't say anything about third love?

Maybe because they gave up.

CHAPTER 20

The next day Christopher and I are called in to the packed conference room. As the doors open I notice there are a lot more suited and booted, grey-faced important-looking people here than I expected; I was prepared for fourteen or so, but there are twenty here already. Some on their laptops typing frantically, others scrolling on their phones, some handshaking and head-nodding earnestly. And nobody has touched the pastries. Not even the custard ones. Very unnerving.

I know that Christopher has been at shareholders' meetings before, so it's no wonder he's relaxed; he knows what to expect. He looks so confident, smiling and working the room with easy opening questions about the drive here, the family, the rugby. I stand by him, trying to settle my nerves and listen as much as possible. This is new ground for me, so I don't want to make a mistake or look too amateur. I pour myself some water and pat my green folder for the hundredth time. Every answer to every question they could possibly throw at me should be in here. As long as I don't get flustered or lose it.

Apart from McArthur and Jennings, there's nobody else here I recognise.

Except for one person.

But she's isn't in yoga pants and a ponytail today. No one would believe that this tall blonde, striking and immaculately dressed in a designer white suit, is the same woman I saw screaming at Christopher in the car park just a few weeks ago.

I watch as she glances up from her phone and registers that Christopher is here. Her eyes fix on him; she straightens and flicks her hair forward over her shoulder as she stands from her chair. Victoria is on her way over.

'Well hello, stranger.'

She leans in, offering him both cheeks to kiss. He complies without meeting her eyes. He's not smiling now at all.

I nudge him to check if he's okay.

'So, of course, I know what you are thinking, Christopher. Why would Victoria, with her crazy schedule, travel all the way from HQ to this little farm town today?' She presses the palms of her hands together and looks us both in the eye in turn as if she is a spirit medium trying to 'read' us. 'The shell-shocked looks on your little faces!' She hunches her shoulders, wiggling a baby finger in my direction. 'And you must be Lily! I'm Victoria Bowery, Head of Talent at Media Core. Don't be intimidated. I was just like you once upon a time. Working my butt off trying to get noticed in a two-bit paper.'

Christopher rolls his eyes and tenses his jaw.

Victoria sidles in closer, lowering her voice. 'I read your bucket list, very cute. I couldn't believe you got Christopher here to stay in anything less than a five-star.' She laughs without any sound. 'Mags mentioned that you'd made some interesting improvements, so I thought I'd come along and check it out. I'm a little magpie like that, aren't I, Christopher? Can't help but snatch a shiny new idea and keep it for myself.'

I never believed anyone could be more patronising than Gareth, but I stand corrected. Worse still, she's drop-dead gorgeous, successful and she's brimming with confidence. She's a tough act to follow.

'I don't want to beat around the bush. Part of my new role is identifying talent across all offices; especially these little overlooked ones. So, you could say I'm here as a scout today, to see if there's anyone that catches my eye that I can poach from you for some new projects we have underway.'

I have no idea what to say. Who on earth would welcome someone who is blatantly out to seduce and snatch *Gazette* staff?

She misreads my blank look. 'Oh I see, well don't worry, I don't always expect there to be diamonds in the rough. I do hiring and *firing*. So if you want me to review your team and maybe make a few suggestions? Maybe some reshuffling? Some accountability measures? Some competence concerns that we can embellish to clear the dead wood? Everything is possible.'

Christopher turns to her. 'Victoria, there is absolutely no dead wood on this team; we need everybody we've got. This office works like a well-oiled machine and they've done an amazing job so far. We appreciate the offer; thanks but no thanks.'

'Okay, but I thought it best that we're all on the same page, in fact, it's best that we all pool information and keep transparent. I mean, we're on the same team, right?'

Neither of us say anything.

'That's not changed, right, Christopher?' Victoria pushes.

'Yep,' he says flatly, the smile gone from his lips once again.

Victoria raises both palms in the air in mock surrender. 'I'm just here to help, don't want to step on anyone's toes.' She looks at me and starts to explain, 'It's just, Lily, you see, there are several big fish in here at the moment. Potential shareholders who can bring big bang for their buck. It's a completely different league to anything you'll have worked with before.' She curls her lip and I watch Christopher watch her. 'We'd really like to get them on board. I know this is your paper and you turned it around, but I also know that it's so easy to completely buckle under the pressure, so if you want me to step in and really nail it down for you   and for your paper of course – I'm here. Ready to step in and take over. Just say the word.'

The cheek! The brass neck! The balls! I'm actually staggered by her arrogance. That she can just walk in here for the very first time, minutes before the biggest meeting the *Gazette* has ever seen and feel like she can take over and claim all this hard work, all the blood, sweat and sacrifice for herself.

I press my fingernails into the palm of my hand to steady my outrage. Maybe this is also part of her plan, to rile us, to sabotage our vibe before we even stand up, so we sound confused and angry. I take a deep breath and reflect the same big smile she's giving me. Whatever way she is trying to undermine us, it just won't work. She wouldn't be here if she really believed we were nothing.

This is our place. Our territory. She is the one who has no place here. I raise my chin and offer her my hand. 'We are very happy, very confident and very excited about today's presentation. Please help yourself to tea and coffee. If you have any further questions, please feel free to speak with Jasmine, our admin manager. She's got an excellent grasp on everything that goes on here at the *Gazette*.'

Victoria bites the inside of her lip and squints at me with one eye. She doesn't want to leave us. She doesn't want to leave Christopher's side at all. I can see her mind ticking over, trying to think of a way to keep our interest. She turns her back to the rows of shareholders and leans in to us both. 'I'm not supposed to tell you this, but the big three are sitting in today. They're looking to invest and expand local news streams. It's part of a new model, a five-year plan to "mushroom". They want a few hundred small, specialist offices globally rather than one HQ in the capital. And the *Gazette* is a hot ticket right now. All three CEOs of Sky Group, GlobalOne and Unitel are here.'

Christopher's eyes widen, and he rubs his chin. I know what he's thinking, that this is his big chance, that if we can showcase to these guys today, they're bound to offer him a position with them. And that's what he's worked for all this time, why he took on the leadership programme, why he left London to come to Newbridge, why he works 24/7 to meet the *Gazette* targets.

'You wouldn't mind excusing us for a moment would you, Lily? I have something I need to ask Christopher's advice on before your presentation begins. A private matter. We go back a long way, you see.' She rests her hand on my shoulder. Then tightens it.

I nod politely, pick up my green folder and move towards the whiteboard at the front. I'm actually relieved, it gives me a chance to compose myself before we begin. I take a long sip of water and rehearse my pitch in my head. Now I know Victoria is going to be listening, I feel more nervous than ever. She's Head of Talent, and as she said, she has the power to hire or fire any one of us. She's also McArthur's protégé; I can tell by the way she mimics her gestures, the way she taps her jawline when posing a question, the way she smiles with her eyes when she is saying something harsh. But I like Mags McArthur. She has given us a chance, and she's fair. I don't get that vibe from Victoria. With her I feel like I've just been robbed somehow. But I'm not sure yet what it is she's taken.

A phone starts to ring. The mortification is instant as I realise that it's mine. I feel the glare of McArthur on me. It should have been on silent; especially as I'm one of the presenters. It rings out again, the tone getting louder. It'll take too long to locate it somewhere in the bottom of my bag, fish it out and then turn it off, so I grab the whole bag and head towards the door, making an apologetic face as I exit.

Typically, the phone stops and the line is dead as soon as I answer it.

The number isn't a contact, and it's a really long number, international maybe? Someone cold-calling no doubt, selling me insurance or PPI cover or loft insulation.

Just as I try to hurriedly turn my phone off altogether, it rings again, the same number. I answer it instantly because I want to give the person me a piece of my mind and ensure they remove my number from any future list.

'Hello? Who is this?'

'Liliana Buckley? Is that you? Marilyn's daughter?'

An instant surge of fear runs through me.

'Yes. Who is this?' I repeat.

'Forgive my manners. This is Maxwell here, your mother's partner. I'm calling from California. I've found your number in an old address book of hers.'

'Is everything okay? Why are you calling me, has something happened?'

'Well, that's hard to say just yet. Have you heard from your mum?

'No… why?'

'Well, she got kind of upset and I've been searching everywhere I can think of, but I can't find her anywhere. And it seems she's taken her passport.'

Oh no.

This is the call I've been dreading. This is the call I used to watch my granny receive. And she gave me very strict and clear instructions before she died on what to do once she wasn't around to respond. Which is now.

Okay. I can hear my granny's voice in my ear: '*So the most important thing is to stay calm, get as much info as you can. You know what she's like, so look for clues, and then act fast to find her.*'

We've always got through it before, she always shows up. Eventually. Well, she always did when my granny was here. But it could be very different with just me around now, deemed one of her great burdens. However, no matter what she feels about me, I'm going to have to find her and make sure she's okay. She may be a pain in the backside but she's my mum. We're all we have now.

'Thanks for letting me know, Maxwell. You said she took her passport? Anything else?'

'Her wallet with all her cards, so I know she has money. But her medication, that's all still here, so I don't think she's got any on her. And that could be… distressing.'

Maxwell is absolutely right. Even if she is physically safe, she could get very distressed and disoriented without her anti-anxiety pills. Even realising she hasn't got them will be enough to send her into a panic.

'I just checked the outbound flights. There are London flights from LAX every hour or so, maybe she jumped on one? I can't get any signal from her phone and no one has seen her...'

'That's really helpful, Maxwell. Thank you for looking out for her. I'll find her, I promise, and once I do I'll let you know. Just leave it with me.'

Before I even have a chance to process what I've just heard and what I need to do next, Christopher pops his head around the door.

'We're on. You ready?'

I shake my head. 'I can't, Christopher. I've got to go.'

He opens his hands in confusion. 'You're kidding right?'

I shake my head. 'I'm so so sorry. I just can't, not right now.'

Christopher runs his fingers through his hair and then holds his head at the temples. 'But this is the crowning moment. Everything we've done, everything we've overcome only counts, only means something, if we get this right, here today. You can't just walk out on all those people in there! You cannot bail on me. You cannot do this to me now.'

Oh my god, I never thought I would be on the other side of those words. Not in my wildest nightmares, would those words be said again in my company, in the *Gazette* of all places, by Christopher of all people.

He walks over to me and takes me by the elbows, pressing our bodies close. 'Whatever it is, will two more hours really make a difference? Because believe me, those hours in there will make all the difference. Don't throw it all away Lily. Just go in there, smash it. Why would you work so hard to get here and then back out on the biggest professional moment of your life? I don't get it.'

In a way he's absolutely right. My mother wouldn't want me to miss out. But my mother isn't missing in action to thwart my success. She's missing in action because something has gone wrong, she's panicked and now she's probably necking bottles of wine in first class, trying to numb whatever terror has seized her and I can't afford two hours. Because if I don't find her, then who knows where she'll end up.

'I'll explain later. But you need to do the presentation by yourself.'

'But I need you, Lily. We need you to present.'

But when you get a call to say your mum is in trouble and when you've promised your dying grandmother that you will always be there for her, no matter what, then everything else just falls away. In this case, even Christopher, even the *Gazette*. Even the biggest day of my professional life.

'No, this is your chance to shine! You need this for your leadership programme. Show McArthur that you deserve it and that you are up to it. You are going to do a brilliant job. I know you can do it. As you said yourself, you were born for this.'

Christopher pales and rubs his eyes. 'No, Lily. You're the Editor in Chief, someone who believes so passionately about the future of this paper! You know this staff and this community inside out. You'll blow them away in there, I know you will. It'd give you the profile you need to move on to the next step.'

I shake my head. 'I'm not interested in the next step, I like the step I'm on. But you, this is your baby. You've got to do it, Christopher.' And with that I grab my bag and shoot out the door.

I've got to find my mother. I already have a pretty good idea where to start looking.

CHAPTER 21

My granny was right, a couple of clues was all that was needed to give me a starting point. Firstly, the passport. This is classic Mum. With the fight or flight instinct, Mum usually does both. In that order. She fights and then she books a one-way first-class ticket home. And she only travels British Airways. So, I drive two and a half hours in traffic to reach arrivals at Heathrow airport. The last time this happened, about two years ago, this is where my grandmother and I found her. She panicked, fled whichever country it was she was in, bought a one-way ticket home and then got here and had no more strength to carry on.

But when I arrive, the last straggling passengers are passing through the gate, which means I've missed her. Probably only by about ten minutes, but even so, I have no idea what state of mind she's in. I haven't really got any leads beyond this point. So, again, I think through my grandmother's sage advice: *'You know what she's like.'* Which of course I do. No matter how anxious or distressed she is, her vanity overrides everything else. Her prime concern on landing will be how she looks. She'll feel puffy and dried out so she won't let anyone see her until she's reapplied her face. I rush straight in the ladies' room.

'Mum? Mum, are you in here?'

I hear a cough. A cough I recognise immediately.

'Mum, it's okay! I'm here! I came to get you!' I keep my voice high and bright. As if this was a normal airport collection service.

'Down here, Lily.'

Thank God.

Thank God, she's here, thank God she sounds okay and thank God I found her. I press my hands together and kiss the sky. *Granny, if you're watching, it worked.*

I quickly text Maxwell and tell him not to worry, that she's here, she's home and that I will take care of her.

I hear sobbing as I move to the end stall. I knock on the door, but it doesn't open.

'Mum, it's me. Can you open up?'

Silence. 'Not yet, honey. I can't go out there yet.'

'It's okay. You take your time.' I take a seat on the toilet in the stall next door and stick my hand under the partition, so she knows I'm there.

She takes my hand in hers. It feels clammy and soft, as if there's more flesh than bones despite it being so small.

'I know you're supposed to be at work. I'm sorry, baby. Will you get in to trouble?'

Of course I could tell her yes, that I'm probably in big trouble. That maybe Victoria will find this a perfect reason to fire me, that I've probably rewound my career by years and who knows if I'll ever get the chance to prove myself again. But I don't. Because I promised Granny, that I would take care of her daughter in the same way that she took care of me. And that woman raised us both to be better than that.

'No, no, there wasn't anything important. Nothing at all. It's fine, really. I'm just glad you're here.'

'You are?' I'm taken aback at the uncertainty, the fragility in her voice. She must have got herself into a right state the poor thing. She sounds so different. Softer and more nervy than I ever remember.

'Of course, Mum. And the main thing is you are safe. You are safe right? You're not in any kind of trouble? You're not ill or injured or anything? Maxwell rang, and I didn't know…'

'Oh Maxwell! How could I... uggh... another screw-up to add to my CV...'

I hear her take huge gulps of breath.

'Mum, if you won't let me in, can you come on out and let me see that you're okay? That you're not hurt?'

'I'm not hurt... Nothing like that... But I'm not coming out. I look like shit. I haven't slept, I have no make-up on. My hair is a mess. Everything is such an ugly mess...'

I hear her blow her nose and collect her breath.

'Have you any paper in there? I'm all out.'

I hand her a roll under the partition.

'So... what happened?' I ask. I need to know if this is something that I can help with or whether I need a professional, and then, whether I need a psychiatrist or a lawyer. 'Mum? Let me help you. I'm on your side, okay. Tell me.'

'Well, if I told you, you'd roll your eyes and say "here we go again, same old story, never changes, crazy old bat..."'

'Well then, what have you got to lose? Try me.'

I hear nothing but sobbing.

'And you're not old, you crazy bat.'

I hear the trace of her laugh. At least that's a start.

'I had a big bust-up with my producer. She wants me to change everything, work faster, work longer... just change this, change that... so I walked out. I broke the contract and I probably owe thousands in recompense, but I can't work with her and I won't go back.'

'We can sort that out. There'll be other producers...' I tell her. She's done this more than once and we've always been able to come to an arrangement.

More sobbing, her voice cracking again, this time forcefully.

'So, I was in a bad place with all that going on. Maxwell suggested we go out to cheer me up, so we went to hear some jazz, an intimate little downstairs place, cocktails and candlelight. Very sweet. Everything was going perfectly. I was on cloud nine.

I caught his eye and I thought to myself, I am in love. This is what being in love is and I know that this is the first time I have felt it – other than you of course – but I realised he is the man I love, the one for me. I was just about to tell him too.'

I'm confused, shouldn't that be a good thing?

'It's okay, Mum, you take your time.'

'He excused himself to go to the men's room. Well, while he was gone, his phone rang. Now this is not the type of gig that takes kindly to a ringing phone! I couldn't believe it, it's so, so unlike him not to put it on silent. Anyway, I had to act quick, so I took it from his jacket pocket and tried to put it on silent, but not before I saw about a hundred messages from a woman called Suzy.'

'Okay.' I can see where this is going now and it's not going to be good.

I hear her take great big gulps of breath again.

'I freaked out! When I questioned him, he said Suzy was a client. I said, then why does she have your personal number and why is she calling so late at night, and how old is she, and is she pretty, and is she single, and where does she live, and you can imagine how this went. He told me to calm down, I told him to go fuck himself, or keep fucking Suzy, whichever, what did I care… and I jumped in a taxi, grabbed my passport and made my way to the airport.'

'And now you're here.'

I climb up on to the toilet and peer over the partition into her stall.

And there she is. My poor mother. Head in hands, bawling like a broken-hearted schoolgirl on the loo.

'I loved him, Lily. I really, really loved him. And now my heart is broken, and everything is ruined.'

'He sounded really worried about you on the phone. You sure he's not telling the truth? Maybe Suzy is a client?'

She shrugs and wipes her nose along her sleeve. 'Doesn't matter now. I've ruined everything anyway.'

'You've still got me. We'll start over. It's what we do, right?' I tell her.

She looks up at me and fresh tears spring to her eyes. But these are not desperate tears, there is a flicker of a smile on her lips.

'You are so much smarter than me. You know how to protect yourself from all this heartache and drama. Now get down from there before you fall.'

'Only if you come out.'

'Deal.'

I climb down and hear the click of her door open.

My slightly bedraggled mum appears in the doorway, a smile breaking her face, her arms open wide.

'Look at you! Honey, you look beautiful. I haven't seen you in too long.'

She wraps her arms around my neck. And I know in that instant that I made the right choice coming here, leaving Christopher and the presentation behind. I see for the first time that sometimes walking away can be as courageous as staying. My mother needs me and there's nowhere else I should be. She sinks in to my chest and I can feel the weight of her sobs. She's right, it has been too long. After all, we're all we've got.

'Take me home, Lily.'

CHAPTER 22

After a hearty bowl of soup, a renewed prescription and Chaplin to keep her company, I'm convinced that Mum is okay to rest by herself for a bit while I nip back to the office to see how everything went. She's in front of the fire with a film, although I can see by her heavy eyelids that she'll fall off to sleep any second. I've shifted some boxes and made up the bed in my granny's old room, so she can have some space to hang her things and make herself at home. For as long as she feels is right for her.

'I'm just nipping out for an hour or two, Mum. We'll eat when I get back. Don't go anywhere or do anything, promise?'

'I'll stay on this sofa, under these blankets. I promise. You go, do what you need to do.'

At the office, I can't wait for the elevator, so I run up the stairs, taking two steps at a time. I need to find out how it all went! And mainly, I can't wait to see Christopher. Driving back from London with Mum made me realise how utterly crazy it would be for me not to give us a chance at making something work, even if he does leave Newbridge. Even if he wants to go back to London, it's not that far. I'm not ready to call time on us. We've just got started. And it feels so right. I'm not looking for just anyone. I want him. And if it means we've got to try and have a weekend-only relationship for a time, then so be it. I can stay with the *Gazette* and look after Mum here in Newbridge and he'll be able to pursue his ambition within two hours' drive from here.

Perfect.

And that's what I'm going to tell him. That I want more. That I'm falling for him. Big time.

As soon as I run in through the doors, Jasmine spins on her heel. She widens her eyes and presses her hands to her chest.

'Oh my God, where have you been! Is everything okay?'

I assure her everything is now under control and ask her to spill the beans. Quick!

She blows out her cheeks. 'Christopher was amazing. He had every shareholder in there in the palm of his hand. Every question, he had the answer. He showcased your features and used them as examples. It was one hell of a presentation and they loved it!'

I knew he could do it. He's been amazing for us, for me. I'm the luckiest girl in the world to have found someone like Christopher, who shares so much of what I love. Why keep it a secret? Why hide this wonderful thing? When I see him, I'm going to plant the biggest kiss on his lips – and I won't care who sees it.

Jasmine continues, giddy with such great news. 'Your ears must have been burning. McArthur then waxed lyrical about you and your passion and drive, about the great efforts made by everyone and how the paper was going from strength to strength and its share value was now at its peak. And then they went into talks and came back with champagne flutes and smiles and told us that, yes, we did it! No final review necessary! The *Gazette* is business as usual!'

Wow. It does feel a bit strange to be on the outside of all this. To hear a second-hand account of something you have lived and breathed and dreamed about for weeks. But even if I wasn't here when the news broke and missed all the excitement of the day, the main thing is that it happened.

And it's still happening! At least I'm in time for the after-party.

On cue, Jasmine looks at her watch. 'Right! It's six o'clock and we've arranged a "Team Meeting" at The Black Boar. Dylan's over there already with a few of them, so come on. We deserve it, that's for sure.'

I smile. I can't wait to find Christopher and congratulate him, I'll only stay for one as I'll need to go back to check on Mum, but I agree, we've earned this, everything we've put ourselves through to reach this moment.

But even though the paper has made it, I still have my final bucket list article to write. My fourth and final feature is going to take some thought… By now I should be able to come up with my own ideas. But how do I top skydiving and extreme obstacle courses and poltergeists?

I don't know if I can.

CHAPTER 23

I settle the tray of drinks on the table at The Black Boar. The place has been transformed for the evening, with a glittery banner reading 'Happy HAG Jasmine and Dylan.'

I catch Amy's eye. 'What's a HAG?' I ask her.

'Joint hen and stag, they wanted everyone here, not separate parties. What a day!'

The atmosphere is electric, the music is blaring, the bar is at least four deep. Jasmine makes a beeline for me, waving an ivory envelope in her hand.

'Wedding invitation time! We're on a budget, so my dad offered to set us up with a marquee at the back of their house, so it's nothing fancy, just simple.'

'And beautiful,' I reassure her, watching her cheeks begin to flush. 'You and Dylan are madly in love and it's going to be the happiest day of your lives, that's what's important.'

'Thanks, Lily. I can't wait. Promise you'll come.'

'I haven't been to a good wedding in such a long time. I wouldn't miss it for the world,' I tell her, meaning every word.

She fans herself with another white envelope but looks at me with uncertainty etched across her face. 'This invite was for Christopher, so I don't know quite what to do with it now. I mean, we'd love him to come, but I guess he'll be busy with his new job now, and Newbridge might be a little too far away to come just for a wedding!'

'What do you mean?' I look up and down the bar, expecting to see Christopher but he's nowhere to be seen. Surely he must be on his way down. He wouldn't miss this for the world.

Jasmine nods and considers the envelope. 'One of the shareholders took him aside and offered him a new position travelling the world, big pay rise, all that. He looked really excited, said he'd never have been offered something like that if he hadn't come to the *Gazette*. They want him to roll out the same model for them across all their media agencies. Are you all right, Lily? You look shocked.'

Christopher is going! Just like that? Without even saying anything?

I shake my head. 'What a day, so many changes.'

Can your whole world really tip upside down in less than twenty-four hours? You bet.

'Yep, they told him his work at the *Gazette* was done and he had to go pack up his things. I told him we'd be here, but he's probably on the road by now.' Jasmine flips the wedding invitation in her hand. 'I'll post it to him anyway; I've got his address on the system. At least that way he knows that's he's invited and that we'd love him to come and he can make his own call.'

Mark sidles up to us and spots the envelope with Christopher's name in Jasmine's hand.

'I doubt we'll be seeing him again. He came, he consulted, he moved on. And now he's landed himself an even better offer somewhere else.'

'He really liked it here!' I say, a little more defensively than I intended. I need to talk to Christopher face to face, find out from him what exactly happened. For all I know it's already too late.

Mark takes a long slug of his pint. 'Someone like him was never going to settle in a small town like this, working on a paper like ours. People like him are cut-throat ambitious. The grass is always greener, there's always another rung on the ladder. They look down on us, happy with our little lives, simple pleasures, not out scheming and turning deals at every corner.'

So, according to Mark, Christopher didn't really care about any of this, about any of us, about me. And I know I haven't always been the best judge of character, but this really doesn't sound right to me. After all, he doesn't know him like I do. He doesn't know how happy Christopher was here in Newbridge and how much he loved the team and how free he felt stepping outside of his old life. Until I speak with him, I just can't figure out what to think, what to believe, what to feel. Other than the aching loss of him.

I make my excuses to go, explaining that my mum is home alone and that I need to get back to her, but really, I'm going straight to Christopher's flat.

Mark licks the cream from his top lip. 'His girlfriend is hot though, I'll say that for him. He certainly gets the women.' Hearing this comment stops me in my tracks.

'Pardon? What girlfriend?'

'I saw him in the car park with some blonde in a white suit, one of the London crowd, then he got in her car and they both drove off into the sunset.'

Victoria.

No way.

I suddenly feel extremely hot. I grab the back of my neck and look around me, not able to focus on anything in particular. I'm trying to say something coherent, but I'm just managing half-sighs and low groans. It's as if someone has come up behind me and pierced me in the back. And I'm deflating. Right here. All my air and energy is just flooding out of my body.

I need to go. I scramble for my bag, say my goodbyes and shoot out the door, muttering to myself in the darkness. With every step I take, I can't help but wonder how I got everything so wrong. Again.

CHAPTER 24

The cottage is quiet and dark when I get home. I can see a thin line of light under Mum's bedroom door and I can faintly make out that she's speaking with someone on the phone. Hopefully it's Maxwell.

I slide out of my work clothes and into my soft, slouchy pyjamas. I pour myself a large glass of red wine and drink it with a toasted chocolate spread sandwich. I switch off my phone, dim all the main lights and lie down on the sofa, Chaplin in the crook of my arm. And I cry.

It's not just Christopher. It's everything. Good tears that the *Gazette* made it, sad tears that I wasn't there to be part of it. Good tears that my mum is okay, worried tears that I have no idea how we're going to get along and if living together under this roof without my grandmother as mediator is even going to work. Good tears that I'm invited to Jasmine and Dylan's wedding, very anxious tears that I will be flooded with bad memories of my own disaster when I hear the wedding march. Good tears that I've had such an amazing time with Christopher, that he did turn out to be truly 'transformational' to me, that I loved every second of being with him and I really felt happier and more confident than I ever have before. But I can't even categorise the tears that are falling at the thought of Christopher walking away from me.

I hear a rapping on my window. 'Lily? Lily? Are you in there?'

It's Christopher. For sure.

'Lily? It's me, it's Christopher!'

'I know,' I call back. I can't help myself.

'I need to talk to you.'

'You are talking to me.' Why has he come here? Why can't he just leave me be? I know what's coming. That pitiful look. That sham apology. This feels exactly like I'm back in the sacristy with Adam. And I promised myself I would never let that happen to me again.

'I needed to see you. Face to face.'

He's outside my house, peering through the living room window, through a crack in the curtains. Damn that crack.

I throw my head back and sling my legs from the armrest of the sofa, walking slowly to the window.

'Lily! What's wrong? Have you been crying?'

I shake my head. 'No. Just tired. I'm really, really tired, Christopher, so if this is your goodbye, then let's just do it quickly, okay?' I want this to be over as quickly as possible, before I get hurt any more.

His faces creases in confusion. 'I really need to speak with you. Can I come in?'

I shake my head. 'My mum's resting. It's not a good time.' I can't bear to hear him tell me that he's back with Victoria. I won't be able to hold myself together and I don't want him to see me like that.

'Well, can you come out?'

The lights of a car flash in the distance.

'Victoria?'

He looks confused. 'Yes. She's just giving me a lift back to London. Looks like I'm all done at the *Gazette*. It appears you don't need me any more! You've done such a good job, they're happy to back off and leave you to it. So, my time is up.'

'I guess congrats are in order then. You came, you conquered, time to move on, I understand. Newbridge and the *Gazette* and everything else was just a stepping stone, like you said.'

'Well, that's what I thought at first, but... Please, Lily, give me two minutes.'

We hear the car horn honk.

'She really doesn't like waiting, does she?' And who can blame her, she's desperate to get Christopher back to London and have him all to herself again after his little foray in Newbridge.

'I need to be at a meeting in London tomorrow and I can't take all my stuff on the train, so I had to jump in with her. Please, Lily, hear me out and then I'll leave. I promise.'

I suppose he deserves that at least. But I also know I have to end this, before I'm left heartbroken again.

I motion to the door and open it slightly, but leave it on the chain.

He steps in closer and reaches out his hands to me. I put mine in my pockets.

'Sky Group offered me a job after the *Gazette* presentation,' Christopher says. 'A really great job and one that means a lot of travel – Japan, Bali, all the places I really want to see. The company's huge and have offices everywhere. Small offices that need a digital presence, just like the *Gazette*. They've offered me a Director post, brand new division, so I'd have lots of freedom. It's everything I've worked so hard to get. I'd be insane to turn it down. I need to take this chance, Lily. I need to go. But here's the thing...' He steps in to me, trying to meet my eyes. 'It doesn't mean we can't try and work something out. If we both want to, I know we'd find a way. That's why we're so good together, Lily. We make ways, me and you. What do you say?'

He cups my cheek with his hand and softly brushes a long tear away with his thumb.

I groan out loud. Squeeze my eyes shut.

Right, I've got this all wrong. He's not running off with Victoria. He never planned to. He wants us to be together. He wants us to give it a shot.

I try to speak but can't for all the garbled tears in my throat.

My heart is churning in my chest. I would so love to believe him. I'd love to jump up and wrap my arms around him and say yes! We can do it!

But then the reality hits me of what it's really going to be like.

Deep down, I know I can trust him. But can I trust myself? Can I trust myself not to live in constant suspicion, on guard all the time, jumping to conclusions every time he's late or on a business trip or Victoria calls or makes a snide comment?

However far I've come, I don't think my insecurity can stand up against this. I was so quick to accept Mark's explanation about Victoria and Christopher, even after everything we'd shared over the last few weeks. I've got scars. I can't just wish them away. There'll be paranoid stalking of his social media every five seconds to see where he is, who he is with, questioning who that girl is in the background, wondering if the next time I see him it's to tell me it's over, that he's met someone else. Or he's back with Victoria. Which may only be a matter of time; she's fixated by him, and it's clear she's not going to lose him over someone as peripheral as me. And the whole heart-break tsunami will overtake me again. But this time I'm afraid it will suck me under and I won't be able to fight my way out.

And it will be so much worse than before because a) I should know better second time around and learn from my mistakes, and b) I know now how long it takes to recover. Adam was hard enough, but getting over Christopher will take a lot of time and a lot of soul-searching. And soul-searching is exhausting.

'Christopher, it's okay. I understand. You're free to go. I don't know why you're explaining to me. It was just a work thing that spilled over, a casual fling, nothing important.'

He stops and stares at me. 'You think that? You honestly think that you're not important to me? Is that why you're acting like you don't care because you think that I don't care?'

I shrug. 'I don't know what to think. I don't want any more thinking. Or feeling or worrying or second-guessing or trying to get in anyone else's head. Been there done that and it's not fun. Believe me, you won't find it fun either, so why bother? You're moving on to better things, I'm staying here with my life, my job and…' I point behind me into the living room, 'my mum's here now too, so I'm pretty full up.'

'So you actually don't care. That's why you didn't want anyone to know about us at the paper?' He runs his fingers through his hair. 'You're serious, aren't you? This isn't important to you. Just a casual work fling.'

'Exactly,' I lie.

He takes a step back from me. Searching my face, trying to read my thoughts. He shakes his head. 'I don't believe you, Lily. I know you. And what you're saying doesn't add up.'

Victoria honks four times. The last honk is extra-long.

I shake my head. 'Go. Please. Just leave.'

I hate this but if today has shown me anything, it's that I'm not ready for this. Will I ever be? Will I ever escape the fear of being deceived? Of being betrayed?

'Just like that, you're calling time on us. We've only just started, Lily.'

And that's exactly why now is the time to stop.

'You can't stay, Christopher, and I can't go. We both know you were only ever here temporarily. This is the right thing to do; you can't miss your big chance. It might never come again.'

He nods, his lips pressed together. He knows I'm right. I wish I wasn't.

'Is this really what you want? To end things?'

I shrug. 'It was just a work fling.'

He shakes his head. 'Don't tell me that the late nights working on the paper, the night we spent at The Shankley, karaoke after the Golden Wok, that that was all just a fling. It was so much more, you know it was.'

'I'm sorry, Christopher.'

'Will you miss me?' he asks anxiously.

I force myself to smile. But I don't answer him. 'Your work here is done. So congratulations and good luck.' And then I shut the door and let him go.

CHAPTER 25

'Who was that at the door, Lily?' Mum asks as she waves me into her bedroom.

'Just a guy from work.'

Which is technically true. If only.

She holds out her hand to me. 'Sit down a second, there's something I need to tell you. I've been carrying it with me and I need to get it off my chest.'

I hold my head in my hands.

No. Please, please no. The absolute last thing I need now is a therapy session with my mum.

But this is her all over. Oblivious to the fact that there might be something big and important and urgent and emotional going on in my life. Oblivious to the fact that this might be a bad time for me. That I may be the one in need of support. That sitting here in my grandmother's bedroom just reminds me of how alone I am in the world. How I used to come here and, without one word, Granny would know something was up and she'd gather me into her. How I remember the scent of her – lavender and lemon peel if she'd been outside, cinnamon and spiced apple if she'd been cooking. She'd rock me very slightly as we'd wait, wordless, for the feeling to surge and settle and soon slip away.

That was the way my grandmother raised me. Filling my life with patience and encouragement and endless loving attention. And I miss her so much. But she is gone. Just bittersweet memories remain. And now Mum is here.

If Mum didn't literally land in the state she was in today, I'd hold my hands up and say sorry, any time but now. My heart is breaking and I just need some space to get over this – alone.

But I'm here as Granny now. It falls to me to be the strong, patient, selfless one. And Mum still looks pretty frail. I take a deep breath.

'Okay.' I sit down beside her, tucking my legs in beneath me. 'It's about Adam.'

I rub my hands down my face. I thought she was going to offload something about herself. Not me! I can't take any more! Can't she tell that I'm not able to deal with this right now? I just want to curl up in my bed and cry. Alone. Get as snotty and ugly as I want to and then tomorrow I can start to move on, start to feel better. At least that's the plan, because it's unlikely tomorrow everything's going to be OK. It's unlikely to be OK for quite a while.

'Can we do this another time, Mum, I'm tired.'

She puts her palms up to me. 'Holding on to everything is making me ill. Please, let me tell you this. I need to let it out.'

I jump up from the bed. 'Mum, I'm sorry for whatever happened, between you and Maxwell, but you can't just show up here in a storm, kick up chaos, disrupt everyone with big revelations of the past just because *you* need to offload.'

She looks at me, stunned.

'I've had enough. Did it ever occur to you for one second that I might not want to know? That I might want to leave all that shit behind? That today may be the worst possible time to divulge something to me that makes me feel even more desperate and tragic and lonely than I already feel?'

Her hands are pressed against her chest. She looks like she's about to cry. She shakes her head. 'Of course, I'm so sorry. Of course, I'll just get my things. I'll call a taxi. I can stay at a B&B. I'm sorry, Lily. I should have thought. I'm sorry.'

I turn to the wall and feel like banging my head against it. How come neither of us can ever seem to do the right thing? How is it we lost our way so badly, not even able to communicate now?

Chaplin pops out from under the bed, tugging at something caught in the carpet. We both look down. A twisting tendril from a royal blue fascinator.

The one my grandmother wore on my wedding day.

My mother frees it from the snagging carpet and lifts it in to her lap.

'Do you think it's a sign?' she says, her face suddenly innocent and wide-eyed.

I shrug. 'Could be. Maybe she's telling us to get over ourselves. To look after each other a bit better.'

My mother nods slowly. 'I know it hurts. I've rehearsed this a million times and, trust me, there's no easy way to break this to you. The last thing I ever wanted was to see you hurt, my darling. That's exactly why I did it, so you wouldn't get hurt! But, believe me, if he didn't come clean, if he didn't tell you the truth before the wedding, then I was going to. Over my dead body were you going to swear your life away to that ballbag.'

I shut my eyes and dig my fingers in to my palms and try to digest what my mother is actually telling me. *She* was responsible for me being ditched at the altar?

Am I seriously hearing this?

I press my wrists to my temples and shut my eyes.

I don't want to hear any more.

I don't want to know any more.

I want to turn on my heel and slam the door behind me and run. Run into the drive. Run into the field. Run into wide-open spaces where there is no one to see and no one to be seen by. But what then? Eventually, I'll have to come back. Come back to her and to this. And it will keep chasing me until I deal with it. Until it's over with for once and for all. But how? How do I even begin to find the words?

I swallow, but it won't go down.

I try again, but this time... this time I lose control. It appears the words have found their own way out.

'Just tell me one thing. ONE THING. What kind of a mother are you? I don't even know why I call you mother, you don't deserve it. I mean it, Marilyn. What kind of a real mother does that? What kind of a mother takes pleasure in abandoning their child, then showing up again years later to destroy everything that's good in her daughter's life? Tell me? TELL ME! Because I'm seriously struggling to understand.'

She takes a breath but keeps her eyes on me.

'Firstly, I take no pleasure in any of this, Lily. Of course, it would have been easier to turn a blind eye, of course it would have been easier to watch you walk down the aisle and look into his eyes and promise to love him forever. Of course, it would have been easier to raise a glass of champagne to your long happy lives together and wish you laughter and babies and a big house and loving stable family. But I couldn't. I couldn't let you sign up to a lie. I couldn't let them fool you like that. I know you may never understand, but I could tell, believe me, I could tell where this was heading. It was all wrong.'

My mother runs her fingers through her hair and talks a long, deep breath. 'You can't out-sneak a sneak. You can't out-cheat a cheat.'

She's talking in riddles now. I have lost her. I am lost.

'What are you talking about?'

'Me. Me and your father. He was married. He was a cheat. So was I. He made promises he didn't keep. So did I. Once you've been there, once you've been that person, believe me, you know the signs, you pick up on the clues, it takes one to know one and I saw it clear as day between Hannah and Adam.'

'You mean you caught them together?'

'In a way. I caught some long glances, the way he straightened up when she was around. The way she avoided his eyes when he was close and then followed him transfixed when he moved away. I hoped I was imagining things, being my paranoid, overdramatic self, hoping that was the case.'

I slide down the wall to the ground.

I'd had no idea. NO idea about Hannah or Adam being together, or that Mum knew. If she'd picked up on it, does that mean everyone had? Was I that blind? That stupid? Was it so obvious that everyone knew except me? Or did I suspect that something wasn't right but I glossed over it because I was so caught up in the wedding? So reluctant to confront Adam about anything?

I shake my head. 'But we hung out together all the time. How could I not have seen it if it was so obvious to everyone else?'

'I kept a very close watch on both of them, but they were even less careful, which made me think that things had reached a new level. When he left the room, she was restless until he returned. When Hannah was in conversation with someone, it was obvious she was only half listening, her attention always cocked in his direction. Hannah was the one I confronted first after the final rehearsal.'

'The night before the wedding?'

'Yes. I followed her in to the garden. Told her I knew. She didn't even try to deny it. She burst out crying. I told her that she was a bitch.'

'Mum! You didn't!'

'Lily she was sleeping with your fiancé for God's sake!'

'What did she say?'

'She said it was all one big awful accident. It started as a drunken kiss on New Year's Eve and then it had spiralled. But she promised that it was finished. It wouldn't happen again.'

I remember the night that I stayed late at the *Gazette* to hit a deadline and told Adam to go a party without me. He came in at 4 a.m. legless. He had an excessive hangover the next day. He was excessively nice to me. As was Hannah. Looking back, I knew something had happened that night.

'She promised me it was over. I told her it better be. She made me promise never to tell you.'

'And did you promise?'

Mum raises her eyebrow. 'No! Since when do I make promises?'

I nearly smile. 'But you didn't tell me. You should have told me! If you had then I'd never have made it up that bloody aisle in the first place! I could have spared myself complete humiliation!'

'But how could I, Lily? I didn't want to screw everything up. I know people make mistakes. I know people fuck up – I had to give them the benefit of the doubt. Hannah promised me it was over. She told me she was sorry, that Adam was choosing you.'

'And?'

'I wanted to believe it, I mean, I even *prayed* that it was over between them and that things were fixed and could proceed as intended. But I needed to make sure. So the next morning, the morning of the wedding, about an hour before breakfast, I hopped in the car, knocked at Adam's hotel room door and who did I discover there?'

'Hannah,' I say. Okay. This is all starting to make sense.

My mother bites down on her lip. 'Adam tried to make up all sorts of bullshit excuses why she was there; everything from lost rings to rehearsing wedding speeches. But Hannah said, "It's no use, Adam, she knows." I lost my shit and told him that he was a snivelling excuse of a man not worthy of my daughter and that the least he could do was spare you further hurt and call off the wedding. Time to come clean. There was no way in hell he was dragging my daughter into a life of lies and STIs.'

Oh my God.

'So Hannah fled, she couldn't take it.'

'Granny said she'd come down with a gastric bug. Vomiting and diarrhoea.'

'Verbal diarrhoea perhaps. And Adam promised me that he'd tell you. Face to face. At your hotel. Straight away. But he didn't, of course, the coward he was. He thought I'd let him off the hook, bow to the pressure of the day. But I waited at the church steps, collared him and warned him that if he didn't call this bullshit off, I would. He waited right until the last moment to come clean. Believe me, if I hadn't been hovering, the bastard would have married you, Lily, and he would have broken your heart into pieces.'

'So that explains it. It explains it all. I never knew why he chose that moment to tell me. He had a gun to his head.'

'I'm sorry, sweetheart. I know it was harsh and I understand if you hate me. But I thought it was better that you hate me than you spend your life with the wrong person. But I need you to know that I love you. And I know how it must look, but I promise you everything I've done, I've done because I love you more than myself... and I couldn't bear to see you get hurt.'

She reaches out her hand and I take it. I sit beside her and curl into her, finally realising that my mother did it for me, to protect me. All my life I spent thinking that my mother only cares for herself but now I'm starting to appreciate that's not the case.

'I'll never forget the day I found out I was going to be a mother. Your granny freaked, of course. But I refused to tell anyone who the father was. Refused all help. I was so sure I could do it all by myself. Growing you inside me made me feel so powerful, so complete. I'll never forget the first time I felt you kick. I'll never forget the first time I heard you cry. It was as if time stood still for just a moment as you entered the world. I'll never forget our heartbeats synchronised the first time I held you. You were breath-taking. The most beautiful perfect creature I'd ever seen. I never knew I could love anyone so much, so instantly, so infinitely. I'll never forget that joy when I heard you say "mummy" that first time. Hearing that from your lips was music to my ears.'

I close my eyes and let the tears fall. Breathing in the scent of my mother. Listening to our breath and our hearts synchronise now. Whatever she's done, she's my mother. And everything she's done, I realise it's because she's my mother, that both our lives are irrevocably intertwined because I am hers and she is mine and, no matter what, we need each other. We have a special love that we both need, that makes us better, that makes us complete.

God, I have missed her. I don't want to lose anybody else. I can't afford to.

'One day I want you to find love and happiness, but until then, never forget that I was the first person you loved, kissed, held hands with, and sought out in the night. And only your granny was a person worthy enough to take my place. Not Adam. One day, there'll be someone good enough, worthy enough.'

I feel tears pool again. 'I used to think so. But it's happened again, Mum. I got sucked in and fell completely head over heels in love and dared think that it might go somewhere, that it might blossom into something, but it's over. Already. Just like that. I just can't seem to hang on to anything,' I confess.

'Was that the person at the door?' she asks me.

I nod. 'His name was Christopher. And I've managed to lose him too; it's all my fault.'

'Enough of that, Lily, it's not your fault.'

'But it must be! How many other people do you know who have been dumped so badly? I mean, if it's not my fault, why did you leave me? Was I holding you back? Did I do something wrong?' A vision of a lone rock bearing my name on it floods my mind's eye.

She wraps her arms around me and hugs me tightly. 'No! No, no way. Why would you think that? I went away to protect you.

To give you a better life, one that I couldn't give you by myself. Because it was for the best. It was for your best. It was hard, but it was worth it, I am so proud of you and who you have evolved into.'

'But I saw my name written on a rock, one of your regret rocks.'

The words come out faster than I can stop them. I've wanted to ask this question from the moment I saw the photo she sent me, but I never really believed I'd have the guts to say it. I never really thought I'd have the guts to hear the answer.

She loops a strand of my hair around her finger, blinking back tears. 'I wrote your name on that rock because I regretted how I've treated you. How can you think I regret *you*? Oh, my darling, you are the single thing in my life that I am proud of. And the regrets I have are all about me and how I've acted. Things I've said and done to you that I really, really wish never happened. And the things I've failed to say and do. They're what I regret the most. So let me start right now, baby. I am sorry. So, so sorry.'

And now I am rubbing my mother's back, shushing her but letting her cry. Telling her it's okay, that I understand. Because, in a way, I kind of feel like I do now.

I'm starting to understand the kind of mother she is. Fierce. Fierce and raw and flawed and selfless and trying to do her best to protect me from anything that could hurt me – even if that's herself.

'It's okay. I get it now. It makes sense. It all makes sense.'

She smiles and rubs her eyes. 'The morning I left, I remember you waking up and running to my side of the bed giddy with excitement, reminding me that it was the first day of the new school year. I will never forget you climbing into bed with me and holding me even tighter than usual as if you knew that things were about to change. That morning I helped you get ready and packed your lunch, dropped you at school and you ran off after saying goodbye without looking back. You were so brave. And I could see that you were happy. And I just sat and cried to myself through the school fence because I knew that it marked the first time in your life that you'd start making memories without me. I knew I was going to miss you unbearably. And I was right, I did. Every day. Every second of every day. But for once in my sucky, selfish life, I was putting someone else before myself. And the only person I've ever managed to do that for is you.

'I had second thoughts when it became real, I thought, no, it's going to be too painful leaving you. That I should stay. But I was out of my depth, I couldn't take care of myself very well, never mind a child. So I stood by that fence watching you with your new friends practising the monkey bars. So strong and determined. And it was at that moment that I knew you were going to be okay and I realised that this day was going to be much harder for me than it was going to be for you. And even though a part of me wished I could have taken you away with me, I knew I had to let go and leave you to be who you were meant to be.'

I always thought my mother leaving me behind with my granny was selfish. But I see now that it was the opposite that's true. That she made the ultimate sacrifice, breaking her own heart to see that I grew up in a peaceful home with a loving grandmother. And she did the right thing. A very selfless thing. And maybe someday, I can find it in myself to do something as selfless as that for somebody else.

We stay curled up on the bed together for what feels like hours. Talking and laughing and singing old songs we used to sing. I hear Mum's tummy rumble and realise it's past dinnertime. I order a delivery and then as I root around my bag for change, my trusty black marker pen finds its way into my hand.

'I have an idea while we wait,' I tell her, twirling the felt tip in my fingers. 'How about we go throw some rocks?'

CHAPTER 26

I wake up the next morning expecting to feel a rough tongue in my ear and some soft purring reminding me to get up and get started. But I can't find Chaplin anywhere. Mum let me sleep and has already put out his breakfast, but his water bowl is still full, his food untouched. I check all his favourite little hidey-places – under my bed, in the corner of my wardrobe, in my left red Converse, under the rose bush, by the fire.

Nowhere. My little Chaplin is nowhere to be found.

Thank goodness I'm working from home today given Mum's return. I'll have to find him. Call out a search party. Take out a double-page spread in the *Gazette*. I can't lose Chaplin. He's got to be here somewhere. I stand by the door and listen out for some kind of hint or clue, hoping for mewling under my car, but again nothing. The only sounds are some birds, barking dogs from the nearby farm and Mum singing along to a crackling record player out back. It's Stevie Wonder and Etta James. I can expect some Aretha in the next hour.

This is a good sign for her, of course. Anytime she gets back to being creative, she gets back to being herself. Her best self.

But as for little Chaplin, I'm still at a loss.

I know I'm going to have to walk down the path to the gate. And from there it's straight on to the road. We're not known for our traffic jams around these parts, nor is this exactly a Formula One circuit, but that can lull people and animals alike in to a false sense of security, believing the roads are deserted and next thing a huge four-wheel tractor takes the bend unexpectedly and that's how accidents happen.

Oh please no. Maybe I should have kept him inside? Maybe I should have curbed his freedom more?

I can't face it if I find Chaplin... unalive.

My stomach lurches at the thought.

So, I turn back on my heel and into the house and start calling him again, deciding to check the garden one more time.

'Still no sign?' Mum says as she wraps her arm around my waist. I know I don't have to explain to Mum about losing an animal. There are tears in her eyes and she's only known him since yesterday. 'I'm sorry, sweetheart.'

Neither of us want to cry. 'Come in and have some lunch. Don't wait out here too long, baby, you'll catch your death of cold,' says Mum as she walks back towards the house. I blink back tears and turn away towards the fields. I just want a second to compose myself, and that's when I see it.

A long dark plume of smoke from the chimney of the cottage across the field. Which can only mean one thing.

Mr Clark is home.

CHAPTER 27

'Hello? Mr Clark?' It's me, Lily? From the newspaper?'

I knock on the door a little louder and I hear some slow activity inside. I huddle my coat around my shoulders. The wind is picking up and I am certain there will be a storm any minute. But then the door opens and there stands Mr Clark, who, despite the gauze bandage around his head, looks much stronger and healthier – and more awake – than the last time I saw him.

'Welcome home!' I say as he ushers me in.

'Thank you. I just got discharged this morning. Nice to be home. And thank you for your texts and updates on Chaplin. It was very nice of you to think of doing so.'

I just hope the news about Chaplin doesn't send him back to hospital. How can I tell him I'm here because I've lost his cat? That's some update.

The fire is crackling and he invites me to make a seat.

'Tea?' he asks.

'Oh, yes please. It's freezing out there.'

I look around the little cottage belonging to Mr Clark. Sepia photos lined up along the dresser in the living room. A picture of Mr Clark with a wife, a son. A proud photo with a teenager dressed as Fagan from *Oliver Twist*, full of smiles and stage make-up.

'Theatregoer I see?' I ask him when he returns with a cup of tea and a plate of plain digestives for us to share. 'Have you been to the Newbridge theatre lately? You know they've got a new director, Julian somebody, and he's really upped their game.'

Mr Clark walks over to the photo and nods his head.

'They're running *Midsummer Night's Dream* from next week.' Mr Clark runs a thumb over the frame of the photo, dislodging some dust. He pauses another moment, then clears his throat before turning back to me. 'I suppose you're here to get the scoop on the lottery win. Well, I'm afraid I'm going to have to disappoint you. I'm going to stay anonymous.'

'That's understandable. You don't want every member of your family showing up asking for handouts, I suppose.'

I meant to say it in jokey way, but I fear it doesn't come across that way.

Mr Clark juts his head toward the photo of the teenager. 'He wouldn't come asking me for anything if I was the last man alive.'

I'm confused.

He picks up the photo and places it in my hands.

'Your son?'

He nods solemnly. This is clearly not a relationship he's used to boasting about. 'Julian Clark, my only son, is the new director. He's moved back. Born singing and dancing, that fellow. No shortage of drama on or off the stage.'

The window rattles with the wind as Mr Clark offers me another biscuit.

'I was very hard on him growing up and, well, he has a long memory. No time for me now, whether I was a millionaire or not. Not that I am a millionaire, mind you, I donated the lot to the hospital.'

I open my mouth, but he raises a hand.

'And before you ask, no, I don't want that in the paper, thank you very much.'

I laugh, but the real reason my mouth is hanging open is because Chaplin has just strutted in to the living room. He is dry, he is clean and is distinctly unsquashed by a tractor.

Mr Clark scoops him up with one hand and begins tickling him under the chin.

'Ah, you've come to say hello and thank you, if you have any manners. I wasn't home an hour and I heard purring on the step. Amazing creatures, extraordinarily loyal. All I had to do was open the door and, sure enough, it was like he'd never been away.'

I give Chaplin a little stroke. Delighted that he's okay obviously, but as much as I'm going to miss him, really happy at the idea that him and Mr Clark will drink tea and biscuits together in front of the fire. I suspect Mr Clark needs Chaplin even more than I do.

I stand to leave. I shake Mr Clark's hand and tell him I'll drop by again for a cuppa when I'm passing if that's okay.

But just before I go, I pick up the photograph of his smiling theatre-mad teenage son.

'Sons and daughters,' I say. 'Amazing creatures, extraordinarily loyal. Sometimes all you have to do is open the door.' And I make my way back across the field, stopping just before I reach home, to look up at the sky. Wondering where Christopher is now. Wondering how he is. Wondering if I will ever see him again.

CHAPTER 28

'Hi Maxwell? It's me Lily. Yes, she's feeling a bit better... Well, she's not really. She won't ever say, but I know she's driving herself crazy. So, if you could just tell me, whatever the truth is, we can take it, as long as we know. What's the story with Suzy, the woman who sent all the messages to your phone?'

A pause. Then in a slow, strong, deep American voice, he answers me as if taking an oath in a court of law. 'A client. Living in Canada. I've never even met her.'

This confirms my cyberstalk. There is a client testimonial on Maxwell's professional website from a Suzy from Vancouver. And the photo matches her social media accounts, so as far as I can make out and without hooking him up to a polygraph, he's telling the truth.

Thank God!

'The thing is,' I say. 'Mum loves you. I can tell. She loves you and she's miserable without you and she's beating herself up for wrecking everything and flying off the handle and not trusting you, even though she knows deep down that she can trust you... Old habits die hard, I guess. She's embarrassed. And heartbroken. And so, so mad at herself. She thinks it's too late.'

'Did she say that? Did she say that she loved me?'

'Yes. More than once. She says it every day. I even heard her say it in her sleep.'

'You know, she's never told me that. That's an awesome step for Marilyn. It's wonderful. It changes everything. I think it means she's ready.'

'Ready for what?' I ask.

'To try again! You know that's all love is, two imperfect people who refuse to give up on one another. And I'm not giving up on your mother. And it sounds like you're not giving up on her either.'

'So it's not too late? For you two?'

'Of course it's not too late. It's never too late to do the right thing. Never! I'm coming over there. Let her know I'm on my way. Tell her she's made me the happiest man in the world!'

I tell him exactly where he can find us and cross my heart that he means what he says. That he really does believe that him and my mum are the right thing. That they don't give up on each other. I've done what I can. Now it's over to them to bridge all the distances between them. But it sounds like they've already started. And I hope with all my heart that my mother finally gets the happy ending she deserves.

CHAPTER 29

'Morning, everyone! Nice to have you back with us, Lily!' Mark struts in, both hands waving in the air.

Jasmine closes a call and says. 'Lily, I need the details for the final bucket list feature. We've got to make it quick as I've got a bridal fitting at three. It's really happening!'

Amy clenches her fists with excitement. 'I can't believe it's this close, just over a month to go. I'm so excited!'

'Right, let's get our schedules sorted and free up some time for Dylan and Jasmine to get themselves ready for their big day.'

I open my desk drawer and take out the two tickets I bought from Mary: front-row seats for the first night of *Midsummer Night's Dream*. 'Amy, can you cover the play at the theatre? It starts at 7 p.m., and I believe it's sold out. Double spread, as many local faces as possible in the pictures, they've worked really hard, so let's support them one hundred per cent.' I hand the tickets to her. 'You'll have company, a friend of mine wants to come too, so can you pick him up at 6.30?' I hand her the scrap piece of paper that I received from Mr Clark way back in the hospital with his address and phone number on it. 'If you get there early, you can have a little cuddle with Chaplin too.'

Amy gives me a thumbs up. We sort through the rest of the tasks for the week; interviews, adverts, promotions, all the usual. This team runs like a finely tuned machine now, everyone knows what to do, when to do it by and how we like it done.

Except for me.

I have one last feature to write for Buckley's Bucket List. And I can't think of anything. I've drawn a complete blank, even though we've brainstormed here in the office and put it out to the public under the hashtag #fillmybucketlist. Which makes fascinating reading. Who knew so many people in Newbridge harboured so many bucket list dreams? The breadth and quirkiness is staggering. Who knew Denise from the bar wants to take a hot air balloon over a Greek island, go on an Icelandic boat trip to see the Northern lights and learn to dance salsa? Who knew that John Boy from the skydiving centre wants to wing-walk. And go into space. Maybe wing-walk in space. And overcome his fear of spiders. And then there's my own mother! She longs to produce her own album independently with full artistic freedom, to visit the sloth sanctuary in Costa Rica and to learn to make Granny's lemon tartlets. Properly.

I smile as I open the Tupperware she sent me in with this morning. Once she shared her list with me, she decided that there was no time like the present, grabbed her apron, made a huge mess before she even started baking, but hey, presto! I pop the last tart in my mouth, wincing slightly at the citrus tang. Still a little bit sharp, but she took a lot of convincing to add even half quantities of sugar and butter and follow the recipe! Believe me, that's phenomenal progress for her. So not at all bad for a first attempt. I reckon this time next week, she'll have cracked it. Maxwell should arrive in the next few days and there's a distinct spring in her step. They're like teenagers, facetiming each other at all hours, messaging I love you's every five minutes. Her mood has lifted again and I realise how much it suits my mother to be in love.

But the contribution that really catches my attention is from a reader called Hannah. 'There's only one thing I really want to do and that's to make it up to a dear friend who I betrayed. I know she'll never be able to forgive me as I will never forgive myself for doing what I did. But I want her to know how much I miss her.'

Tears stream down both my cheeks as I read and reread her words. Especially the last few lines. I can't bear the idea of Hannah wasting her precious life beating herself up over what's past. I think we both deserve to leave it behind and start afresh. I type into the comment box below her words and press 'reply'.

'Hannah, consider it done. My elbow healed nicely so thanks for taking care of me. Wishing you all the best in your future. Lx'

I twirl my pen in my fingers and stare down at the blank screen in front of me. Surely, after all these amazing suggestions, surely, after putting myself through three really tough bucket list challenges already, *surely* I can think of something authentic. No McArthur or Jennings steering for local or commercial angles. No Christopher pitching suggestions to hook in a new readership…

I drop my pen.

That's my block right there.

No Christopher.

I miss him. I miss him here in the office, his energy, his creativity, his smile. I miss him everywhere.

Right now, everything should be fantastic. The *Gazette* is in full flow, my team are amazing. To be honest, Amy's taken everything I've thrown at her and run with it. She could run this place as Editor in Chief. My relationship with mum is getting stronger every day, small steps, but I'm starting to see a time when we'll be able to just sit together and chat like a 'normal' mother and daughter. Well, maybe not completely normal but a normal that fits us. Everything I wanted has come good. Except I'm not feeling it. And sitting here, in silence, stuck, working alone on something Christopher and I used to work on together only makes me feel one thing. The aching loss of him and all the empty spaces where he used to be, which will be forever void without him.

I even went to the Golden Wok by myself last night and ordered the satay. It was terrible, but it made me smile. And then my eyes welled up at the thought of him. When I got the bill, my lone fortune cookie read, 'If you wish to see the best in others, show the best of yourself.'

Ah! And then it hits me.

Everything a bucket list is truly supposed to be. It's not about an individual event. It's not contained in a fleeting moment or single snapshot. It's about bringing a change – changing the way you feel, changing your perspective. So, yes, each task itself is worthwhile, but the magic starts once it's done. When you go back to your old life and say, hold up, wait a minute – *I'm different now*. I did something so far removed from what I thought I could do, that I'm going to do things differently from now on.

I pick up my pen and start scribbling in my notebook. The words flow so quickly that I can barely write fast enough.

This is it. I've got my bucket list item. I've got my final Buckley's Bucket List article. And it's not only a result of the changes in me, but it might even have the potential to change everything. Because I've lived keeping quiet, I've lived swallowing back my thoughts and ideas and keeping myself to myself. But look where that got me with Mum for so long. With Adam. With Hannah.

With Christopher.

Time for a change. I'm going in for the biggest exposure to date. The most terrifying item I can think of. But I've got to chance it, because it's too great a risk to let it go.

Buckley's Final Bucket List
No. 4 – The Big One!

I thought it was fitting that for my last feature, I attempt the hardest and most scary thing of all. To be upfront and honest about my feelings. Face up to the possibility of rejection. Go public and not be ashamed. So, this one is for everyone out there who's been so hurt by someone, who's thought, that's it. I've had it. I'm never letting that happen again. For this bucket list task, I don't even need to leave this seat at the *Gazette*'s offices. No parachutes, no muddy fields, no ghosts. Just me and this blank page. Here it goes.

In life, we are constantly losing people. One day somebody wakes up and they just don't feel the same way, or maybe it's you that feels you've grown apart from them. When we lose somebody, we tend to lose a piece of ourselves, but sometimes that piece is bigger than you expected it to be. Sometimes, someone you didn't even realise you loved gets away from you, and it's tragic and painful and that empty space they left never gets completely filled.

So, to the one who got away from me, this is to you.

It has been some time now since you left; not years or even months, but it feels like forever to me. Some days, I still expect you to walk in any second with coffees and a new big idea. But I know that you won't and that leaves me so heartsick and flat. What I find the saddest about what happened between us is how nothing went wrong except my lingering fear that something *would* go wrong, that disaster was inevitable, that heartbreak was always around the next corner. We got along, made each other laugh, enjoyed the time we spent together. No big betrayal. No dramatic clash of morals. And when you decided to go your own way, I took it as a rejection, even though you asked me to come. Because I knew I couldn't come too. I wasn't ready to give you my whole heart and trust you with it. I didn't think I would be able to love you, knowing that I might end up hurt again.

When I first met you I never expected to have you in my life the way I did. I never even realised I loved you until you were gone. But it's funny how things work out sometimes and, then again, how they don't work out at all. And it hurts me every day that we weren't able to figure it out, that I only saw ways and reasons why we *wouldn't* be able to stay together and continue to be as happy as we were. It especially hurts how nothing is the same, and it might never be again. Sometimes I don't know what's worse: knowing I lost you or knowing you'll never come back.

I never want you to compromise your dreams and I understand that you had your reasons and you needed to do what you needed to do. I hope you understand that I had my reasons too. But I know now that my reasons came from fear, nothing more. I know now might be too late. I'm doing my best every day to be okay with that. To not blame or beat myself up. To try and take this experience and make me better. Braver. Bolder.

Because I wish I'd fought harder. I wish I hadn't given up so quickly.

Losing you was hard – it still is. I didn't just lose a piece of my happiness, but someone who became my best friend. You're probably long gone from those feelings, and maybe you will live the rest of your life without ever thinking of me again. For all I know you'll meet someone else that you love more than you could have ever loved me. I like to think that one day we'll meet again and you'll choose the worst thing on the menu from the worst restaurant in the world. And I'll still have a wonderful time because I'll be with you. If you can forgive me, you know where to find me. And this time, I'm ready.

Lily xx

CHAPTER 30

One Month Later

Mark twists the white rose in Dylan's buttonhole. 'How you feeling, buddy?'

'On top of the world,' Dylan says without an ounce of sarcasm. 'Been waiting for this day since the moment I saw her.'

I look to Mark and see his bottom lip tremble.

Dylan smiles and wraps his arm around him. 'Ah, man! Don't start me off!'

Thanks to too many nights at The Black Boar, everyone's invited – including my mother and Maxwell, who turned up as promised on our doorstep in his cut-off denims and cowboy boots and has officially moved in with us, which has been a delight. Denise the barmaid and Mary the cleaner are dolled up to the nines, both trying to out-do each other in the hat stakes. Mr Clark, a friend of Dylan's father, gives me a wave. It turns out that the night Amy accompanied him to the theatre was a major turning point for him and his son; a gesture of pride and acceptance. Mr Clark gave Julian and his cast a standing ovation at the end of *A Midsummer Night's Dream* and that marked the beginning of a new relationship for them both, a fresh start with a focus on their shared future. He looks ten years younger in his beautiful tailored blue suit, standing proudly by Julian and Luiz as they hand out the bubbly and welcome everyone on arrival. The whole town is here. Except of course the one I miss the most. It's been a month now since I published my final feature and I've not heard anything from him. So I know I need to accept his decision. Accept that it wasn't to be. Maybe I'll forgive myself for that someday. But right now I still hurt for kicking myself.

However, the *Gazette* is a good news story. It continues to go from strength to strength and I can honestly say that I love being Editor in Chief of the fastest growing regional paper in the country. We're up for a Community Champion Award at the end of this year based on our digital campaign to save the library from closure. We gathered in tens of thousands of signatures via an online petition in just a matter of days. The old Mayor backed off very quickly once he realised what we could do and how strong the voice was that we represented. He lost the election because of it and the lady who replaced him is marvellous; she's lined our streets with flowers and benches and has plenty of exciting plans such as bringing back the Folk Festival and making it bigger and better than ever. A welcome breath of fresh air for Newbridge.

The bridal chorus begins, and I watch Jasmine walk up the aisle, her arm looped into her father's. His eyes are wet with proud tears and she is beaming with happiness. And she really is the most beautiful bride I have ever seen. I don't feel any of the angst I feared I would. I know now what I felt for Adam wasn't true love and clearly what he felt for me wasn't either. Mum was right to do what she did. She managed to protect me after all.

Dylan turns around to meet her and she picks up her pace to a skip. She slips her hand into his and, in that moment, love looks like the most natural, most easy emotion in the world. Just as it should when you've found your happy ever after.

Soon it's time to kiss the bride and then the party begins! The seats are cleared, the band set up and the dance floor is readied for action. The drinks are flowing and Amy clinks glasses with me as we stand around waiting for the new bride and groom to take the floor for their first dance.

Jasmine has been extremely decisive about every aspect of her wedding, from whether she was veil or no veil (no veil), hair up or down (down), dress short and high-neck or long and backless (short and backless), to the various flavours of her wedding cupcakes (chocolate, vanilla, red velvet). I can see that vision fully realised now and it is a truly beautiful affair, which reflects both her and Dylan's personalities perfectly. Even the little fondant groom atop the wedding cake has delicately painted tattoos up to his jawline. It is real and charming and original because it's theirs, and for everyone here who loves them, that's a real treat.

But there's one thing that has remained a secret just for them. The song for their first dance. Mark has a fiver on the fact that it's some kind of death metal anthem. Amy thinks it'll be a high-energy choreographed hip-hop number – the kind that usually go viral. I haven't a clue, but whatever it is, it will be as perfect for them as they are for each other.

Just then, we hear a loud bang and the lights cut. There's some shuffling, some confusion until we realise it's probably nothing but a blown fuse. We are in a field after all, more than likely powered by a generator the strength of a hairdryer. A tinny beeping noise comes from the amplifier by the plyboard stage, followed by a loud screech before the sound also cuts altogether.

Amy sucks in her breath and whispers in my ear, 'With no electricity, we have no lights and no music. Do you think they'll be able to fix it? Is there anything we can do?'

Before I can answer, Jasmine's dad claps his hands above his head. 'Appears we've lost power, folks, generator a little overwhelmed – chat amongst yourselves and we should be back for the couple's first dance very shortly!'

I glance at Amy. 'Poor Jasmine. She's planned everything so perfectly and I know that this is the part she was most looking forward to.'

And that's when we notice Mark begin to light the candles at the tables and dot tea lights around the dance floor. Soon everyone follows suit and the whole room is lit with a gentle, flickering golden hue. It looks beautiful and I feel tears prick at my eyes as I watch everyone come together, friends and family from both sides, the elderly sitting in their chairs, giving instructions to the children carefully carrying tea lights from one table to the next. Everyone working together to save this special occasion, to make sure that nothing gets in the way of making this one of the most memorable days in their lives.

A hush descends. I expect it to be Jasmine's dad giving an update that the power should be resumed shortly. In a way, I kind of want it to stay like this; intimate and personal with a dreamlike quality due to the light and shadows of the candlelight. But he doesn't say a thing. Instead, I hear a single, crystal-clear a cappella voice soar over the din.

Dylan steps onto the dance floor, holding out his hand to Jasmine. She smiles as she curls into his chest and they begin to sway. To my mother's lone voice singing – no backing, no accompaniment, no clutter. Just her and the words to their first dance.

It is breath-taking.

I pass Amy a tissue to dab at her eyes, so overcome she is with emotion.

'I can't believe that's your mother. It's per— it's so… per-fect,' she manages in between hiccuppy sobs of joy and Prosecco.

Once mum hits the chorus, Jasmine waves everyone in to join them. Couples swing in from the sidelines until they are surrounded by a heart-shaped crowd, all swaying and twisting to the best first dance set I've ever heard.

And that's the moment I feel a tap on my shoulder.

'May I?'

I know that voice, but it can't be. Not here, not now, not in Newbridge.

I turn around and he's there. Christopher.

'That last article…' he says.

I nod, my face breaking with happiness.

'Appears the one that got away couldn't stay away, not after reading what you wrote. Did you really mean all that?'

I take his cheeks in my hands and I raise my lips to his and I'm staring right into his eyes, my fingers on his skin, in his hair. Everything else falls away and we are suspended, held somewhere quiet and timeless, like the moment between two breaths.

And then bang. His soft lips are on mine and I can taste him, I can smell him, can feel him lighting up every nerve in my entire body. We stop, to smile, to open our eyes, to drink each other in and then we kiss again. The next kiss is the kind that breaks open my chest. I feel my heart swell and soar at once. This kiss steals my breath and then bowls me over. This is the only kiss I'll ever need. This is the only man I'll ever want. This is it. 'Yes. I meant everything. I'm ready. I'm ready for all of it.'

And, for once in my life, I don't want to be anybody else but me. I feel this is what my story was meant to be all along. I want to go wherever life leads me, without fear. And this time, I know I'll be strong enough.

'Shall we?' I ask him, offering my hand, and with smiling eyes, we swirl on to the dance floor.

Together.

A LETTER FROM COLLEEN

I want to say a huge thank you for choosing to read *For Once in My Life*. If you did enjoy it, and want to keep up to date with all my latest releases, just sign up at the following link. Your email address will never be shared and you can unsubscribe at any time.

www.bookouture.com/colleen-coleman

I hope you loved *For Once in My Life* and if you did I would be very grateful if you could write a review. I'd love to hear what you think, and it makes such a difference, helping new readers to discover one of my books for the first time.

I love hearing from my readers – you can get in touch on my Facebook page, through Twitter, Goodreads or my website.

I have thoroughly enjoyed writing about Lily and discovering her journey with her. The research I undertook for this book really did challenge me and take me to very muddy places that I never expected to go! A huge thank you to the Mud, Sweat and Wine Cyprus Legion Team: Nik, Jess, Rebekah, Bekki, Kerrie, Suzanne and Lindsay. You girls were amazing. Thanks for pushing me through – mainly from behind! Just like Lily, I found the camaraderie eclipsed the pain. Thank you for a real peak experience that I'm never likely to forget (or recover from).

There are times in life when we are committed to pursuing our passions. Every fibre in our body is focused on doing what we love. At other times, circumstance and necessity mean that we put our dreams aside and do what needs to be done! It is during these moments that we can easily forget what it is that makes our hearts sing. There are many other reasons why we may leave our passions behind. Someone in our lives may keep telling us that our passions are childish and unsuitable – until we finally believe them. But just because you've had to shelve it for a while doesn't mean it no longer exists. Life is too short to stop doing what you love, and it is never too late to rediscover your favourite things. So if you gave up singing, painting, writing, running, or any other activity or interest that you once loved to do, now may be the time to take up that passion again. If you don't remember what it is that you used to be passionate about, think about the activities or interests that you used to love or the dreams that you always wished you could pursue. I know this first-hand, as this is what led me back to writing. And now, four books in, I can hardly believe what joy this passion has brought me.

And it's not only our passions that make life worthwhile, but companionship. An animal companion, like Chaplin, can often mean much more in terms of a special friendship beyond simply being a pet. I know this from my own cat and dog, Lola and Stella! A donation from the sales of *For Once in My Life* will be given to supporting animal refuge charities. So by simply buying this book, you have helped our furry friends receive a little relief, a little comfort, and a little nudge to say that their welfare matters to us, so thank you from the bottom of my heart.

Many thanks to all of you, who email me, message me, chat to me on Facebook or Twitter and tell me how much you enjoy reading my books. I've been genuinely blown away with such incredible kindness and support from you all.

Thank you to my wonderful friend Trisha Sherwood for proofreading every book so far. You are a complete angel and eagle-eye. I am so grateful for all you do. Thank you to Clair and Lyndsey and Kaisha, who support me endlessly and send me the most gorgeous messages and reviews and who are real-life inspirational superwomen. There are so many things I love about being an author. However, my favourite has got to be this immense connection with people all over the world, from so many different walks of life, and feeling that I truly have friends everywhere. Thank you to Nicola, Jamie and Mark for sharing their skydiving stories as I was too chicken and to Caroline for being the best friend a girl could ever wish for.

Team Bookouture, Abigail Fenton, Emily Ruston and Jade Craddock have made my dreams come true and encouraged me every step of the way. This book would just be a tangled mess of words without them. They truly know how to read in between the illegible lines and bring out the best in me and the characters. I am indebted. You are magicians.

And thank you to Julian, Elizabeth and Sadie. You make every day the best adventure of all.

Thanks, happy reading and until next time,
Colleen Coleman xxx

 CollColemanAuth

 @CollColemanAuth

 www.colleencolemanbooks.com